The Dreamcatcher Fallacy

K. B. Nelson

A special note to sensitive readers:

This speculative fiction story contains explicit
and story-relevant relationships between adult
men over the age of eighteen and is intended
purely as fantasy for *mature readers*. *Please do
not continue this novel if such material offends
you.*

This is a work of fiction. All characters and
events portrayed in the book are either products
of the author's imagination or portrayed
fictitiously. Any resemblance to actual persons
living or dead, business establishments, events or
locales is entirely coincidental.

The Dreamcatcher Fallacy

Cover design by Kathy Haug
You can contact Kathy for cover design ideas at:
http://ferncreekassociates.com/

Acknowledgements

A special thanks must go out to the people who cheered on the early drafts of this book: Del and Marilyn Beyer, Brian Beyer, Karen Brody, and my writing mentor from college in Michigan (you know who you are) who all showered me with both humor and patience through the many stages of writing this novel.

Thanks also to my family who must live with me when I manifest unbridled obsession while working on the novel of the moment. You keep me firmly rooted in reality.

I am thankful for the Bainbridge Island Speculative Fiction Writers Group, who, for fourteen years, has championed both this genre and the people who love to write such things.

Finally big hugs and hats off to my dear friend Kathy Haug who can start with a raw and wordy book-cover idea, a fistful of graphics, and make it all breathe together.

Other Titles by K.B. Nelson

The Dreamcatcher Fallacy

Children of the Great Reckoning Series

Firewall Book 1: Ianto

Firewall Book 2: Samu'el

Architect

Operator

Coming soon: Folds of the Script

Prologue

Locked here in my cell, I have far too much time on my hands. I want to stop the hate that is chewing a hole in my gut, but I no longer know how. I suppose my forced addiction was meant as a kindness, but the numbing of emotions by the drug called *cziana root* is not much better than the awful rawness of my mind.

In this, perhaps I am a masochist.

Staring at the metal beams of my room, I often ponder the far-flung agricultural and mineral planets that have become both lifeline and chain to our dying world. The world's near cousin, Rialga, has perhaps a few more decades before it, too, will have nothing for its restless winds to blow about but sand and soot. Its red-hued continents always come quickly to mind, even when I sleep-- that place where I was captured and the place where I had to leave my lover behind. Such sunsets on Rialga, though.

That, at least will never change, even with the death of all that is green there.

Terrantata is also constantly with me, the newest of the supply-planet jewels, only ten-thousand humans digging toenails into its skin, raking their little teeth over the stalks of the jungles. But they are ten-thousand souls bred to be true human beings, waiting their chance to break from the confines of their structured society. I know because I sent them there, and they will one day provide the nudge that will topple kingdoms.

Planets are the things of large vision, though. Inevitably, prison also means too much time to nurse a sorrowful distaste for the waning power of the Core Families. They seem tied forever to the original home of humankind and still act as if they held an influence that truly mattered. They could have prevented the travesties I have witnessed if they had only opened their eyes early on. But with dependence comes a narrowed vision. How sad now to see these unaltered humans at their dinners and business meetings and pre-bought legal proceedings, playing the near politics because the real scope of life is simply far beyond them now. How they fiddle about, one hand on the door to this world, the other in each other's pockets and still think themselves quite mighty and grand.

But in truth, I spend most of my precious time feeding my rage about this sprawling Company that has dragged me back to Earth and into this dungeon. They are the ones who had originally dared to designed whole new sub-species of "humans" to take over the jobs that the normal or non-company personnel (or NCP's as they have come to be called) would not or could not do.

It is the Company who births us, owns and sells us, and decommissions us at the end of our useful years. It is headed now by the oh-so-perfectly molded Administrator classes created within its own walls, their leashes, in turn, held by the still-human Core or so their advertising machine helps the worlds believe. Accountant, product designer, executioner and mortician—those are the roles I have always seen in their genetic template, but then I nurse my hate with such words; it gives me the will to live year after long year in a room without windows, perfectly isolated--until I have begun to savor being such a perfectly poisonous creature.

There is no outside eye anymore in all the cosmos capable of observing what the Administrators do to their human genetic products, no balances, no checks on how much more they could change us, both within and without. They have already ripped individuality from their soldiers and freed them from the wisdom of physical pain, bred a kind of autism into their high-science techs even as they destroyed their tendency toward creative impulses. For themselves, they have designed minds constantly nimble with numbers and data, but without any receptors for the useless information that once informed such niceties as empathy.

But of course, as one of their products, I can see this from within the belly of the beast. My time with my all-too-human lover, Krystine, opened my eyes to what had been lost, and to what would continue to be lost if I did not choose to act.

Oh, yes, I see clearly. Humankind, genetically modified and not, has become as barren and desolate as its home world. In the end, I am as committed to my course of action as surely as the Administrator classes are to their own. I know my job—to bring back the ancient genetic lines of humanity, and set loose a viral judgment on them all.

And I have that singular luxury of time to truly hate myself as well. That I will be forced to use my own son as an agent of destruction surely will damn me for all time. But I have no other options. I must reset the double-helix within us all and breathe a vicious and pregnant wind of change over the Cosmos.

I pray that God, if such exists, will pardon me for my own hatred and hubris.

No. I retract that statement.

No more reconciliation, no more bowing to any power. For surely God Itself has given me the prophet's clear seeing, the warrior's sword and a poet's unblinking vengeance.

No, the only thing I really pray for is a way out of this addict's hell that has become my life. One day, my last words will fall on my son's ear—"I have delivered thee unto Hell with but a cup of water in thy hand."

Use it well, my son, you who are my vision, and my weapon.

James Illion,

Genetic Specialist Tech Grade 8

Historical Journal Entry

Recovery Data,

Company Central Historical Archives

High Security Holding Cell
Company Central, Earth Complex

James Illion, Tech Grade Eight for Earth
Company Central, slumped his shoulder against
the door of his cell. He struck at the heavy metal
with his fist, and then slid down its cold surface
until his long legs folded beneath him. The edges
of his belt buckle shoved into his bare stomach
and he leaned into the dull pain, surrendering
himself to it. For a moment, it gave him a focal
point.

But he could still feel the other's presence,
pressing on his skin.

Cheek hard to the door, James splayed one
brown hand across the reflective surface. His
fingers, delicately turned but with ragged,
chewed nails, flexed against the door.

I am finally going crazy.

He lifted his head and stared at the slightly warped image of his own face. Dark purple smudges stained the skin beneath his bloodshot eyes. His dilated pupils pressed the irises into thin rings of golden brown, making his eyes seem almost black. James blinked and felt the dry heat, burning as always. His black hair, chopped severely short, stood in stubborn little spikes across the top of his skull. He touched his image with his fingertips. *Was my hair long once, or am I only dreaming? It's so hard to tell anymore.*

He swallowed and stared at the skin that clung to the bones of his long face, and tucked tight beneath his high cheekbones. His lips cut a narrow swath of lighter color through the day's worth of stubble. *Krystine, you would not recognize me anymore. I don't know myself anymore.* Shaking, he shifted himself around and leaned his head back against the door.

The single plastic chair creaked beneath its occupant's weight, the sound sharp and insistent. James shut his eyes and pressed his hands over his forehead. "I'm begging you, Muligan. Is that what you want? For me to beg? Well, I am now. I need my music. I can't work without it—it carries me, don't you understand?"

"I'd never ask you to beg, James. That would be uncivilized." Muligan's voice always had a flat quality to it, an awful patience that ran fingernails over the normal cadence of ordinary speech.

James slowly rolled his head up. His hands fell limply into his lap, his head cradled by the door behind him. "What would you know about being civilized, Muligan?"

Administrator Muligan smiled. His legs, shoved straight out across the floor, crossed at the ankles. An expensive brown turtleneck, tucked fastidiously into black pressed pants, seemed at odds with his thin, messy hair and sleepy eyes. It was that gaze that always infuriated James. That, and the slender tube that drooped from his slightly parted lips. The poisoned part of James knew intimately how cziana root deadened the emotions, dampened the shifts and moods that stress brought out in a human. It suppressed feeling to the point where each day went smoothly forward, gray and dull and changeless. *And dead, just like you and I, Muligan. But at least you had a choice in the matter.*

Muligan raised one eyebrow, quirking his otherwise round, slack face. "You're fascinating

14

like this, James. Look at you. You're so deliciously raw. Everything's on the surface, every emotion, every witty comeback just pops out, unedited. I would have thought three years here would have..."

"Four years!" James knit the fingers of his right hand into the stubs of his short hair and pulled his other arm tight against his stomach. "You know very well it's been four years, Muligan." He glanced around his room then, mostly to avoid the satisfied smile the other man cast at him.

A simple mattress, spread out on metal brackets, hunkered on the wall to his right. At the foot of the bed, an open doorway led into a cramped bathroom. Someone had removed the actual door, leaving ragged and accusing holes in the frame. His black plastic workstation stretched across the entire left wall, littered with used syringes and stubby glass vials. His specialized keyboard lay buried beneath a wad of dirty clothing.

My world now. This is all of it.

James made a sound something like laughter, but the coarse gasp of breath behind it mutated it into the sound of despair. "My god, Muligan. Do you have any idea how mad a man can go in a fifteen by fifteen foot room?"

"Some," Muligan replied. He took the root out of his mouth and held it in a practiced, two-fingered grip. Its normal silvery-blue had already shaded to the sickly gray of a nearly empty stick.

James kneaded his stomach with his fingers. His neck hurt and a headache clamored behind his eyes. *So tired.* He could feel his jaw quiver, clicking the backs of his teeth together. "My music. You've taken everything else from me. Why this? And why *now*?" He pulled on his hair again, and then slid his palm back down the side of his rough face. "What have I done to deserve this? I'm meeting my quotas, aren't I? My eye is as good as always. I know I've caught more than my share of template flaws this last quarter. So why take the music now?"

"Because you've been a bad boy, James." Muligan straightened a little in his chair. He wove the root through his fingers, a deft trick of under-over, and then slowly replaced it in his mouth. "You're not taking your prescribed drugs."

"That's not true." James gripped his stomach with both arms then. He stared down at the floor, at the lines of cables that ran beneath his workstation to the wall hookups. Blue lines and red lines twisted there like an umbilical cord.

"You're lying to me, James. You're in withdrawal right this moment. I should know— I've been through it a time or two myself." Muligan chuckled, an awful, fabricated sound, and then leaned his weight forward. "Besides, I have a vid-disk of you last night, listening to...what was it? Tchaikovsky? You were crying, James. People who take their root don't cry."

James jerked his chin up in frustration, smacking his head back against the door. The impact echoed a little in the base of his skull and radiated down his spine. He lifted his eyes to the ceiling. *Surrounded by metal. And everywhere my own face thrown back at me. God, Krystine. What I would give for just one wet leaf. Just to hold it in my hand, feel the veins running under my thumb.*

"I had to feel the music again," James whispered, still staring at the ceiling. "Really feel it, like a human being is meant to. I couldn't let you take that away from me. I won't."

"And I won't let you torment yourself with all that noise until you are stabilized again. Until you are back on cziana root, your music retrieval passcode has been revoked. It's that simple," Muligan said with a weak shrug.

"Stabilized?" James cried. He rocked

forward, clutching his stomach. "Four years you've thrown that at me. There's nothing wrong with me. There never was!"

"Nothing wrong with you?" Muligan actually sounded amused. He lay back in his chair and shook his head. "Nothing wrong? You're a classic case, you know. Just like all the other Ancient Recovery Products. Moods shifts, trouble with authority, job tasking glitches."

"Stop it."

"Why the upper level Administrators ever started messing with the old Tech Grade genetic templates, I have no idea. Better to have let history remain history."

"Stop it!" He pulled his knees into a tighter ball and drew his breath over his clenched teeth. "Stop talking to me like I'm some kind of goddamn machine. I'm not a product, I'm a man."

Muligan snorted. "Come on, James. You're no more a natural human than I am. This place is womb and parent and God to people like you and I. You were designed and made here, James, and you *will* die here."

"No." James opened his eyes and glared at Muligan. The other man watched, smiling around the edges of his root.

"No, what?"

"You can take everything else from me, but not my humanity."

Muligan shrugged his shoulders as if suddenly bored. He pulled the cziana root out of his mouth and tossed it to the floor. His arm held the flinging gesture for a moment, his first finger crooked, his thumb flicked out, then let the movement go. "I can't take what you never had, James."

James curled what was left of his fingernails into his own skin. His eyes burned dry and hard in his skull. "Get out."

Muligan merely smiled at him.

James rose shakily to his feet. He put his hand out against the door to steady himself, then shuffled two steps forward. "You heard me, Muligan! Get out!"

"In time."

Muligan stood then and moved over to the workstation. He fished into his back pocket and pulled out a small vial filled with a pale blue fluid. He set it down firmly. "New stuff. A little stronger distillation just for you." Head bent slightly over the vial, Muligan looked up through the sprinkle of his eyelashes without raising his head.

James faded back toward one wall, his arms clutched over his belly.

"You have to stop fighting me, James, or you'll stay in here for the rest of your life. Do you understand that? If you'd just work with me, I could extend your privileges with a clear conscience." Muligan tapped the vial with one fingertip. "Try this. Who knows? If you respond well, maybe I could even get you stationed back on Rialga. Someone named Krystine would like that, don't you think? Unless she's already found herself another Tech to screw."

"You son of a bitch," James whispered.

Muligan smiled and pulled the cell's passkey out of his pocket. He walked to the door, then stopped and looked straight into James' face. "Be careful not to take too much of that cziana. It *could* kill you, you know." His muscles shifted around his cold eyes, folding out another smile that did not reach their brown flatness. "To lose a Tech Grade Eight with your long years of experience would be very unfortunate, don't you think?" He pressed the tab on the passkey without taking his gaze off James. The door moved aside.

"Very unfortunate," Muligan repeated as he slipped past James and left. The door clanged shut behind him.

James gave a strangled cry, stumbled to his chair, lifted and heaved it at the door. It crashed just to the right of the frame and bounced against the floor without leaving a mark. He spun wildly, and his reflection mocked him everywhere he turned. Giving an inarticulate cry, James fell to his knees, both hands pressed tight to his temples. Gravity pulled him forward until his forearms smacked up against the floor. "I can't. I can't." He fell over to his side, curling his limbs up close to his body. The cold floor sucked greedily at his clammy skin.

"Oh, god, Krystine. I can't do this anymore." He shuddered, feeling his stomach knot. It sent little tendrils of burning liquid up his throat and with it, his anguish rose, bitter and devastating. "Four years, Krys. Four years and they never even let me say good-bye." He gulped at the air, and pulled himself tighter.

"You've got to help me, Krys. Please, help me." *Can I even remember you, the way you really were?* He tried to draw Krystine in his mind, shading her hair auburn, her eyes green, trying to remember the feel of her waist against the palms of his hands, the spicy smell of cultivated Rialgan flowers on the soft skin of her neck. That ghostly scent alone held the image together, even when it tried to buck and flutter in his mind.

He clung to the shifting image, willing it to feel real, begging it to stroke his hair, touch his lips. "Tell me I'm still alive, Krys. Tell me I'm more than a Company product. You tell me, and I'll listen. Please, just tell me."

The image of the woman in his mind clarified. He could imagine the warmth of her skin as she took his hand, smiled, and then leaned her head against his shoulder. He sobbed, mentally clutching her to him. "You're so tired," she said. "As soon as you finish your work, then you'll be able to really sleep, James. Rest now, and then finish it. Finish it all."

James slowly let the ragged edges of his consciousness slip away beneath her shadowy touch.

———

James jerked awake. The cold drove him, groggy and still nauseated, off the floor. He dragged himself to the bathroom sink and splashed some of his carefully rationed water over his face. No sense in turning the light on; enough flooded in from the outer room for him to see. For a moment he just leaned against the hard edge of the sink and let the precious water drip over his dangling fingers. It was his only luxury.

He had to push himself back into the cold glare of his room. "Lights, down sixty percent," he murmured. Deep within their ceiling recesses, they automatically dimmed. *Better. Better.* James swallowed back the aches and insistent roll of his stomach as he crossed to his workstation.

He brushed a shirt off his antiquated keyboard, and pulled it across the hard plastic surface until one rounded corner bumped up against his thigh. Without bothering to straighten it, he typed his entry-code with one hand.

The entire left wall flickered, and then lit up with a dizzying genetic template display. Color-coded lines linked series of numbers in a tangled abstract schematic of life. In the left corner, the flowing red product designation read Number 1011, Batch 16-2240, L-Group.

James reached up and tenderly touched the wall. In response to his contact, the number sequence beneath the pads of his fingers flared a rich shade of green. He slid his hand along the metal and the numbers slid with him, shifting into new positions. He withdrew his touch and walked along the edge of his display "Yes," he murmured absently. *Now you'll be able to hear Tchaikovsky the way he should be heard, with your whole soul. Or whatever you choose to call such a thing.* He had set up the whole template to cascade like a gym filled with dominos, one switch tickling the next, on down protein sequences that would be impossible to trace in the early stages of development but would have a cumulative effect on the fetus. He hadn't been stopped by the Company because what he was doing was so subtle and had certainly never been attempted before. Quality control would miss it for a very long time.

He prayed it would be long enough. The Administrator element within this, his last work of art, was the shakiest part of the whole creation. The ultimate success or failure of his entire life hinged on a decision that would be triggered by the smallest package of genetic information. But it was all he could do.

He backtracked along the edge of his station, his eyes flicking over the riot of numbers and lines. A small smile tickled his lips. "That'll finish it, I think."

Abruptly, his stomach knotted itself into a hard ball. He bent sharply over, feeling his skin flush hot. The screen lurched and the lines and numbers warped, shimmering. He groaned and tried to steady himself against the workstation.

His hand bumped against the vial Muligan had left.

Trembling, he picked it up and shook the liquid a little. It sloshed up against the sides of the container in choppy wavelets. James closed his sweaty hand around it and looked at the complex data stream on the wall. "You win Muligan. But so do I."

If he did not take his own life, another man would soon come and do it for him. He knew his executioner's name, his blue-gray eyes and blond hair. Death, from the moment he had been captured, had always been inevitable. This way felt clean, though, ending life mostly on his terms and not at the hands of a one-time friend. They were still united in their vision, though. And that would be enough.

James fumbled on his desk for a needle and syringe. He speared one end and emptied the entire vial into the thumb-thick plastic cylinder. With his first finger, he tapped the air bubbles to the surface. He caught the hint of irony in the gesture, and laughed in a short bitter explosion of sound. *Like it will make any difference now.* A moment later, the needle sunk into his flesh and he winced as always with its bite. He tossed the empty casing onto the floor, barely noticing the clatter on metal.

Leaning heavily on his arms, he studied the schematic again through both the bright glimmers of pain and the gathering cziana fog. *If the genetic production directory overrides that I acquired still work, he'll have a chance. Just a chance, but that's all I can give him now.*

James drew his lips up, a quivering compromise between a smile and an expression of despair. *This form, this mind, this is all I can leave to you.* He pulled the keyboard to him and pressed the numbers that would send the template to the production directories. Within hours, the soup of lines and numbers would begin to dictate the formation of living tissue.

Happy Birthday, my son. And someday, I hope you can forgive me.

He pressed the last number, and the screen went dark.

Chapter 1

My job description is really quite simple.
Oversee the many streams of data, maintain
the predictability of the Company genetic
lines, and moderate change when necessary.
It is the last bit that intrigues me the most,
for when does anyone within the Company
admit to a flaw that would necessitate any
change? It is certainly not part of our current
business culture.

Prime Andrea Annon
Company Central's Administrative Lead
Earth Complex

Administration Hall
Company Central, Earth Complex

Tech Grade Four Warrin Tilley rubbed his fist against his sweaty forehead and eyed the figure that sat just beyond the open doorway. The tiny data capsule in his pocket jabbed its sharp point into his chest and he pulled it out, rubbing his thumb over the top of its glass-like surface as if it was his favorite amulet. The empty Administration corridor sucked up his heavy breath, trapping it in the knobby cream carpet and abstract wall weavings. Finally, there was nothing to do but tap on the expensive wood frame of the open doorway.

"Come." Prime Andrea Annon absently gestured with the tips of her fingers. Her dark mahogany desk wrapped around her like a wooden amoeba, more curves than corners. The monitor area seemed to hang in mid-air, all light and numbers that shimmered a bit with her breath.

Warrin swallowed and bobbed his head at her in greeting. As he crossed to her desk, he noticed that the brief image of himself in the Astazia metallics had run the gray of his uniform into the planes of his face. He knew those off-world wall hangings were enough to pay for him several times over.

That alone made him feel slightly ill.

Andrea hadn't even looked up. "One moment please." She stared intently at the screen before her, her mouth pulled down at the edges of her lips, her face too long and narrow to be called truly beautiful. Her thick brown hair might have been styled to lessen the severity of her features, but instead, the twin waves pinched her face between them. Finally, she seemed to reach an end point on her data screen and looked up Warrin. "Let me guess. You have some tech anomalies for me to sign off on."

Warrin started to smile, decided otherwise and ended up with a lopsided grimace on his face. "Yes, Prime. Here." He handed her the data square. Her dark, steady eyes, startling against the pale skin of her face, unnerved him still more. "I was ordered to obtain a termination OK for number 1011, Batch 16, current year, L-Group."

She gazed at him, as if expecting more.

He swallowed.

"Who is your department head?" she asked.

"Barry Reighton, under Administrator Muligan...Thomas Muligan," he answered quickly.

"Of course. Muligan." She slipped the data capsule into a small hole on her desktop. A light blue aura lifted from the small tech, displaying a hand-sized screen filled with numbers and a spider web of crossing lines. The light washed over her features, further shadowing her eyes.

Warrin stood there, unsure of whether he should step up and interpret the data for her.

"This report shows that the fetus is still viable," she said at last. "I'm not inclined to terminate at this late date. You *do* know the costs associated with bringing an L-Group product this far along, yes?"

Warrin blinked at the barest echo of strain in her voice, even though he knew better than to attempt to guess its reason. Prime settled back in her chair, her hands a knot of fingers in her lap.

"Yes," Warrin replied hesitantly. His eyes shifted to the data image for a moment. The desk, too wide to lean across, forced him to gesture vaguely at the blue light. "But notice that there is a significant departure from expected norms present here as well. This fetus is not anything like his L-Group cohort."

"Yes, I see the differences, but I don't see any life threatening ramifications." She pulled her fingers apart as if she were dispersing the patina of tension that had been there. "What I am more curious about is why the physio-irregularities are showing up at all. The rest of this particular L-Group batch appears to be maturing within projected parameters."

"Muligan agrees with your basic observations," Warrin said. He swallowed at the lump of nervousness lodged in his throat. He hated interacting with people like this, particularly people who could have him decommissioned on a whim. "Due to the information we have, he suggests this may have been a mistake, a glitch of some kind."

"Indeed," she answered. He could feel her eyes raking him. "Tell Muligan that I expect a full analysis and backtrack of the genesis work on this fetus because I don't see a mistake here. This is careful, blatant manipulation. I'm sure he sees it, too."

"Manipulation? Why would anyone willfully alter..."

She silenced him with a sharp rise of a single eyebrow. "I can read genetic templates, Tech Four. I'm deeply familiar with all our product lines, and I can tell the difference between a coding error and purposeful craftsmanship. As to *why*, that's Muligan's job to speculate about, not yours and not mine."

Warrin cringed.

"I am curious about one thing, however," Andrea continued. "Has Muligan gone ahead and tagged the Techs who would have had access to this genesis work?"

"Not that he's shared with me."

"Of course." She returned her gaze to the

31

screen. For one moment, the Tech thought she had dismissed him, but then she continued, her voice lowered in throaty concentration. "This little accident is actually quite a piece of art." She waved the data around with her fingertips. "Notice the splice indicators in the sub-section here? Whoever did this was attempting to graft together two, maybe three different sets of Company-engineered genetic material. L-Group code, certainly, and..."

She stopped her musing abruptly and looked up at him so sharply that he felt his heart smack up against the ribs in his chest. Her eyes overpowered the rest of her face; he couldn't look away from them. "Give him my message. Tell Muligan I want that analysis today, in person, along with the tech responsible for the template work on this product."

Warrin hesitated to ask the next question, but Muligan was almost as off-putting as Prime in his own way. To bring him bad news would be highly distasteful. "What should I tell him about the termination orders?" he asked in a small voice.

Prime frowned. "What are you not following in our conversation? Tell him the termination request is denied."

Warrin felt his shoulders tighten beneath his lab uniform. "In case of such an answer, he instructed me to request a removal of this particular fetus from the L-Group development center when it reaches self-supporting status." The breathy quality of his voice distressed him. He managed to disengage from Prime's eye-lock and dropped his gaze to her shiny desktop. He felt so exposed without the press of his lab equipment on each side of him and the hum of jovial lab conversation in his ears.

"Tell him no."

"What?" he burst out. He jerked his gaze back to her impassive face. "Prime, L-Group was designed as a homogenous collection of male units. Any physical aberration would threaten the stability of the Group, let alone the development of the unusual individual. It would be easier to attempt to retrain the aberration into a Tech or low-level Administrator position. With all due respect, how can you..." He broke off as Prime straightened in her chair. Her fingers wrapped around the arms of her seat, claw-like. He felt the blood rush out of his face.

"I will not approve removal of 1011 from his Group," she repeated in a low and carefully controlled voice. "Tech Grade Four, although I appreciate your candor, I am quite aware of L-Group social dynamics. Please convey my orders to Muligan. And tell him that any further communication from his department should come through normal data channels. If you are wise, you'll tell him this immediately. You are dismissed."

"Prime." Warrin brought his fist to the side of his temple in frantic respect and half ran from her office.

—

Andrea leaned her chin against one small fist as she again studied the genetic template. The pressure felt good, grounding her in a reality that had become oddly tenuous. She tapped her fingernails against the wood surface, but neither holding her aching head nor the random movement would change what she saw in the data now.

My genetic template. Mine. I recognize the pattern. Did Muligan miss it? Surely he would have thrown that in my face tonight if he had seen it.

"You bastard," she whispered, as if the data itself somehow violated her. "You slimy, evil, Tech Grade Eight bastard." The soft overhead lights shone down on her desk. Not a fleck of dust marred its rich surface. She slammed both hands down on it and drove her fingers into the finish as if she could mar it. When she lifted her hands, only the oily smudges of her fingertips striped the surface. *Perfect. My record as Prime has been perfect. Now what am I supposed to do with this?*

Her eyes tracked back to the data as if dragged there. *I have a son, that's what these squiggles and numbers really say. I have a son, thanks to you. But why? What were you doing?* She ground her teeth until her jaws let out little flairs of misery. *Was this a way to protect your little creation? Did you think that I would keep this unit alive because I would be able to see myself in it? One order, and I could wipe him away. One simple order. That would be logical. Practical.*

But she couldn't do it.

She could feel herself tremble with fury. Something far beyond her control froze her hands and chilled her usually agile mind. The data merely waited, patient as always.

A son.

She tipped her head back and lifted her eyes to the raised swirl pattern on her ceiling.

Something soft, some kind of a feeling like

the beginnings of amusement tickled at her belly then. And its presence confused her. Rage, yes, that emotion she understood. But the melting edges of the anger, where it drifted into a kind of wonder, even a muted kind of elation, these made no sense to her at all. *What am I feeling? It's dangerous. I know it is. It will affect my judgment. It will compromise the Company and my own position. I should kill it.*

Kill it? Why not use easier words like terminate or even abort?

She laid her hands over her flat belly, feeling herself breathing. A smile almost came to her lips before she licked it away with a scowl of disgust.

A son.

Andrea at last shoved all the emotions back. She moved her data storage codes around, locking it down to any other prying eyes. Muligan's tendency to dig out discrepancies was bad enough, and the child would raise questions. If she were honest, he would trigger a great many questions, in fact. She didn't want any of this easy to peruse. *You win, James Illion, Tech Grade Eight bastard. But this will be our little secret.*

Ours alone.

—

Thomas Muligan slouched in the office chair with his hands folded across the shiny red swath of his sweater. He studied Andrea through his half-open eyes, and then let them wander over her richly appointed walls and gray-blue carpets. Even after her imperious summons, he had waited until late evening to show up at her office.

He liked to irritate her. It was one of the few amusements that touched him anymore.

Andrea stood up and navigated her way around the curves of her workstation. "What do you mean the Tech Grade Eight responsible for the aberration is dead?"

Hands pressed back against her desk, she shifted her weight and waited for his answer as if her very proximity would change his report.

Muligan raised his eyebrows and shrugged. "Dead. Suicide. How much do you want spelled out for you, Andrea?" He rubbed at his lip, a mannerism instilled by years of cziana root addiction. He performed the gesture lazily, allowing just a hint of an old-fashioned fop to glimmer through the motion. Muligan purposefully looked past her and pushed a little at the mousy brown hair slicked back from his rounded forehead.

"Suicide, Muligan? Do you realize how mathematically rare it is for a Tech Level Eight to take his own life? We bred that out of them decades ago."

In a calculated way, he shifted his gaze back to her and smiled.

Andrea crossed her arms over her slender midriff. The pressure creased her white shirt. "Out with it. You aren't telling me something, and I have very little patience for your games tonight."

Muligan shrugged again. "The report is on your unit. You tell me."

She ran her fingers sharply through her hair and turned to gesture the screen up and around. Muligan let himself settle into the old routine, forcing her to test the limits of her tolerance for him. She seemed to read the report carefully. By the shift of her head, the lift of her shoulders, he could tell she had started at the beginning and was reading through again.

"Are you sure these findings are accurate? This is high-grade Tech material, not just random low-level composites. Did he...did he introduce his own genetic code into an L-Group medium?"

"There you have it. I ran the series twice to

be sure. There is no doubt that significant strands of this genesis template match up with the dead Tech Grade Eight."

Prime wandered away from her desk, her fingers laced behind her back. He tried to catch her gaze but failed. He finally contented himself with the warped image of her face reflected in the metallic Astazia wall hangings.

"A form of self-preservation?" she asked at last. "Is that what we are seeing here?"

He nodded, but she still hadn't looked up at him. "It would certainly appear so. And perhaps of more interest to you, this particular Tech Grade Eight was part of the ARR program your illustrious predecessor insisted on dabbling with. I could find you L-Group assault weapons that would be less dangerous."

"The Ancient Recovery and Reintegration program...that might explain this particular Tech's mental aberration," she said. It fascinated him, how she could ignore him so completely at times.

"What I wonder about," Andrea continued, "is why didn't we catch this work earlier?" She ambled across her office, and pressed a black button set unobtrusively into her wall. A compact bar turned itself out from the goldish metal and she ran her fingers over the fronts of the delicate decanters, finally selecting one and pouring out a splash of the pale wine into a waiting glass.

Muligan waited patiently until she looked at him for any kind of feedback. "We had trouble with this Tech before." He itched at his wrist, where the sweater cut a little too tight. "We had to retrieve him by force from Rialga about five years ago now. You can read the particulars in his file. But he seemed fairly stable after we got him back here and under drug therapy."

"Drug therapy?"

"Cziana root in modest doses."

"Of course. Your drug of choice." She took a swallow of her wine.

"If I can do anything to avoid terminating an expensive Tech Grade Eight, especially one with his talent, I do it. Working in full isolation, he still saved us nearly 450 million credits last year alone in template control. He had a gift for identifying production variants."

"A rare gift indeed," Andrea muttered to herself.

Muligan smiled and laced his fingers together, settling them on his stomach. "Enough of a very dead issue, then. Sign the orders and let me terminate this little creative flair of his, and the whole issue can be neatly filed and done with.

"Why would I want to do that, Muligan?" He blinked then, surprised at her answer. If he wasn't mistaken, she was purposefully baiting him.

"Come, Andrea," he prodded her. "You are aware, as well as I, that the Ancient genetic components make any synthesis unstable at best. As admittedly talented as he was, this Tech Grade Eight was a prime example of the mental and emotional hiccups associated with the entire ARR project. Nothing of value will come from this unit. Cut your losses now and dispose of it."

"That old line again, hmm, Muligan? Everything is about cost management and quality control. Are you not even a little curious about this unit? I expected more from you, God knows why." She slipped back to her desk, and dropped into her cushioned seat.

He lifted a hand, and flicked his fingers at her in a mock salute. "I am ever your humble servant, Prime. But the suicide death of this Tech merely underscores my distaste for the ARR program as a whole. Its units are dangerous and should be brought under permanent censure. Death has always been the most permanent of solutions after all. Why are you so squeamish about these things?"

She smiled then, and he did not fail to catch the hint of condescension on her face. "So, now you're off the subject of this particular unit and back on your ARR crusade again? Death is often only a waste, Muligan, an expensive solution for a small mind. There are still ARR units functioning in the field with no strange mental side effects or behavior issues. Commander Drew of L-Group is one such man, and he has always proven exceptionally stable in all his duties. And the Terrantata Colony is primarily an ARR group you yourself had a hand in forming. They are making terrific progress. I've approved a new mining project for that world, and they'll begin shipping refined materials by the end of next year."

Muligan rubbed at his forehead, then flopped his hand over the edge of his chair. A mild wave of irritation ran through him, a sure sign that he needed more cziana soon. "Terrantata was useful because it allowed us a dumping ground for a large number of our ARR units, nothing more. And yes, Commander Drew is an admirable example of good science and conditioning. But this 1011 represents a different sort of problem entirely. It is the product of an unstable Tech, not part of a carefully monitored and preplanned experimental batch. Let me clean this up. Please."

"No. Not yet, in any case."

"Will you at least let me remove him from his batch and group?"

"No."

Muligan took a deep breath and pushed himself out of his chair. "Why do you insist on displaying such classic Administrator arrogance?"

"To balanced your classic Tech-brained departmental shortsightedness," she returned.

"The danger is real, Andrea."

"He's one unit, Muligan." She leaned forward to retrieve her wine glass from her desktop. "And I have work to finish this evening. Please alert me when he is taken from the development chambers. It will be interesting to view him in person."

"Of *course*, Prime," Muligan replied. She did not raise her eyes at his insolence and so he let himself out without further comment.

Chapter 2

It was not that I hated the Ancient Recovery and Reintegration Project as such. It simply felt to me like an evolutionary step backward into the chaos of the individual and the messy dance of non-hierarchal "people" that had led to the founding of the Company in the first place. To put it succinctly, the ARR Program would simply be bad for business.

Administrator Thomas Mulligan
Historical Archives
Terrantata Research Library

L-Group Nursery and Developmental Section
Company Central, Earth Complex

Deep in the bowels of the Company Nursery Center, a child cried and gasped, rending the air with tiny red fists. The hum of machinery, hidden behind the Company logo wall murals, evidently served as a very poor lullaby. A flustered unit nurse tapped vainly at the plastic separating him from the common circulating air. On either side of him, babies twitched uncomfortably in their sleep, jerking with every piercing wail.

Prime Andrea stood very still in front of the observation window, her long arms straight and proper by her sides. Her hair was pulled up in a neat bun, shot through with delicate Asian holding sticks. Muligan reclined against the frame of the window, toying with his ever-present cziana root. He was dressed for a night at the games in a loose cotton shirt and deep green vest that hung nearly to his knees. The tile floor hurt the bottoms of his feet, but that very sensation brought a kind of pleasure as well. He glanced from the baby to Andrea and smirked. "All this waiting for that little dark thing? Good lungs, as they used to say. Notice he's the only one bawling, Andrea? Your little experiment is off with a bang. Or should I say, a howl?"

"That's enough, Muligan."

He chuckled and chewed lazily at the Root. "Like some cziana, Andrea?" He extended the gray-blue twist of his tubule toward her.

She glared at him and strode over to the communication access. "Nurse?"

The man looked up, distracted at first and

then paled as he recognized his visitors. "Yes, Prime?" he asked, straightening noticeably.

"Pick up Unit 1011. Hold him," Andrea commanded.

"Excuse me, Prime?" the nurse asked, taking a half step toward the observation window. His confusion showed all over his wide face.

"Hold him!" Andrea repeated impatiently.

Muligan snickered and slowly turned so he could bounce the back of his head gently against the glass.

The nurse still hesitated, flushing through the pale skin of his cheeks. "As you wish, Prime." He turned to 1011, popped the cubicle and awkwardly scooped the baby up. For a few minutes, the tirade continued unabated, and the sound of the voice seemed even more magnified by the walls of the nursery. The nurse continued to glance helplessly at Prime, patting the baby's stiff little back with an unpracticed hand.

"God, what a noise." Muligan pushed off the wall and walked a slow and exceedingly precise circle in the corridor.

Andrea ignored him.

Gradually the screams dissolved into rhythmic cries, less shrill and piercing and began to trail off into small hiccups. The baby relaxed his tiny body against the nurse at last, shuddering and shivering but at least quiet.

Andrea activated the pickup. "His name is Joshua. Do you understand?"

The nurse nodded, wide-eyed still.

"Sure he understands," Muligan stage whispered, without stopping his slow ambling circle.

"You will devote yourself to this child each day. He is to be held as much as seems appropriate, and the hours of contact logged." Andrea carefully pronounced her words as if the man beyond the glass was incapable of coherent conversation.

But he nodded his understanding, and if he had questions, he swallowed them quietly.

Andrea stepped back from the glass, crossed her arms and turned to face Muligan. He halted at last and smiled at her. "Well, where are your snide comments?" she asked.

"I thought you were so set on training him strictly as an L-Group Unit." He affected a wide-eyed, questioning look.

Andrea raised her chin a little. "I'll be sure to resume normal protocols with him as his nervous system is able to cope."

"Cope?" he chortled. "This is all too much.

You're waiting to see if a military-designed unit will learn to *cope*? How absurd can you make this?"

"Look at it as an experiment, Muligan," she countered. She started down the hall, her soft-soled flats slapping the floor in muffled taps.

Muligan drifted in her wake. "I'm not used to seeing you so free with your compassion, Prime."

She stopped then and swung around to face him. "I have no *compassion* as you call it for that child. None whatsoever."

Got you. He smiled serenely at her. "Well, it seems to me..."

"You are a blind technocrat," she snapped. "Absolutely blind to what we potentially have in that child." She shoved her finger up against the green of his vest, stabbing home each word. "He just imprinted on that nurse, an adult not even close to L-Group genetically. He should have been arching his back and fighting away from the man." Andrea pushed him back with one last thrust of her forefinger.

Muligan examined the root he was holding, and then looked up into her fierce brown eyes. "You cannot possibly call what we just saw imprinting behavior. It was a normal reaction to discomfort arising from the chemical soup in that thing's brain, " he responded. He replaced the root in his mouth. It was another kind of pleasure, really, seeing her get angry. He had almost forgotten what such emotions felt like internally. It was very, very hard to get angry when stuffed full of root. Still, seeing her like this, he could almost capture the threads of the feeling in himself.

"Normal!" she snapped the word out. "That's exactly what I am trying to tell you. L-Group babies don't cry like that. He craved contact. That's something new, something we might be able to build on, to *use*."

"So it craves contact! So what? That's not useful for a damn soldier, Andrea. There is no way that is the beginning of a useful skill set, unless you want a Batch sex toy. It only means that this baby is carrying around all those damn aberrations I have been trying to warn you about." *There. A close approximation of her tone, correct?* He always meant what he said when they went toe to toe like this. He just couldn't seem to find the right sort of energy to put behind his words anymore.

"You just don't get it, do you?" Andrea asked, shaking her head in exaggerated disbelief. "Use that addicted package you call a brain and try to think creatively. I for one would welcome the opportunity to market a military-class unit who may have more intuition and be more trainable in Tech areas. In short, be a little more like an Admin-class product, but with teeth. I can imagine an L-Grouper who is capable of serving as a bodyguard and companion, who can operate outside of normal L-Group strictures, who can bond with his employer. Do you realize the financial potential of such a thing? And the political clout it'll bring my administration if the experiment is successful?"

Muligan drew in a long breath, fiddling with his Root. "I recognized the Administrator genotemplate in the report, Andrea. No, don't look so shocked, I can read those things as easily as you. But the presence of such a mix of genetic stock usually results in wildcard behavior patterns. He may not be trainable at all, and certainly may not bow to whatever you have in mind for him. That's the cost to put alongside all your ideas of a payoff."

"All beings can be controlled. I'll find a way. Or create one," she countered.

"You're the one who doesn't see. That child is different, Andrea, from the tips of his dark hair to the length of his bones. He's going to be about four to six inches taller than anyone in his batch, and I haven't even begun to speculate about his nervous system, reaction speeds, intelligence ratings. He's going to be like fitting a damn NCP into one of our labs—it never, ever works smoothly."

"I don't agree. Even Non-Company Persons can be integrated and influenced when you find the right tool to use with them. We've been doing it for years in the outlying colonies. We'll just have to find the right combination of stimuli that work with him. He'll be raised here. He won't learn to question authority like an NCP would. He'll *be* L-Group; he just will have a few more endowments, that's all." Her brown eyes snapped with excitement.

Muligan stared at her. Even divorced from her delicious and undiluted feelings, he could sense the danger. It was all there, in every sweet bit of data concerning the child. He could see the varied avenues this newborn could take, might take, see them in a glance that carried neither malice nor admiration. How could she not see the same thing?

"In the scenario you've just painted, he may be even more dependent upon his Group because he is different," Muligan found himself cautioning her. "Or the admittedly constrained individuality that has been bred into Admin-class units may keep him from being an efficient killer. There are lists of variables here, Andrea. You have no idea what you are playing with."

She smiled at him, her lips tight and her eyes hard. "Maybe not, but this Company was originally constructed on experimentation and taking chances. I haven't come this far without being able to analyze potential accurately. And I see so much potential here, Muligan. Stop sparing with me and look at what he could mean to the Company!"

"Why do you think we haven't continued this kind of genetic mish-mashing? In a worse case scenario..." he began.

"God, Muligan!" she finally exploded. "He's just one unit. Even if things don't work out, even if I have to terminate him at twelve or twenty standard years, what in the world is he, *by himself* mind you, going to harm?"

What in the world? Exactly. He almost shuddered as his mind began to list the possibilities, and then became so entranced with the gut wrenching emotion that he nearly lost his train of thought. And that sent a spear of exquisite pleasure through him. Time for more Root, that point at least was clear.

Andrea leaned closer, looking him full in his eyes and he came back to the conversation rather unwillingly.

"I've tolerated you so far, out of respect for our Admin cohort, but I will not let the Company suffer because of your lack of vision, Muligan. Even though I deeply value your ability to sift data holistically, I remind you that I have never, ever needed your permission to pursue the development of this child."

Muligan tipped his head at her, exquisitely aware of the edges of tension in his body. Lovely thing, tension. His mind crackled with pleasure inside. However, it was time to let the argument and emotions go. Pity, just that thought siphoned the adrenalin from his system, leaving him blank and ready like an old-fashioned computer screen. "I've always trusted you," he said. "I hope that never changes."

"It won't," she assured him. Then she spun and continued up the austere corridor. He dropped the spent cziana root to the floor and followed.

You take the round. But we're not done here, Andrea. Not by a long shot.

Chapter 3

I watched him, always, trying to be objective. From toddler to shy child, from awkward teenage to towering young man, I waited with a kind of sick intensity for him to fail me. He never did, even though his life and upbringing would have broken most units. Joshua 1011, child of mine, child of James Illion, you have been resilient if nothing else. So grow on, grow up, and let's see what we can make of you.

Prime Andrea Annon
Historical Archives
Terrantata Research Library

19 Years Later...
Lunar One Mock-Up Base
South Dakota Sub-surface Training Facility
Continental Regime

Joshua 1011 eased himself down onto the dusty

floor and ignored the soft gray patina on his hands and heavy-knit pants. He stared through the green aura of his light-sensitive contacts, playing with the odd and abbreviated rainbow of light that shimmered over everything. The narrow room was cluttered with chunks of ceiling tile and a tangle of air conditioning and heating conduit pipes. For a moment, he curiously watched the antiquated fluorescent tubes as they trembled a little against the sagging ceiling. Twelve other men lounged around him in various positions. Some perched fastidiously on the metal tubing, some leaned against the walls and chatted easily with their neighbors. All sported the simple black uniform that identified them as L-Groupers. And all shared the same body type and coloring: white-blond hair, pale skin, grayish eyes and medium framed athletic bodies.

All, that was, except for him. *I am the dark shadow of L-Group* he mused with a tight smile that didn't show his teeth.

Pressing back against one cracked wall, Joshua adjusted the emergency breathing tube against his cheek. The plastic rubbed a little against the high cheekbones of his face and pulled at the wisps of dark hair tucked behind his ears. He tugged a bit at the tight neckline of his uniform. *Ignore it all* his training insisted. But the air filtering in through the breathing unit tasted of chemicals and his special ordered uniforms never seemed to keep up with his growth.

Joshua dropped his fingertips to the explosive pack at his narrow waist and traced its sharp edges with his thumb. On the other side of his harness, his antique journal snuggled itself between his sidearm stunner and its spare power cells. He gently ripped the Velcro aside, looking through his eyelashes to be sure he hadn't drawn any particular attention to himself. His journal, as he liked to call it, was really a simple handpad with a hardcover for protection. With a single press, the quirky screen popped into view and exposed a screen-homed keyboard. Taking a final glance around him, he bent his head closer and began to press the letters with his pinky.

The man to his left shifted. Joshua could see the long legs out of the corner of his eye. He knew better than to look up at his Batch commander, Adam. The lithe blond man sat with him occasionally at the mess, always an arm's length away, and only speaking as if to himself. In the training center, they ran together a few times a week, but never close enough to touch. Joshua had learned that if he attempted to communicate, Adam would rebuff him by simply walking away. They had carried on this strange sort of friendship for years, a kind of familiarity and contact that was not.

"Hard to believe the real thing, Lunar One, is on the moon. Place feels like a rat cage. Lets just hope we never get popped up there." Adam's voice came out as a whisper. Joshua knew he was not expected or encouraged to reply. The blond man shoved off the wall then paused and looked down. He met Joshua's look of polite attention with a faint smile, then turned back to his duties.

Joshua watched him unobtrusively as he made his rounds, checking the equipment on his batchmates, laughing and lightening the mood with other L-Groupers. Adam, like all the command-designated soldiers stood some two to three inches taller than the other men. His face looked almost delicate, though, with thick eyelashes and gray eyes that could shade nearly lavender at times. He moved with long, graceful motions, naturally balanced and elegant.

And lethal, of course.

Joshua laid his head back against the wall as he watched Adam bend yet again to speak with a man named Garrick. *Why would it be so wrong for you to speak to me like that? What would be so terrible, Adam?*

He flicked his gaze across the floor toward the men assigned to his team. The blonds sat so close that their shoulders brushed. Their frames half-slumped against the plastic-sprayed wall behind them in an attitude of total nonchalance. The taller Alec leaned closer to Michael's ear for a moment and then sat back smiling happily.

Joshua swallowed and pulled his arm tightly to his stomach. God, how he envied their ease, their smiles, their casual contact that hinted at more intimate things.

As if he felt Joshua's stare, Alec abruptly glanced up. He nodded, cool, with no light of welcome in his gray eyes.

Joshua looked back at his journal, and jabbed vindictively at the antiquated keyboard and sent a string of X's flying across the faintly green view screen. His twenty years with the Company's feared L-Group had molded his mind and body but had also given him something else— something he knew could only be called loneliness.

He typed that word out twice, the first time slower than the second. The keys were cramped even for his fine-boned fingers. The words hung after the string of X's like tapering banners. All of L-Group was so similar, so bonded, so much a kind of singular organism.

Except for him.

The barest hint of a shadow fell across his old journal and he looked up. Brandon glowered down at him, his lips locked around a sneer. "Lonely? Poor little baby." He leaned his shoulder against the wall, his arms crossed over his chest, but his gaze lewdly raked Joshua's lap.

"Back off."

"You should really put in for Body Unit detail. Not that any self respecting L-Grouper would touch you without a dose of cziana root and proper shots, but the novelty of it could prove entertaining."

Joshua looked resolutely at the floor.

"We've been speculating about whether your cock is as long and skinny as you or if you have one at all. So maybe you could..."

Joshua exploded off the floor, and shoved his journal hard beneath Brandon's chin, knocking his blond head against the wall with a satisfying crunch. Brandon grabbed awkwardly at Joshua's throat, but snagged only air. Joshua kicked his feet out from under him, and the other man fell hard at his feet. He stepped back then, balanced and ready, still gripping his journal in his left hand.

It was all over in less than a breath.

Brandon came to his feet in a rush, his face flaming and his fingers curled deep into his palms. "You freak!"

"Brandon!" The voice exploded behind Joshua's left shoulder. Adam's tone, cold and absolutely in control, checked the other blond. The commander wove around Joshua, who still held Brandon's furious glare.

Adam thrust a finger in Brandon's face. "You fuckers never learn do you? He said back off. I think that's a good suggestion, don't you?"

"He's asking..."

"I don't want to hear it!" Adam roared. The room went wholly silent as the group fed off the small spectacle. Slit eyed, their lips open a bit in a kind of lust, the men focused on the two combatants. Their expressions wicked the worst of the red fury out of Joshua, letting him find some measure of control. *We're letting off steam, scapegoats of the others. I can feel it. We're being used, Brandon, but you don't get it.*

"Go find yourself another piece of wall to hold up, Brandon. Or so help me I will turn you over to corrections when the training mission is over." The other man, his lips still twitching and wrinkling like a dog's, growled and spun back to a far corner of the room.

Joshua stood very still, hating the eyes on him, hating the lingering euphoria and dread that hung in his veins like a kind of drug. *Not one of them can take me anymore. Not one. All they have is words and looks now.*

Unless they decided, as a group, it was again time to teach him a lesson.

"Sit down, Unit," Adam ordered him coldly as he went back to his spot.

The words stung. Joshua moved sluggishly to his patch of wall and slid down into the dust again. He snapped open the journal again, but didn't type. A tidal wave of emotions ran through him again—hatred, frustration, the awful but familiar byproducts of the separation, even isolation, he had always lived with. His fingers shook with it all. *They'll never really accept me. Never. But by God one-on-one they will never hurt me again, either.*

The room rustled and then everyone came to their feet as their mission leader, Tony, strode purposefully into the room. Joshua eased his journal back into place on his belt.

A full ten years older than the other men in

the room, the command designated L-Group commander stared at his men, his square forehead fringed by the ever-present blond hair. His eyes, however, were intensely blue. The muscles in his jaw bunched, making him look brutal in a way that Adam never would with his fine, narrow features.

Tony scanned the faces, and then prowled along the edge of the exposed piping until he occupied a central position in the room. The dust itself seemed loath to cling to his impeccable uniform.

"The orders for the mission have come through," Tony announced, his voice bouncing off the crumbling walls. "All targets have been programmed into your tracker units and your detonators have a standard three-minute count. The entire operation will be timed and evaluated, gentlemen. That means get it done clean and neat. Questions?"

He paused, but they had been through the simulations many times before, back at Central. "Alright. Alec, Michael, Joshua, you're up first."

Joshua dropped to the rear-man position on his team. They didn't even glance at him, but he could feel the ripple of their discomfort, maybe their embarrassment at being group with him.

Tony's eyes traced their battle harness, their faces.

For a moment, the senior commander focused on Alec. The two men seemed to contend with each other for a moment, a battle of unknown origins. Joshua let a little frown pucker his forehead, reading something other than the typical military bravado there. For a moment, Joshua was sure Tony would say something, but instead, the commander pointed to the door. "Begin."

He trailed the other two into the dusty passageway, vaguely relieved that his team would go first. The sound of their footsteps bounded off the low ceilings of the hallway and eddied away into the regularly marked intersections corridors.

Joshua settled easily into his long, loose stride. The precise slap of their feet against the floor raised a soft cloud of dust that fluttered out and away from them.

Minutes later, Alec bent his head over his tracker as they jogged along. The red corridor lights began to give out as they passed intersection 52. Finally, they were forced to slow, picking their way over rubble that time and other training exercises had dislodged. At the next junction, Joshua turned with his teammates into a hall of nearly unbroken blackness. His sensitive contacts strained to pick up the sparse light, and finally he could just make out a series of downed panels and shattered glass. They slid over the crunching refuse, hands trailing the wall a bit for an extra sense of balance.

The target was a system relay room that, in a fully functioning base, would have been a vital and protected communication nexus. If this were a full combat exercise, Joshua knew they would have expected to meet with an organized resistance here, but this run was a simple real-time run to get used to accurately placing the explosives.

Nonetheless, they approached the room cautiously as they had been trained. The room glittered with lazy dust currents. The tall conductor tubes in the middle of the space shimmering through his contacts, a green and hulking presence within.

Michael shifted the explosives off this belt. "What do you say I take this first one, boss?"

Alec grunted at the patently playful slang, but a little smile edged his lips. "Go."

Joshua crouched opposite Alec, just outside the doorframe. He rubbed at his eyes with the back of his hand. Damn the dust anyway. Maybe the oxygen pack wasn't such a superfluous addition after all. He lifted his eyes to the four information cylinders, running from floor to ceiling that dominated the center of the room. Each was thick as a man, and set with myriad readout screens. Michael carefully attached the hand-sized pack to the largest columns. "I'm setting the counter," he called over his shoulder. "Max blast array...should take out the whole tube system. Might take out a lot of the room above this, too, but shouldn't get to much lateral damage if the specs were entered in the preprogram correctly. Get ready to move on three...NO!"

The explosion ripped through the little room, slamming Alec and Joshua backwards. Joshua kicked out and flung himself further into the corridor and landed hard on his stomach. He scrambled to cover his head as an avalanche of debris crashed down on him, pinning him face down on the floor.

Joshua scraped frantically at the smooth surface with his bloody hands, gasping. He tried to shove at the chunks of metal and concrete, but no matter how he strained, he could only reach immovable, tortured metal. The rubble settled with a low screech and he screamed as the debris bit deeply into his legs. For long moments, all he could do was retch and writhe. Dimly through it all, he remembered he was not alone.

"Alec!" he twisted his upper body around to his left, searching through the gyrating ripples of dust for the other L-Grouper.

Alec lay trapped just a few feet away from him. He turned his face toward Joshua and reached out a torn hand. A thin curl of fluid snaked from his nose, over his lips and chin. He opened his mouth, but only a rush of dark blood came out.

"Alec." Joshua swallowed hard. He choked on the dust as he strained to reach the other man. He couldn't quite touch those broken fingers. A moment later, the hand dropped back to the floor and the dimming gray eyes slid away.

Joshua stared at him in disbelief, and then buried his own face in the crook of his arm. Memories of broken bodies he'd helped clear after the last United Cal Territory quake awoke from where he thought he had caged them, and taunted him with their smell, their tattered skin and their terrible fogged eyes. Worse, he could feel the pain building in his legs and spine, could feel his hipbone grinding into the cold floor.

Shock. Shock is what kills.

He closed his eyes, trying to breathe slowly, shutting out the pain, shutting out Alec's slack, bloody face. *They will come. They will come soon.* He listened to his breath in the silence and clung desperately to that frail thread whispering over his lips and bared teeth.

By the time the rescue team arrived, he was no longer totally coherent. He dimly watched them dig at the wreckage, levering up the heavy chunks to pull him free.

He found himself startling a little at the faces that drifted in and out of his line of vision, hands doing efficient jobs without any sense of compassion in them. A lance of pain thrust him almost to consciousness.

"Stop...the...the pain..." he panted.

Commander Tony loomed over him, studying him with cold gray eyes. "Pain, Joshua?" He glanced around and then leaned closer, his lips nearly brushing the edge of Joshua's ear. "Did you see, when it happened? Did you *see*?"

Joshua tossed his head, twisting with the growing agony, not understanding the question. "Alec...Michael...dead in the blast. Faulty set-pack. Too much juice."

A voice drifted from further off, not a conversation he had tried to hear, but it came to him anyway, unbidden. "You're wrong. Had to be an accident. L-Group doesn't kill its own."

"Yeah, but he's not L-Group. Not really," came a low and bitter reply.

Something sharp jabbed into Joshua's arm, and he thankfully let the meds silence and darken it all.

—

Commander Tony crouched on his heels in the dust. A handpad lay at his feet, one corner of its plastic case shattered. He picked it up and cradled it in the palm of his hand. The silence here felt good; the work crews would return tomorrow to dig what was left of Michael's body out of the wreckage. Only their tracks in the cloying dust remained, like a tantalizing after-image of flesh and blood men. He raised his eyes to the shattered room and breathed deeply, the nose-tube that dragged at his nostrils and cheek only a minor irritant.

He smiled into the chaos.

With a flick of his wrist, Tony flipped the hand-pad open and touched the activation key. It bravely glimmered to life, displaying the last entry. *Loneliness* it read. He frowned, turned the pad over in his hand, then returned again to the screen. He scanned the words upwards, past a string of X's, past the Lunar One heading. Where the text changed from single word inanities to fuller paragraphs, he began to read.

I am aware that beyond the physical differences that separate me from my group, I think completely differently than my batchmates. I won again at Tel-Menar this evening; it has become easy for me. But I find I am beginning to fear the joy that comes when I humiliate one of them; I fear the satisfaction. This cannot be honorable, these feelings of jubilation and revenge, but I do glory in it. And that further separates me from them all in the end.

Tony closed the journal with a quick snap of his fingers and stood. "Joshua," he muttered. He stared at it a moment longer, his jaw clenching so hard that knots rose beneath his cheekbones. He hurled the piece of machinery against the wall. It rebounded with a hollow whack, and hit the floor, the outer casing riddling with fine cracks.

His eyes fell to the spot where Alec's body had been pulled from the rubble. He strode over, glowering down at the rusty-brown stains on the cement. "What did you feel, Alec?" he whispered fiercely. "Tell me. Did you lay here bleeding and finally think of me? I dreamed I would know when you died, here, in my mind." He touched his forehead with one long finger. Tony crouched again, in slow motion. His fingers traced long lines in the dust as if he could sift Alec from it. "I waited for the feelings, but nothing came. In the end, you robbed me of that, too, the ability to connect with you." Tony rubbed the dried blood and dust between his fingers, lingering over the sensation. He brought his fingertips to his lips and closed his eyes. "It doesn't matter, though. No more Michael, Alec. No more you. I win."

"Win..." the hall echoed back his thoughts.

Tony raised his head with a frown. He scanned the rubble, the flickers of light at the end of the tunnel where a lone light panel still functioned sporadically. Slowly, he turned his gaze to the floor again. "You knew I wanted you dead, didn't you. You saw it this morning when you looked into my eyes...you *knew*."

"Knew..." the hall echoed inside of his skull.

Tony's eyes drifted to another spot on the floor and his face hardened until his skin glowed an almost transparent white. His mouth worked, tongue and lips wrestling with emotions that refused to become words. Fists clenched, arms rigidly bent, he threw back his head. "No!" he screamed. "Him? You shared your last minutes with him? What did you tell him? What?" He threw himself to his feet, backing and stumbling down the hall, his voice rising in the empty corridor. "It won't work, Alec! No one will believe him! I'll kill him! Do you hear me? I'll kill him like I killed you!"

"Kill him..." the corridor reverberated.

Tony froze.

"Like I killed you..." something whispered from the wreckage.

Tony hunched his shoulders, his eyes flickering wildly. "No." He pressed his hands against his ears and drove his fingers, claw-like, into his scalp. He scuttled up the decimated hall in a jerky, uncoordinated run.

Chapter 4

The lack of L-Group's ability to recognize pain as pain has been an interesting psychological issue to study. In some ways, it maximizes their functionality, this tendency for them to sense only cold or in some more unusual cases, a kind of pleasure when they are injured. Not only do their bodies continue to function in situations no NCP could tolerate, their minds remain wholly focused on the business at hand. But we are getting more and more data that suggests that their aggressive sexual encounters may, in fact, be traced to the same characteristic. That may, in the future, require more fine-tuning by our Genotemplate Tech Grade Eights. For nothing can so disrupt a Group's functionality as the personal dynamics within it.

Psychtech Report
Company Center Research

Company Central, Earth Complex
L-Group Med Labs

The circle of boys jeered at him, shoving Joshua
from one side of the moving enclosure of their
bodies to the other. Their young muscles shone
beneath the lights, but their faces were aged with
hate. He could feel their fists, punching his naked
stomach, his shoulders, then grabbing his wrists,
shoving him face first onto the white tiles of the
Arena shower room. Someone snatched at his
shoulder-length hair and jerked his head back.

"Cut it all off!" one boy screamed.

"Yeah, all of it!"

Joshua struggled madly. He felt the strands of
his own hair rip out at the root as he fought. He
struck out with his foot, hearing a yelp of pain.
The hands slackened on his wrists. He twisted,
crazed, wanting to hurt them. With a final
wrench, he tore free, flipped to his back, and kicked
up into the nearest naked stomach. The impact
landed with a solid thump and the young L-
Grouper fell back with a sharp exhale.

The opening was all he needed. He leapt to
his feet, his stance low, his eyes set and hard in his
skull. The circle retreated, more wary now, but the
smiles came back to the pale faces, lips pulled back

from white, even teeth. They were L-Group. They
understood battle.

If they all came at him at once, he would go
down again. He knew that, even as he stood them
off, his long hair sliding over his naked shoulders,
his fists clenched. And they would take liberties
with a great deal more than his too-long hair.
"Come on!" he screamed at them. "Come on!"

They did.

Joshua jerked up in bed with a cry. He heard
the startled gasp at his shoulder as someone
scuttled back. He cast around him wildly, the
sweat streaming down the sides of his face. No
circle of boys closed in on him, no laser cutters
prepared to hack at his hair and scalp. Only the
cold metal room of the familiar med-center
bounced his ragged breath off its walls. He
turned his head, staring at the med-tech who
cowered a few steps away, his pasty face and gray
hair making him look like a pale caricature of a
human.

Then the pain hit.

He dropped back against the pillow with a
hiss. "How bad?"

"Bad. But the mend is proceeding well," the
med-tech said, his voice still a low quavering
thing. "Body defenses have responded within L-

Group norms. You'll be back on your feet in another day."

Joshua nodded and clenched his eyes shut. He sent his breath down deep into his legs, into the raw heat in his muscles and bones.

"According to your records, your pain receptors are more active than in other L-Groupers. I can get you something for the pain. It'll help you sleep, too."

"No," Joshua gasped out between his clenched teeth. "I've slept enough."

"But..."

"Get out."

"Now look, Unit..." the tech began.

"Leave me alone!" he cried. Behind tightly shut eyes, he heard the quiet curse, the door sliding shut, leaving him in silence. He arched back into the pillows and threw one hand across his face. The techs never understood his inner battles. They always wanted to bring the drugs, the painkillers, the sleeping meds. Awake and aware, he could control this level of pain. He *would* control it.

Breathe. Feel the pain and know that you feel discomfort only because it is something new. Make it part of you. Make it normal, and the sensation of pain will stop.

He let the breath drive the tension away. "I am L-Group. This pain is not real," he murmured. "I am L-Group. This pain is not real." Over and over he muttered the mantra, breath and words flowing together. And as it always did, the pain receded and time ceased to have meaning.

—

Two days later, Joshua slipped through the outer command offices on shaky legs, barely glancing at the sparse furnishings. He could hear transports, both private and large carriers humming beyond the walls. He tapped on the doorframe to the inner office, feeling the vibration in his knuckles and wrists as he struck the metal.

"Come."

Joshua opened the door and hobbled into the office. He stopped just in front of the desk, laced his fingers behind his back and widened his stance. His legs ached, and he quickly knotted his hands, willing the sensation down.

Commander Drew, head of the Company's L-Group operations, waved his data screen aside and folded his arms on his desk. Off in one lonely corner of his workstation, a violet dropped its fuzzy leaves against a stained white coffee cup. His office walls, simple by the standards of any age, sported only an abstract painting of lines spiraling away from a tiny red dot. It rose behind the commander as a wild backdrop. The other walls gathered close, gray, and bleak around the metal desk. Joshua stared at the painting for a moment until his eyes burned a little and the sensation forced his eyes back to Drew.

"What happened out there, 1011?"

Joshua blinked, startled by the intensity of Drew's gaze. "Sir, with all due respect, I've been answering that questions for days now. If you've read the reports, why are you asking?'

"Yes, I've looked all that over," Drew said patiently. "And I've read Tony's reports as well. I'm asking you, as the senior officer of L-Group, if anything *unusual* happened at the training base prior to the accident. Any little thing at all?"

Joshua shook his head. He could feel his legs shaking as the repaired muscle tissue tried to respond accurately to the new nerve and chemical impulses. It would go away in a few days, the med-techs had assured him. At least the bones hadn't been so badly damaged that they needed replacing; he had gotten off with just a fuse patch. His genetically enhanced body, the inner recuperative elements that made L-Groupers far superior to NCP troops, would take care of the rest.

"It was a standard training mission, Sir," Joshua found himself saying. "Nothing out of the ordinary occurred prior to the accident." He looked full into Drew's face, hoping the man could read his sincerity.

Drew shifted his slender frame back into the chair with a sigh. According to L-Group rumors, this man had come up through the ranks much faster than the standard command designated units. To Joshua, he radiated an assurance and cool detachment more reminiscent of the Administrator classes.

"Tell me you aren't protecting someone, 1011."

Joshua frowned in confusion. "No, Sir. I have no reason to protect anyone."

"Not even yourself?"

Joshua felt a little heat rise into his cheeks. He clenched his hands hard behind his back. "What are you asking, Sir?"

"Did you set the explosives to go off on your team members?" Drew posed the question calmly and even reached to retrieve his coffee mug from the edge of the table. He took a sip, and then set it down with a grimace. "Well? Are you hoping someone will answer for you?"

"No," Joshua said, his voice bitter and emphatic. "I should not have to remind you, Sir, that L-Groupers do not kill other L-Groupers." The shaking in his legs grew worse and for one terrible instant, his left knee began to buckle. He shifted his weight to the right, furious that Drew might interpret his body language as a subtle admission of guilt.

"There are those," the commander frowned, "who say you aren't a real member of L-Group. That the strictures that bind these Company products together do not apply to you."

"They're wrong," Joshua retorted, feeling the blood pound in his temples. He immediately regretted his quick flair of temper. More and more he found himself reacting without thinking, like a slow burning itch in the middle of his brain kept him in a constant state of irritation. The pain added to that itch, making him feel more than a little off-balanced.

Drew sighed, a sound that echoed the soft sag in his shoulders. He shoved the coffee mug away from him with a nonchalant and practiced hand. "I'm not your enemy, Joshua. I happen to believe everything you are telling me. I've seen you fight, you know. It would have been easier for you to break their necks in a Tel-Menar match. Nice and official that way."

Joshua opened his mouth to protest, but Drew waved him silent.

"The fact remains that a great deal of evidence points to a purposeful manipulation of the explosive units. If you remember anything significant or maybe even something just a little off, you notify me at once. And only me. Understood?"

Joshua nodded. "Yes, Sir." The older man's words made him feel both awkwardly young and relieved. *He believes me.* And Drew had noticed him in Tel-Menar, had seen how good he'd become. He shifted his weight gingerly back to his left leg, anticipating a dismissal.

But Drew surprised him.

The man purposefully turned away from Joshua and leaned back in his chair. He seemed to stare up at his strange painting. "You were pinned for over an hour, I understand. How did you manage it?"

"Sir?"

"How did you manage to survive? The med-center said you shouldn't have. You lost a lot of blood. That alone should have taken you out."

Joshua shook his head, not wanting to recall the ordeal. "I went someplace in my mind where I could wait. Someplace safe, where time isn't the same." The words sounded vague, silly even to him. He wondered how Drew could ever understand the feeling of standing alone in one's mind, of fleeing the outer world with nothing but breath and a tenuous control. L-Groupers didn't do things like that. They didn't have to.

Drew pivoted his chair around. "You feel pain, don't you? And standing here, you can't concentrate enough to really block it, can you?"

Joshua nodded, slowly, as if someone had grasped the back of his head with an unseen hand and shoved his chin down in a stiff affirmative. "As noted in my personnel records."

"Are you aware what we feel, when we are injured?"

"*We* being other L-Groupers." He couldn't help himself.

Drew raised his eyebrow but didn't answer.

"Cold. I...I think that's how it was once described to me."

"Yes," Drew answered. "Cold, and with some, it takes on a kind of dull pleasure." He flexed his fingers before his face, and then laid his hand flat on his desk. "You've found on the Tel-

Menar courts that we aren't exactly immune to impact-related injuries, though. Scrambles our brains a bit. I've read the civilians envy us, our unique reactions to pain. But sometimes..." Drew shook his head and stared down at his own hand.

Joshua watched him, his own breath light and high in his chest.

"You've tried to deal with your pain like you think an L-Grouper would, like you don't really feel what is there?"

"Maybe." The commander's words struck too close to home.

"How long have you been doing this? Finding this inner way around the pain?"

Inner way around the pain? Joshua turned the phrase over in his mind, wondering why he was so transparent to Drew. "I've tried to find ways around pain for as long as I can remember."

"And who taught you?"

"No one. I guess I figured it out myself."

"How?" Drew asked. He almost whispered the question.

Joshua dropped his gaze to the floor. His heavy black hair fell forward across his cheeks, and he shoved it back behind his shoulder. "I think I used it for the first time when I broke my arm in a training exercise," Joshua said.

"When you broke your arm, or someone broke it for you?"

Joshua swallowed. "I broke my own arm. Fell badly."

"Was that the time you suffered a radial fracture? And a broken nose, a cracked rib, laser burns on your scalp, some more internal injuries of personal nature? When you fall, you really do it right, don't you? But please, by all means, continue."

The heat in Joshua's face escalated to a throbbing burn. His leg muscles screamed. He could feel cold fingers of sweat tickle beneath his armpits and down his spine. "If you already know so much..."

"I want to hear it from you." Drew's voice carried just the barest whip-flick of impatience.

Joshua stared at him stonily. His commander raised his eyebrows, waiting.

"It took some time for help to come after that particular *occurrence*," Joshua murmured. He felt his eyes shift from the commander's face again. "I learned that if I concentrated on breathing, just breathing, I didn't feel the pain as intensely."

"And is that true for other kinds of pain, Joshua?"

"Sir?" He blinked back the ache in his legs, not sure he had heard the question correctly.

"Never mind," Drew replied. He reached for his coffee cup again and turned it in a precise circle on his desktop. "Do you see anything, when you breathe like that?" he asked quietly. "Visions or nightmares? Anything?"

"No. I hear my breath. That's all." Joshua forced himself to swallow the cottony dregs of moisture in his throat. *What game are you playing with me, Drew? And why?*

The commander abruptly shoved his mug away. "You're dismissed, 1011." But his voice still held the echo of unasked questions.

Joshua snapped a quick salute and walked clumsily from the windowless room. He hated the stiffness, the pain. It made him feel vulnerable.

But not as vulnerable as the man who waited for him in the front office.

Adam.

The L-Grouper nodded to him as he replaced his plastic passkey in the hip pocket of his uniform.

"Good evening, Commander," Joshua murmured. He hovered by Drew's door, unsure whether to simply move around his batch-mate or remain where he stood. Adam actually smiled at him, the expression lifting his face and brightening it.

"You still look sore," Adam noted casually. The L-Grouper stepped out of Joshua's escape path and gestured to one battered chair. "Sit before you tip over."

Joshua hesitated a moment but as his knee tried to buckle again, he gave in and eased himself down on one chair edge, trying to make it look less like a near-fall than it was.

"I've always heard the post accident interrogations were hard to go through," Adam said. He cocked his head a bit to the side, and smiled again. His black uniform clung to his almost too-slender frame, and his large eyes and sharp cheekbones gave him an almost feline appearance. Joshua had learned to notice all the little differences that separated L-Grouper from L-Grouper and even clung to the realization that they, too, were not entirely alike.

And he had studied Adam for years, knew each line of his face, every motion of his body.

"It wasn't so bad," Joshua said uneasily. "Just monotonous." He looked into those gray eyes. "Were you waiting for me, Sir?"

Adam shrugged his shoulders beneath his

black uniform. "Yes, as a matter of fact. Commander Drew asked if I could take you in hand for a while. I thought we could start training tomorrow morning, but take it slow. We could play some Tel-Menar if you're up to it later in the week. Might be nice to beat you for once." Joshua didn't miss the predatory flicker in Adam's eyes.

"I'm not sure I'll be ready for Tel-Menar. My legs are still pretty weak."

Adam's face quirked, as if Joshua's admission was something he found amusing. "Well, we'll see how it goes. You must feel rotten if you are turning down the chance to flaunt your staff skills."

"Not exactly legendary," Joshua murmured. "But thank you."

Adam seemed to let his face fall into lines of supreme indifference then. He stuffed his hands in his pockets. "Look, my job is to get you going, get you involved in what you like to do so those legs heal faster." He stopped a moment, and Joshua nearly shivered as those gray eyes traveled over him.

Adam seemed to read his expression. "This isn't friendship I'm offering you, 1011. I'm following orders, that's all."

Something in Joshua recoiled, hot and embarrassed by the tone of Adam's voice. *Just orders. Of course. Why would things ever be different between us?*

"I understand, Commander. And thank you." He rose to his feet, brushed off a quick salute without meeting Adam's eyes and limped from the room.

Chapter 5

I cannot say it aloud, because it would pass from lip to lip like a virus in the barracks. But I can think it, staring at the ceiling from my loft's mattress. I find Joshua 1011 wholly beautiful, his darkness, his smile, his raw and sometimes stupid courage. I have always known one day I will take whatever opening I get, and hold that long hair in my fist and kiss him hard enough to bruise. Even if I have to give him up the next instant, it would be worth it. And I hate myself for such thoughts, because he is everything L-Group is not, and I should not desire him so. It is just another part of me that is different and wrong.

Commander Adam
L-Group Batch 416

L-Group Training Center
Company Central, Earth Complex

The fourth floor of the training center pulsed with early morning runners. The high steel arches above the track supported a series of crystalline skylights and L-Groupers paced themselves through the alternating patterns of sunshine and shadow, their blond hair one moment dazzling, the next just softly illuminated. Adam and Joshua worked the outer edge of the track, leaving the inner lane for the sprinters. They ran stride for stride, fists lightly balled and backs straight.

Joshua snuck a glance at Adam. His batch-mate moved with a kind of economy, wholly and unconsciously beautiful. The sheen of sweat on his bare chest only highlighted the grace and power of his movement. Joshua secretly enjoyed watching Adam here and everywhere they had been for nearly a month. He could easily picture the man; head braced against his hand in concentration, his hair jutting through the edges of his fingers as he studied the Tech layouts for their next training mission or laying flat on his back on the Tel-Menar court, laughing at his own mistake. He remembered the warm light in

Adam's eyes when Joshua had finally kicked the top half of the punching bag after two long weeks of humiliating attempts. The young commander caught Joshua's gaze and smiled even as he picked up the pace.

He couldn't ignore the other L-Grouper eyes that passed over them, but he liked to think they were more accepting of him. Still, when a faster runner slowed up, and trotted backwards for a few strides, he tensed. The other man yelled at them, "you ready to answer all those questions we have about his other *staff work*, Commander?"

Joshua, prepared to shrug it off with a lifetime of practice, heard only a guttural curse from his running mate. "You son of a bitch!" Adam leaped forward, a lean and angry arrow straight at the man who had thrown the jibe. Joshua turned with him, following in Adam's wake. In less than fifteen strides, Adam caught the other man and shoved him hard against the plexiglas inner wall of the track. The two went down in a mass of twisting arms and legs.

Adam seized the other man's throat with his long fingers and dragged the L-Grouper to his feet. He slammed the struggling young man against the wall and that section of the partition shuddered with the impact. Joshua dove between them, putting his back to the hapless soldier's flushed face and thrust his hands hard against Adam's chest. "Let him go, Adam! It's just barrack talk. Just barrack talk!"

"I'm going to fucking kill you, too! Get out of my way!" Adam snarled.

"Leave it! Now!" Joshua shoved him hard again, backing him away from the other dazed man by sheer force. Adam finally ripped himself away, tearing at his own hair with his fingers, still seething.

The blond man behind him slid down the wall as Joshua turned to help. But he was still conscious enough to slap at Joshua's proffered hand. "Stay away from me, you freak." He tried to clamber up the wall, wobbled, and almost went down again.

Joshua raised his hands, palms out and backed away. A little knot of men gathered, helped the other man to his feet, their elbows roughly pushing Joshua aside.

He let them.

Adam was pacing the outer edge of the track like a caged animal. He glared at Joshua, his hands flexing in agitation. He pointed a stiff finger into Joshua's face. "That's the trouble with you, Joshua. You take it all and take more, again and again."

"That's not true. It's just that I pick my battles, Adam. That was just lip. We should both be used to..."

"Used to it? I am a command-designated unit. I shouldn't have to take that kind of shit from anyone. Neither should you. Take that guy's head off next time, and that will make them shut up for good. That's an order!"

Joshua stared at him a moment, then turned away. "I'm heading for the showers."

"I'm not done here."

"I am," Joshua retorted.

"Don't you fucking walk away from me!"

Joshua turned slowly back, his eyes snapping to his commander. "Yes, Sir," he replied. For a moment, he was sure Adam would strike him. In fact, he wanted the blond man to try. They contended silently a moment. Then he forced himself, willed himself, to soften. "Adam, why are you doing this? Jumping on that guy like you're a maniac? They're going to lock you in solitary Refit for a month if you don't settle down."

"That's my problem, not yours," Adam retorted.

"What are you doing? I mean, running with

me, throwing yourself at that guy. I think I liked you better when you played your little games. What is it you want from me?"

Adam glared at him but said nothing, his chest heaving with his stifled emotions. He walked forward, his gaze hot and focused and stopped just inches from Joshua, looking up into his face. Joshua felt his height keenly, only a few inches, but it separated the men like a wall.

"There have been times when you wanted to kill one of us. Or maybe the whole damn batch. Am I right, 1011?"

Joshua blinked, his mind scrambling to keep up. His hands trembled at his sides, and he knotted them into fists as he searched for some measure of steadiness. "Yeah. You'd have to be an idiot not to get that. But L-Groupers don't kill other L-Groupers."

Adam stared at him for a moment. His eyes, palest gray against his flushed skin, went wide as if Joshua had said something both funny and profound at once. Then, the edges of his mouth twitched and Adam threw back his head and laughed.

Joshua frowned, suddenly groundless in the rapid mood change. He let his hands go helplessly slack at his sides as he watched his batch-mate.

"God, you're too much," Adam chortled. "L-Groupers don't..." and he laughed again. "Leave it to you to quote some part of the soldier's morality manual in the middle of a fucking fight."

Adam's bright laughter floored him, and something in him shifted uncomfortably. How could this behavior be normal? The fighting, the yelling, that he understood. But standing under Adam's laughter, somehow shoved outside it, that both confused and burned him.

"Showers it is. Then breakfast." Adam turned away from him, evidently assuming Joshua would follow.

And after a moment, he did.

—

The L-Group personnel quarters lay deep underground along the far western edge of the enclosed Company complex. A limited access area, complete with laser security and long tunnels of gray metal walls, it conveyed nothing other than offhanded simplicity and a clear message for others to steer clear. As any given batch aged, the Company allowed each soldier a modicum of privacy in the form of a cramped and bare apartment, although the men still took their meals together in a common mess hall.

Joshua followed Adam through the security maze and trailed him up the ramps to his room.

Adam, a towel and his running shorts folded haphazardly over his arm, dug into his uniform pocket for his passcard. He dropped it and Joshua immediately stooped to pick it up for him. His batch-mate accepted it without thanks and automatically keyed his door. He had been quiet most the way in from the mess, his pale brow furrowed and his eyes far away.

He turned to go, but Adam reached out and touched his arm.

Joshua hesitated a moment, then followed the other man into his apartment. The little room, barely twelve by twelve feet sported a simple loft with a battered green-gray couch beneath it. A water bottle snuggled between two of the cushions. On the left wall, a door led into a tight bathroom, and on the right, the Company logo splayed across the bare metal walls in a series of interlocking circles, each a different color designating the various departments. Joshua visually traced the black L-Group circle with his usual vague mix of belonging and disquiet.

Adam threw himself down on the couch and dropped his head back. "I lost my temper."

Joshua perched at the far end of the sofa. He wished for a moment that he could relax into the cushions like Adam, but old habits died very hard indeed. He could feel dampness gathering in the palms of his hands, but he was too self-conscious to even wipe them on his pants. "It's OK, Adam. Happens. We're all a little live-wired."

"There are times when I feel like I can't breathe at all," Adam whispered without raising his head off the couch.

Joshua glanced at him uncertainly.

"Sometimes following orders—I just want to throw it all back in their faces. Or drive one of the 'lectric transports right into one of those damn Company logos. Live-wired? Hell, I'm not wired like *anyone* else, Joshua. I feel things, dream things..."Adam broke off, his eyes closed, his cheek bones pressed cruelly beneath his fine skin.

Adam's words made him uncomfortable. "Have you talked with the psychtechs..."?

"Damn the psychtechs!" Adam exploded, rolling forward, his arms braced over his knees. "They've never been L-Groupers, so how are they supposed to know what we can and cannot feel?

Yes, I've tried to talk to them! They always end up giving me a little blue pill, or a yellow one, or goddamn rainbow handful of them. And I flush them, every damn one."

Joshua wondered at that moment how he could gracefully extricate himself from Adam's apartment.

Adam fell back, as if spent after his little tirade. He lifted one hand and flexed his fingers. The overhead lamp shone through the tips of his fingernails. "Commander Drew is a weird one, too."

"What do you mean?" Joshua asked, unsure he was following the turns of the conversation. He finally shoved himself back into the corner of the couch as if it were a defensible position.

"He wanted to know what I dream about."

"And what did you say?" Joshua asked.

"I told him I dream about being out in the open, away from all the walls. And do you know what he told me?"

Joshua shook his head.

"He said I should try going to a place like that, a field say, in my mind when I am awake." Adam clenched his fist, driving his illuminated fingernails into the shadow of his palm. "I told him I didn't understand what he meant. How can anyone dream wide-awake? He's crazy, like me, like...like some of the other commanders. I know it." He opened his palm and Joshua could see little half-moons of blood where he had driven his own nails into his skin.

Joshua started to rock forward, then decided not moving might be the better plan.

Adam stared at the wounds. "I can't feel what I am supposed to feel. This should hurt, shouldn't it? He thrust his palm out at Joshua. "You could feel this, couldn't you?"

"If you want me to go..." he murmured, ignoring the question. He knew he should walk away. Safer, once he closed the door behind him.

But Adam abruptly rolled to his side, and reached out to grasp Joshua's wrist. "No. Don't go."

Joshua swallowed, his eyes on the white fingers wrapping the darker skin of his arm. He didn't try to pull away.

"Come here," Adam tugged.

Joshua didn't move for a moment, not sure he had actually heard the invitation implied in word and gesture. His pulse ratcheted up and his mouth went dry. He looked into Adam's delicate face, into the gray eyes that regarded him with unflinching intensity. The long tendons of the other man's neck shifted as he leaned toward him. "God, don't make me order you to do this," Adam whispered.

Joshua leaned forward and let himself be pulled into a bruising kiss. Adam, without releasing his wrist, placed his fingertips against Joshua's face, as if shielding him from the blood in his palm. The fingers traced back, cupped the base of his neck and pulled him in even tighter. He thrust his tongue into Joshua's yielding mouth, darting, exploring, his fingers knitting finally into his dark hair.

For a while, Joshua hung weakly in Adam's hungry grasp, letting the other man do whatever he wished, even as the kisses began to feather over his chin and down the long line of his throat, even as Adam's fingers began to shove his uniform shirt up over his nipples. He'd never been kissed before, had certainly never kissed back. He felt painfully awkward and self-conscious, even as he felt his own cock rise, heard his own breath turn deep and hungry.

Then Adam's head sank toward his chest, his perfect white teeth nipping at the tender nubs there. Joshua threw his head back with a low moan, finally wriggling out of the death grip Adam had on his wrist, only to feel the other man grab his shirt with both hands and lift. Joshua raised his arms to pull the uniform top totally off, but Adam twisted the fabric around his wrists and shoved hard with his torso and hip, demanding Joshua put his back to him.

As soon as he shifted, he could feel Adam's hand on his crotch, grabbing his cock and balls through the heavy fabric of his pants. His hands were pinned behind his neck and he could feel the hard, warm length of his batch-mate pressing along his spine. He arched into Adam, thoughts tumbling together and dissolving into incoherence.

It was about sensation now, Adam's tongue on his back, tracing down his hot skin, Adam's fingers ripping at his belt and zipper, stripping his pants off his hips and finally Adam's hand closing around his package, squeezing, tracing and stroking in long, firm motions. Touch, glorious touch, without battle, without any trace of anger or distaste. He wanted to roll over, to free his hands, to touch Adam back, to feel all of him.

"Don't move," Adam whispered in his ear. Joshua heard the sound of the other man's uniform rustling off, falling away. Something cool and slippery touched his hole and he dropped his forehead to the arm of the couch, his chest painfully full of his thundering heart. And then, Adam was sliding in, just a bit, very slowly, his hands gripping Joshua's shoulders. He felt hot, full, the condom a little sticky and burning. He felt for several breaths as if he would rip wide, but the sharp pain passed quickly and then Adam's erection seemed to reach up to the base of his heart before sliding back.

The blond eased into a gentle rhythm, worked in and out, silent except for the quickening of his breath, and the vise grip of his hands that nearly encircled Joshua's neck. It was revelation and belonging, it was contact and being claimed, and each movement drove Joshua closer to his own climax. He suddenly could feel Adam jerking deep within him and he cried out with the sensations.

He wanted so badly to come as well, but Adam grasped his cock hard, freed his arms and pushed him over onto his back. The blond man knelt and took Joshua deep in his throat, then withdrew a bit. His tongue licked and played over the edges of his dark head, stabbing at the small slit there, his hands reached up and twisted at Joshua's nipples. Then, he took the cock deeply again, and Joshua could feel Adam's throat working all along his shaft. When he came it was hard, almost unexpected, and he grabbed the back of Adam's head as if he could grip the sensation forever.

For a long moment, Adam simply crouched with his head against Joshua's thigh as their breath evened out. His hand stroked Joshua's soft inside thigh, but he was trembling and jerky, his gestures anything but languid. Then he rose and without a word, without a glance, stalked to the bathroom and slammed the door shut.

For a long time, Joshua just sat there, naked and empty and a little sore. When the shower kicked on, he closed his eyes for a moment, willing the hurt and anger and confusion deep into his gut. Finally, he quietly stood, dressed, and let himself out.

Chapter 6

They cannot help but obey. It is both hardwired into their natures and then the response is further conditioned through years of training. Fuss, talk back, blow up, act out sexually, these are fine ways to let off the constant steam they seep in, but once they are given a command from a man of higher rank, that is the end of tension for them. Go! And they go, without question or remorse as if relieved to be aimed and fired at last.

NCP L-Group Observation Notes
Core Libraries, Earth Node

Tel-Menar Courts
Company Central, Earth Complex

Joshua read the digital summons for an early evening Tel-Menar match with only a dull sense of resignation. He was tired, and a kind of heavy depression was settling over him, working its darkness into his bones. In the end he simply fell into bed, after setting his data pad to wake him in time for the match. There were studies he had to see to, tech reports to go over, but all he wanted was for his mind to stop replaying his sexual encounter with Adam.

And sleep seemed the best way to do that, hang all other duties.

It felt like he had barely laid his head on his pillow when the alarm jerked him out of bed. I was hard to move at first; his body ached and his throat seemed knotted around itself. But eventually, he forced himself to shower and made his way to the stadium.

When he arrived at the Tel-Menar courts, he sat down heavily on the faux-marble bench in the changing room. White enameled lockers surrounded him, and somewhere a showerhead dripped small fortune into its drain. He let himself lay back on the bench with groan, swiping at his forehead and irritated to find himself sweating so heavily. A deep pressure lurked behind his eyes and every twist of his neck was shot through with a little finger of pain. The body aches were growing, shivering down his spine and settling deep into his thighs. He tried staring up at the crystalline skylights overhead, tried to direct his breath into his belly and ride the illness out.

It did not help that Adam's face appeared again and again before his mind's eye, and his gut replayed the morning tryst to the point of agitation. It made no sense to him now, the physical closeness, or the Adam's erratic behavior prior to it.

He finally stood on shaky legs and opened one of the lockers. He never dressed here; it felt sacrilegious somehow. The perfect white lockers, the skylights, everything around him was detailed and richly appointed, nothing like the L-Group compound. This was the land of the Administrator caste.

Inside the locker, he tapped the control that brought up a full-length mirror on the back of the cabinet. He surveyed his outfit with a critical eye, tracing the neat buttons that ran along his left side and plunged finally into a tight cummerbund. The padded white outfit washed out his features a little and highlighted the deep blue smudges of skin beneath his eyes. An empty Velcro patch on his left arm would soon bear the colors he had been designated to wear for the evening. Any color was OK as far as he was concerned. He wasn't nearly as superstitious as some L-Groupers, but then, they didn't win as much as he did, no matter what the color.

"Data screen on," he murmured. The projection mirror flickered and then displayed the Company logo. "Please enter your request." The voice that emerged from the locker's speaker pronounced the words slowly enough for a two year old to understand.

"Tel-Menar doubles, tonight. Who's playing and what are the color designations?"

"There are no doubles scheduled for tonight's Administrator court."

Joshua frowned. "List events please."

"First event, Tel-Menar single combat. Joshua 1011, L-Group Batch 416, playing blue. Adam, Command class L-Group batch 416 playing red. Second event..."

"Hold and close," Joshua interrupted the feed. The data link complied, returning to the mirror that reflected far too much glaring whiteness. "Singles," he muttered. Joshua closed the locker door and drifted back to the bench. Singles meant quick, furious staff work, no color-floor strategies. Two men, face to face with few formal rules, offered the Administrators an opportunity to rate their product lines' coordination or track endurance changes within a batch. The entire court monitored both players, and stats ranging from heart rates to hot-spot bruising could be easily monitored from the comfortable viewing areas. But for the players of a single's match, it would be a long and brutal half-hour unless someone was forced to yield before time.

And at their age, that rarely happened.

His mind seemed to stop, and a trickle of sweat rolled down the side of his face. Joshua let it go.

He didn't hear Adam's step but something like fingers playing over his neck startled him. His batch-mate, a changing bag slung over his shoulder, did not even look at him. Instead, he crossed silently to a locker, jerked it open and began to strip.

"You're early," Adam finally murmured in greeting.

"A bad habit of mine," Joshua replied. The light shone on Adam's bare shoulders and feathered down his spine. Joshua looked away, clamping down on the emotions that seethed just below the surface of his brittle control. "Adam..."

"Stop," Adam interrupted coldly. He tugged his arena gear on with sharp snaps of his wrists. "None of it happened. Not you, not me, nothing I said to you. Do you understand?" Adam turned then, as he buttoned the collar tight.

Joshua opened his mouth but no words came out.

"Why are you sweating, 1011? Because you took liberties with your Batch Commander?" Adam savagely tightened his cummerbund. "Or are you just scared I will beat the shit out of you tonight? Because I just might." Adam kicked the door shot and the boom echoed in the small changing area.

"You really are crazy," Joshua finally whispered.

"I'm going to enjoy this match," Adam continued. "Oh, here." He tossed Joshua a fabric circle of blue.

He snatched it from the air without dropping his eyes from Adam.

"Would have matched my eyes better," he said. "But then again, red is an old color for purity. L-Group purity. The real blood line."

"I don't understand..."

"You never did. And you never will," Adam answered. He turned his back and started down the corridor to the arena.

Joshua hesitated a moment, shaking, trying to make sense of things through the growing fever in his mind. Finally, he simply followed in Adam's wake.

—

Four men could have walked abreast through the arena entrance. The carpet ended abruptly, mutating into a black pebbly surface that helped ensure good footing. A glass-fronted locker, embedded in the left wall of the entrance contained the Tel-Menar staffs and helmets. Each weapon was just over four feet long, with smooth grips and a slender construction. Adam pulled out one staff and leaned it against his armpit as he pulled his helmet on.

Joshua hovered by the right wall, waiting for Adam to move aside. He stared hard at the ground, swallowing convulsively every so often. Sweat beaded on his forehead and dripped from the few black strands of hair that had come loose from his ponytail. The weapons rack seemed to shift, as if the light itself bent and shimmered. Only the wall seemed secure, and he put out his hand to steady himself. *Breathe. Pain passes, all pain passes. I'll go to the Medcenter after the match. Probably just a flu variation that other L-Groupers will never catch. This has happened before. Breathe.*

Adam finally moved aside, swinging his staff in slow circles and rolling his shoulders and neck beneath the crisp white uniform.

Joshua pushed himself off the wall and selected a helmet from the display unit. He fit the Velcro strap below his chin and then reached for a staff. He shut the glass door with care, turning the brass handle. His fingers left little smudges on the metal, and he felt his eyes linger there, as if moving them to the next task at hand required a special effort.

Deeply aware of the tremble that had climbed out of his hands and into his arms and thighs, Joshua took up his position behind his batch-mate. Adam turned toward him then, but he held his ground, his jaw clenched and his fingers tight around the staff.

He could feel Adam's eyes roving over his face, as if he were trying to memorize his features. For a moment, the blond's hard face softened. He touched Joshua's lips with just his fingertips.

Joshua twisted away in confusion.

Adam lowered his hand to his staff. "What I said in the locker room; I didn't mean it. There are a lot of ears in there, catching the locker room talk. And I won't forget. Not ever."

Speechless, Joshua stared at his batch-mate as the battle-ready mask of his skin reclaimed the sharp lines of his face. Adam nodded once and turned back to the court. "So it begins."

They moved together into the brightly lighted arena. The Administrators had darkened the enclosing circle of high-impact glass walls, but Joshua could still feel the observer's eyes on him. He took up his position, his hands sliding on the smooth staff, trying to find his perfect balance point. *Loose grip, open shoulders.* Joshua swallowed, and found it hard to complete the automatic movement, as if his throat muscles had somehow stopped coordinating with one another.

Adam took up his own still stance on the arena floor, a fighting style that mirrored his own. Usually L-Groupers were in constant motion, using their natural, nervous energy to mask moves of intent. But not Adam. Like Joshua, he stood his ground with just a trace of a smile on his face, as if baiting him.

The small smile lifted and became a familiar predatory gleam in his eye. They bowed to each other, and then the dance began in earnest, their steps controlled as they began to circle each other.

Adam sprang to attack first as Joshua knew he would. His staff, carried chest high, exploded on Joshua, who back peddled, flashing his own weapon up in a smooth defensive arc. The impact of their staffs jarred through his arms, searing lines of agony into the very bones of his hands.

Adam flashed in close, following up on his attack. Joshua released one hand, snapped the staff low, and managed to land a glancing blow on his shins. Adam stumbled right, trying to get his feet back beneath him.

Joshua let him go, and opened a little more space between them. The lights burned his eyes and drove little daggers of pain into his temples. He shook his head, trying to clear his vision.

Adam warily circled back toward him, looking like a pillar of light against the darkened glass and black floor. He swept forward then, his hands sliding to one end of the staff and swung it hard. Joshua countered, his breath suddenly catching and hoarse in his ears. He blinked rapidly, trying to focus. Adam pressed the attack; his face twisted and flushed, his staff a stabbing blur.

One vicious drive slipped through Joshua's

defenses and caught him hard in the chest. He bounced off the glass partition and gasped, frantically trying to drag air back into his lungs. Adam twirled the staff, wrists crossing, and then slapped one end upward. Joshua drunkenly raised his own weapon to deflect the blow, but it flew out of his fingers and hit the pads with a dull thud.

That ends it. That's a match. I haven't lost so quickly in years... He stumbled, one hand extended. *Damn, I'm so sick.* He ripped the helmet from his head and started to sketch a bow as the sport dictated. He barely registered the movement blurring toward him, and then Adam's staff smashed full into his face. He crashed into the glass wall again, slid down in and rolled face down onto the floor. Ears ringing, he tried rise, but his arms gave out beneath him.

Adam backed off, his staff still twirling in agitation in one hand. "He's no L-Grouper!" he screamed into the darkened glass and finally thrust the staff in Joshua's direction like a spear. "Are you blind, all of you? Do you think L-Group doesn't *know* what happened? Do you think we don't *know* he killed two of his own batch-mates? He is a monster!"

Again Joshua tried to push against the mat,

and again his own muscles refused to obey him. Blood was filling his mouth and trickled in a thin stream from his nose.

Adam swung the staff around him, as if he were pointing at all the observers he couldn't see. "If the Administrators won't take revenge for the deaths of Alec and Michael, then I will! If you want that thing to live another day, you get him out of L-Group! He doesn't belong! He never has!"

Joshua struggled to raise his head. The cords in his neck burned and it felt like a hand had closed tight around his windpipe. *Get up. Get. Up.* But his body would not obey him.

Adam strode over the black-pebbled surface and shoved Joshua's head to the floor with the sole of his foot. "Stay down, you stubborn idiot" he hissed. Then in a louder voice, a voice that carried, he cried out as if to an audience. "How does it feel, Joshua, to hope you can trust someone, maybe like Alec and Michael trusted you?"

He could take no more. Joshua struck at him, but his blow went wide and wobbling. The movement drove home little lances of white pain behind his eyes.

Adam snorted in derision then knelt. His

voice, the barest whisper, touched just the edge of Joshua's hearing. "I'm sorry." A moment later, he leapt to his feet and gave way.

Joshua caught the blurry movement of two other forms in the arena. Their med-tech gray uniforms barely registered as they knelt beside him, and even their touch seemed almost unreal. He couldn't see or hear Adam anymore; his pulse roared in his ears, and all light seemed to be narrowing.

One tech rolled him over. He was dimly aware of a bioscanner humming into the bones of his chest. "High fever, severe nervous system disruption."

"Source?"

"Scanning, hold on." The gray uniform rustled against him "Got a positive synthetic compound reading. "What the hell is going on? This man had been drugged," the med-tech muttered. "NCPs kill each other, not Company units."

Joshua stared up into the man's foggy face, trying to make sense of the words. *Drugged? Who drugged me? When? Adam?* He could hear is own breath growing more ragged, his heart rate ratcheting up and shaking his whole torso.

"Condition?"

Joshua latched onto the deep tones. *Senior Commander Drew? Here?* For a moment, he remembered the man backlit by his huge spiraled painting. Then it all slipped away again, unreal.

"Cheekbone and orbital is shattered, Commander, but that's not the real issue. We've found a synthetic protein string in his blood-work. How close internally is he to L-Group norms?"

"Close enough."

Close enough? Did Drew really know that for certain? I have never, ever, been close enough. Joshua could dimly hear a flurry of activity beyond the arena glass and his mind imagined terrible faces grinning in at him, their teeth more like fangs and eyes glowing with the light of a kill.

Then his muscles began to twitch, little tremors racing through him. He clenched his jaw then screamed as this own broken cheek seemed to shift beneath the skin. The twitches turned to jerks and then he was twisting against the floor, half-crazed with the tidal wave of pain and involuntary movement.

"This synthetic has a lethal interaction with base adrenalin! I need a sedative and NOW!"

Long corded fingers pressed his shoulders

back against the mats. "Calm, Joshua. I know you can do this. Just like Lunar One. Don't fight it. Relax into it."

Joshua forced his eyes open, even though Drew's image jumped and fuzzed around the edges. He tried to cling to Drew's even voice, to the feel of those strong hands trying to hold him still against the floor.

He barely felt the sedative needle pierce his skin, just one tiny stimuli in a world of movement and pain. But Drew held on with an absolutely focused will, and Joshua stayed with him, breath by breath, as his own body twisted around his heart.

Slowly, slowly, the greater jerking stilled, falling to mice-footed tremors tickling over his bones. He rolled his head away from Drew then and he noticed at a great distance that they had lifted the opaque filters over the walls. Everyone there in the observation gallery was silent, still.

Waiting for me to die.

One man leaned forward a little, his thin lips working on a blue cziana root. The Administrator tapped something into his handpad and then set back with a cool smile on his face. Nothing like pity, fear, or horror touched his features. Joshua let the image go, let the terrible, cold face blend with all the other faces in his memory.

"And they think they've designed a perfect order," Drew whispered in a low and furious voice. Joshua tried to look at the commander, but his body ceased to obey him. Perhaps he had not heard right; Administrators were never challenged, never spoken against. Surely it was the sedative. His every perception was dubious.

"I want him in a private room. Lock-coded door, my ident only. If anyone wants to see him, they come through me and that includes medstaff. Understood?"

Joshua did not hear the response, and darkness finally washed up and over him.

—

Muligan ran the first two fingers of his left hand over the wall as he drifted along. The Administrator passageway, newly carpeted, still smelled vaguely of chemical sealers. Andrea would have the whole area air-exchanged tomorrow no doubt. He looked curiously at the freshly installed triangular lights that offered up their soft, yellowish glow. The sconces smacked of her tastes, and reminded him that her hands were everywhere except where they were most needed. It was almost like she was nesting.

Muligan didn't bother to announce himself. He keyed the lock with his passcard. She valued her privacy, yes, but she valued his insights even more.

He glanced at her empty desk, and then drifted to the door of her inner apartment. "Open," he murmured serenely, "Passcode Admin 02, Muligan." The entry way etched itself free of the expensive metal Astazia wall and slid obediently aside for him.

Her apartment, dimly lighted and rich with deep autumn browns and brass fittings suited her perfectly. Andrea sat on the floor before her wall-sized vid-display, raptly watching the screen. Her woven black robe pulled up tight to her knees, the collar nestling just below her ear. The fireplace off to the right and the huge window overlooking the star-port opened the space up, letting it breathe.

"Evening, Andrea," Muligan said.

She raised one hand, silencing him without even bothering to look at him. He ambled to the couch and slouched into a position where he could see both her and the display.

A man crouched there on his knees, his eyes

open and staring, tears streaming down his face. If he knew he was being recorded, he certainly didn't seem to care. He wore a standard Tech Grade Eight uniform, blue-gray with a green pin set in the collar of the turtleneck shirt, but the clothing sagged on his lanky frame. He lifted his hand a little from his lap, his fingers crooking as if he was ready to pluck a tiny, imaginary flower. In the background, music blared, an ancient classical piece. Tchaikovsky, Muligan realized, recognizing it by the complex mathematical sequences more than by tone.

"That's Illion," she whispered. "I just found this file the other day; someone buried it pretty deep."

"I know who it is, Andrea," Muligan replied. "If I remember correctly, this was just days before he killed himself. Revolting, isn't it?"

"I've watched this twice now. His eyes are tracking, like he sees something that's not there." Andrea leaned forward as if her proximity would clarify her curiosity. "What could he possibly be looking at?"

Muligan chuckled then. "You won't like the answer."

She swiveled around to look at him finally. "You asked him about this?"

"We discussed his behavior at some length actually.

"And?"

Muligan raised his eyebrows a bit and wrinkled his nose. "He said, 'I watch the pictures that the music paints for me. Wonderful, terrible pictures.'"

"Music can't paint images," Andrea murmured. She turned her attention back to the display. "Psychosis, then. That's what we're seeing here." But her voice lacked conviction.

The image of James Illion brought his hand to his forehead in a fist, and then lowered it, still clenched, to his lap. His face, alive and flushed with emotion, seemed drawn with equal amounts of pain and pleasure.

Muligan found himself looking away. "I don't want to stay too long. I just dropped by to let you know your little L-Group experiment took a beating in the arena tonight."

'Meaning?" Andrea asked without turning from the display.

"I mean someone drugged Joshua 1011 and his batch-mate, Adam, messed him up something wonderful in a Tel-Menar match. He may not live."

Andrea spun on him then, rising to her feet.

"Who the hell would…"

"Would have been a good match to bet on tonight, against the favorite of course. Ah, hindsight. The synthetic proteins in his bloodstream should have killed him, but Drew was there, somehow calmed him long enough for the sedative to do its work. Joshua is in the private room at the medcenter, limited access, Drew's sole jurisdiction. I find that *fascinating*, don't you?"

Prime Andrea planted herself on the little square of carpet staked between her feet. Her jaw worked and her eyebrows pulled down sharply over her nose. "Who is behind the drugging?"

"We don't know yet. Most likely Commander Adam; they were seen together at morning practice, and Joshua was logged into the commander's private quarters for some time this morning. After that, he spent the rest of the day in his own quarters. Do you want me to follow through with an Admin inquiry?"

Andrea shoved her hands into the pockets of her robe and walked over to her picture window. She seemed to fight with herself for a moment. "I don't think we need to interfere at this point. It's an L-Group matter. Drew can handle it as he sees fit."

"OK," Muligan replied.

He could see her eyes, reflected in the glass. The green and orange lights of the spaceport drew long lines of fluorescent auras in the sky. "Any kind of long-term damage to 1011?" she finally asked quietly. She raised her eyes to his own reflection in the glass without turning toward him.

"I think it's too early to tell." Muligan hesitated a moment. "You knew this might happen. It's what I've been telling you all along. He's not L-Group; he knows it, they know it. And if he did kill Alec and Michael..."

"Good night, Muligan," she cut him off.

"Andrea..."

"I said good-night."

He allowed himself a delicious, self-righteous sigh and hauled himself off the couch. At the door, he half-turned to her. "You're playing with a dangerous toy, Andrea, pretty as he has become. Could be that L-Group will take him off the board itself."

She didn't reply, even though he could see her shoulder rise a bit toward her ears. He smiled at his little triumph and let himself out.

Chapter 7

*I must not vary from the acceptable
parameters of behavior set by the Company.
Being aware of them has been a double-edged
sword. I know what is safe and what could
get me decommissioned; the lines are quite
clear and so I can anticipate and frame any
actions I take. But when I am forced to move
beyond those imaginary walls, I am hyper-
aware that I endanger not only myself but the
entire human species that James Illion wishes
to birth. That irrational sensitivity has
become sobering in the extreme.*

High Commander Drew 379
L-Group

Medcenter Private Rooms
Company Compound, Earth Complex

Joshua twisted his head away from Drew in a
movement just short of insubordination. He
half-heartedly lifted his fists into the air, but the

white padded manacles at his wrists snapped his arms back and down. Four weeks of bondage had worn raw patches into his dark skin, but he could no longer find the energy to give a damn. His body still continued to jerk and play, and the bindings kept him safe.

And caged.

His private room, cold and bare of any kind of artwork and furnished only with a single metal chair, pressed on him, drove him further into a nauseated despair. "I'm not a Tech, Commander." An invisible hand still gripped his vocal cords. He could barely force simple words past his lips, and his voice sounded all wrong, higher and tighter than it should be.

Drew sighed and sat in the low folding chair. His black uniform made his pale face almost waxy and inhuman, particularly under the med-light's glare. He folded his hands in his lap and watched Joshua with his yellow-flecked gray eyes. "I'm not asking you to become a Tech, I'm asking you to try to get some extra training. A soldier with skills above Tech Grade two would be a great asset to L-Group. We need competent wake staff on our transport ships who are also trained soldiers. We need people with your obvious talents."

Drew's positive tone grated on Joshua, but the emotion died somewhere in his chest. He watched the intense lines of the commander's face spiral inward until all his energy seemed to focus in the space between his startling eyes. "If you really needed people like that, the Company would have bred them. You really just want to keep me from my batch-mates, don't you?" Joshua could hear the hollowness in his own voice. *Take it all away, Drew. Why do you play with me?*

The spot there, the small wrinkle, twitched. "I'd be lying if I said that wasn't a benefit just now."

"You think they'll kill me. But L-Groupers don't kill other L-Groupers." Joshua turned his head, adjusting his vision to stare through Drew's chest. He could hear the sarcasm in his own voice, the only punch he could throw.

His commander leaned forward over his bent knees and sealed his palms together over empty space. "Have they ever really considered you part of L-Group, Joshua?"

It was an empty question, and surely Drew knew it. *He's read all the files, he knows how many nights I've slept in the medcenter. He's seen how many times I've eaten alone, months in a row. He*

realizes how differently I process pain, how
differently I look and move. And now, the
monster, the oddity, is chained in the bowels of the
Company at last, helpless and broken and
consigned to retraining to keep him useful. To
keep me useful. But why bother?

"The Techs identified the protein strands as a possible by-product of Rialgan pneumonia," Joshua forced out. "I reacted to the vaccine before. This is probably some kind of delayed response to that previous shot."

"Joshua, we've been through this. It's a synthetic. Your body didn't make it; you ingested it or it was introduced somehow into your bloodstream. Adam poisoned you for God's sake, probably when he fucked you."

Joshua closed his eyes to the brutal observation. "Leave me alone."

He could feel Drew watching him. And for a while he was content to sit wrapped around in silence. When he finally opened his eyes again, Drew still occupied the metal chair, his dark uniform shirt rising and falling with his even breath. His face was an impassive mask of extreme patience, a kind of waiting that ceased to know or care about time itself.

Fine. I can play that game, too.

After a full half an hour, the continued silence and stillness finally struck at Joshua in a way words could not. "OK!" he half-screamed in his choking voice. "Adam tried to kill me. Is that what you want me to admit? That we fucked and ten hours later, he was ready to watch me die? Is that what you want me to admit to you so you can get out of here and leave me the fuck alone? Well there, I've said it!"

"Yes," Drew responded to the string of curses with a slow nod, even though his eyes flashed with something like repressed anger. "I did want to hear you say it, but not because I am being cruel. You need to talk about this, *we* need to talk..."

"Why?" Joshua cut him off with a flat voice, and stared up at the ceiling "What does it matter?" *I'm tired of it all. So very tired.* "Those days with Adam were all a lie, like my whole life here. There's only a hole in me, and everything falls into it eventually. I've waited for years, and I still don't understand any of it. I don't understand and I don't care anymore."

The metal chair creaked as if his words had finally hit a mark in Drew. "I know you were drawn to Adam and he to you. And I also know you can't understand why he is still walking around free, as if none of this happened. I can only tell you that I have handled the situation as I have because Prime Andrea Annon ruled this as an L-Group matter. She is convinced that Adam was forced, possibly against his own will, to frame you for the murders of Alec and Michael. And I concur with her. Adam free and moving through his routine may reveal who aimed him at you, who put the drugs in his hands, who orchestrated the whole thing."

Joshua heard the quiet force growing behind Drew's voice, the vocal tension that said what words alone could not.

"I've seen what the Administrator class does to off-beat units like you. Usually when they show the slightest variation from expected norms, they are terminated. Period. But you? Prime is *intrigued* with you, and that has preserved your life from the time they pulled you from your fetal canister. Or maybe even before that. You're special, Joshua, not a freak, not a monster. And I for one want to find out just how special you are."

Drew finally got to his feet and waved a data screen into light and life, just off Joshua's shoulder line. "There is also something else I want you to consider," Drew said quietly. "Your behavior from this point on will reflect on me as well."

"Meaning?" Joshua asked. The fatigue was gathering again, making it hard to concentrate.

"I'm what they call an Ancient Recovery and Reintegration unit. Just. Like. You." Drew let the words hang there in the tight little room.

Joshua rolled his head a little, trying to see something *off* in his commander, some sign that he was other than standard command-designated L-Group design. He'd heard the rumors of course, that the ARR program had been disbanded because it produced units who were sometimes not just physically different but who were occasionally deeply unstable. He searched the fine lines of Drew's face, but all he saw was the L-Group brand of blond hair, gray eyes, light frame. *Why don't I look like that? Why these dark eyes, this straight black hair, this narrow face and hawk-nose. I am just a shadow here, a shadow against their lightness.*

"Prime will watch us both now. I took swift measures to protect you and they were noticed. That makes me a little suspect. You will need to exercise control, Joshua, be more self-aware and careful. We'll work on it together, you and I. I don't want to give her any reason to stop protecting you. And I would prefer to stay out of her line of attention as well." He sighed a little, and pressed his hands against his slender hips. "There will come a day when we will talk at greater length about the ARR program, but this is not the time or the place. All I can say is that in the long run, the way things have worked out, even the nature of your attack, might eventually prove a blessing for you."

Joshua resolutely shut his eyes. He pressed his lips tight to his teeth. He didn't care that Drew was watching him dig into the darkness that surrounded him. As far as he was concerned, the commander was just taking up space, a cardboard cutout, not particularly irritating or very restful either, a ghost presence against his senses.

"So, I'd like you to start reading for Tech level three certification. Just small bites. Rest every few pages. But with that little progress, maybe you'll feel..."

"Get out," Joshua said, almost under his breath.

Joshua heard Drew move abruptly to the headboard and could feel a breath of raw tension enter the room. "What did you just say to me?" Drew growled.

"You heard me fine," Joshua replied.

A brutal slap seared into Joshua's face. His head snapped aside with it and a spreading warmth fingered out over his barely mended cheek.

"Do you want to try that again?"

Joshua rolled his head to face him, the blond man's eyes glaring hot and furious into his own.

"Because I am through with your self-pity."

"Kill me, Drew. It's what they really want. Hell, it's what I want." Joshua's face throbbed, but even that felt vaguely distant. He even sort of liked the pain he realized. *Pleasure from pain? Could I be reduced to that?*

The commander's face went pasty white. His jaw muscles bunched in tight clumps beneath his glowering eyes. Abruptly, he jerked the wrist manacles free, seized Joshua by one arm and dragged him from the bed. Joshua scrambled for balance, his feet slipping on the cold floor, his body unable to respond. Drew shoved him face-first into the floor tiles.

"You want to die? Then do it yourself! Do it!" Drew screamed at him. "Ten pushups ought to run that poison in your system right back into your heart like a goddamn bush knife!"

With a ragged cry, Joshua jerked away

from the relentless pressure of the hand against
the back of his skull. He scuttled back against
the bed frame and pressed his spine into the cold
piping that ran along the edge of his air mattress.
One of the manacles shivered off the bed, and fell
across his chest. His heart ached, seemed to
twist and hiccup beneath his ribs. He threw back
his head, without trying to cover his nakedness
and the cry that broke from him shuddered his
whole frame. Another tore itself loose, then
another. Hand clamped beneath his left armpit,
his heart leaping and burning in agony, he cried
in great choking sobs.

Dimly, he felt a blanket fall across his lap
and the strong grip of another man's arms around
him, holding and rocking him slowly. "You don't
want to die, Joshua. You don't want to die.
You're better than that, better than *them*. You'll
see it in time." Drew's head leaned against his
own, but his grip never slackened.

Later, he was not quite sure how Drew
managed to get him back into the bed. The
hated cuffs lay in a twisted mass on the floor. A
cool hand combed his sweaty hair off his
forehead, and then the fingers touched his
breastbone. "I'll check in on you in a little while.
Tech reading starts tomorrow. It's not a request.

It's an order. And a better chance at life than you've had for a long time, Joshua."

Joshua didn't respond, didn't move. The soft pressure of Drew's hand lifted, but then he reached up and snared his commander's uniformed wrist. Drew let him hang on for a time, and then gently disengaged himself without a word.

He held on to the memory after Drew left. It was his only lifeline. And he would cling to it, for as long as it kept the darkness at bay.

—

Adam crouched naked on the floor, his knees pressed into the carpet and his hands flat and stiff upon his own thighs. He kept his eyes down; that's how Tony preferred him. He watched the other man brutally unlace his own black boots, jerk them off and heave them into the corner. The metal wall rang with their impact.

So close, the walls of these rooms. Everything pressing in on me. Everything. But Joshua is alive. Alive. It's enough. Adam carefully swallowed, trying to study the nap of the gray carpet beneath his knees. He could barely tolerate being alone in his own quarters, let alone crammed into one of these cans with another man. The smell of the other became obnoxious; their breath seemed to compete for the very air. *"Urban-batch L-Groupers aren't claustrophobic," the pyschtech had laughed. "And where did you hear that term in the first place? Stick to L-Group strategy reading and leave our field alone."*

Tony stood and started pacing. *He always has to move when he thinks. Always. He's as caged as I am.* The revelation gave him a moment of satisfaction, a brief escape from the walled hell he found himself crouched in. He could imagine the anger glowing in his commander's brilliant blue eyes, his square-cut features made harsh with his tension.

"He's going to live." Tony hissed it like a curse. "You could have killed him in the arena. Changed the face blow to an upper cut under his chin and broken his neck clean. Why didn't you?"

Adam blinked. "I thought the drug..."

"You weren't supposed to think! You disobeyed direct orders. Disobeyed! And then you made sure that they'd pull him out of L-Group with that little show of yours." The pacing feet abruptly planted themselves just a short stride away. "You protected him. And now I can't get anywhere near him. Do you have any idea what I should do to you?"

Adam chose to remain silent.

Tony started pacing again. "You're my body-unit. That counts for something with you, doesn't it?" he asked a moment later.

"Yes, Sir," Adam murmured. He breathed carefully through his nose and kept his eyes cast down.

The taller blond strode in front of him. Adam watched in a kind of dread fascination as his legs collapsed neatly down, knees hiding shins and feet. "Look at me, Adam."

Adam raised his face up the fitted uniform to Tony's uncompromisingly masculine face. The man stared back at him, as if his look alone could beat Adam for his failure with Joshua. Tony shifted, and suddenly he was holding his knife. Scratches marred the ebony handle of the weapon, but the blade shone flawlessly in the artificial light. The commander drew the razor edge down across the pad of his left pointer finger and thrust the neat gash under Adam's eyes. "I can't feel this as pain. I know I am cut. I can see that I bleed. But it just feels cold. God, I want to feel it just once so I know I'm real!" He drove the knife into the carpet next to Adam's knee.

Adam held his gaze on Tony's face, even though he would have given anything to contemplate the ugly carpet again. The commander's eyes, shiny and hard with emotion, abruptly went flat. He pulled the knife free of the carpet with an expert jerk of his wrist and then looked at his finger. The cut had already stopped bleeding, the edges pulling toward each other. Tomorrow, only a light scar would remain on the pad. And a day later, nothing. *The Company make its products to last*, Adam thought bitterly. He could feel sweat trickle down his back, and he knew Tony would like that.

The knowledge gave him no pleasure.

"Did you know that Alec was different, Adam? That he could feel pain? I used to cut him and just watch his face. Try to feel through him, what has been denied to most of us. And it worked for a while. It was like I could connect to him, like I was *inside* his head and body." Tony blinked quickly, but his voice was almost mechanical. "He and Joshua together, in the rubble. They shared this thing, their thoughts, their pain. And Joshua knows what I did. I am sure of it. He'll tell others, it's only a matter of time. And then, I'll be decommissioned. Sent to the incinerators."

Adam knew better than to speak.

"You don't believe me? Then let me tell you this. I know you are like me, Adam. That's why I sought you out. I know you go places in your head that no one else talks about. That you see things that move where nothing real exists." Tony's voice became hollow, distant. "Do you know that Alec still comes here at night? He crouches where you kneel now and he holds out his hands as if he could heal me with a touch, then pulls away and leaves me cold and aching. He clings to me, everywhere I go, not seen, no, but I can *feel* him. And he told me there is a man who knows all my secrets, all the little secrets. And who do you think that man might be?"

Adam swallowed convulsively and clenched his hands tight around his thighs. "Joshua. You think its Joshua."

"If Joshua talks, they'll kill you, too. You know that. They know you've been together. They'll know you're tainted. I'm just trying to save you, don't you understand?" Tony reached out and touched Adam's lips, then abruptly grasped his hair and jerked his head forward. "You will kill him next time. Or I'll make your life a living hell." He shoved Adam back so hard he nearly fell.

For a moment, he could almost feel Joshua there, the clean sweat of their workout clinging to his dark skin. He could remember how white his own hand seemed against Joshua's rich brown, how his fingers tangled in long, black hair. He could still feel his lips, his tongue, hungry in a way that he had never experienced with another L-Grouper. He wanted more, wanted Joshua again. Yes, his whole self was tangled in the other man. In that rush of sensation, he had a glimpse of how Tony must feel, how he could be haunted by a presence not *here* but also never very far away.

In an instant, Tony had righted him, had drawn him into a kiss that was more a kind of an assault than a gesture of love. Tony put a hand on each shoulder finally and thrust Adam back again. "Tell me you understand."

"I do," Adam murmured. "I understand."

At least that much was true.

———

Prime Andrea Annon raised her head as the tall L-Group commander entered. He inclined his head, all graces observed. "You asked to see me, Prime."

"Drew. Yes."

The man walked toward the visitor chair within measured steps. "May I?" he gestured at the seat.

"Actually, I could use a stroll," Andrea replied. She smiled warmly as she rose, and noticed the composure on his face slip a little. He straightened slightly, his hands laced behind his back.

"Whatever you wish, Prime."

She smoothed her soft burgundy sweater as she made her way around the edge of her desk. He waited patiently for her to pass by him. His stiffness suddenly irritated her. "This isn't a parade review, Drew. You don't need to be so damn formal with me all the time."

"Yes, Prime." But nothing in his stance changed.

She rolled her eyes when she was sure he couldn't see her.

He followed her out into the hallway, just behind and to her left. She stopped abruptly and turned toward him. "Give me your arm, Commander."

"Prime?" A little frown carved itself deeper into his forehead. His skin looked so very pale and vulnerable above the collar of his black uniform.

"Oh, God. Here." She grasped his arm and linked it to her own. "Get the picture now?"

He swallowed visibly, his throat spasming over his small Adam's apple.

She gently propelled him down the hall. The evening dims came on as they walked, bringing out the brassy highlights in the walls. The carpets swallowed the sound of their footsteps. His warmth felt good against her arm, even though she could feel the tension flowing from him as well. *Too long since you've taken a lover into your bed, Andrea. Far too long.*

"So, is he going to pull through?" she asked him.

"Who?" Drew asked guardedly. He flushed a little, and the color was actually good on him.

She smiled sadly inside. *Oh, Drew, don't fret. Your most precious secret of all is safe with me. I know you've always liked women; I understand that this simple contact awakens things in you that you must never admit. It's not L-Group after all.*

"Joshua 1011. Is he recovering?" she repeated.

"Yes, I think so." Drew kept his eyes straight forward, his face smoothing out again into nearly unreadable lines.

Prime allowed a little hard edge to creep into her voice. "Come on, Drew. I want more than a vague 'I think so' from you. I'm taking a tremendous chance, leaving him so completely in your care. You know that, don't you?"

Drew paused in front of one of the hall windows and gazed out over the spaceport. The sky was already watercolor washed with its lights. For a moment a kind of longing sifted over his face, then just as quickly disappeared. He disengaged himself from her and she let him go. He put his hands hard and flat on the window ledge. "I almost let him die today. Who can say if that was a kindness to keep him breathing?" His eyes never left the sprawling spaceport.

"What do you mean?" She leaned against the window frame, watching him in the oblique.

"He said he wanted to die, so I gave him the room to find out if maybe he wanted to live just a little bit more." Drew finally turned to look at her, frankly and without apology.

"That was taking a rather liberal risk." *And playing with the life of my son, Drew. My son.* She gripped her arms tightly over her chest.

"Permission to speak freely, Prime?"

"Cut the military crap, Drew."

142

He grinned then, a surprisingly human expression as he glanced at her sidelong. "Yes, Sir." He put his back to the window and crossed his own arms over his chest. "He's not L-Group, Prime. He never will be. The mold you've tried to cram him into won't fit. He's James Illion's son, after all."

Prime straightened, her arms falling heavily to her sides. "How do you know that?"

Drew frowned, his head tipping a bit, as if sharing a secret with her. "I met James Illion on Rialga. We were both stationed at the same base for over a year. Joshua's resemblance to him is remarkable and unmistakable. I never knew what happened to James when he was arrested, but whatever did, this kid *is* his son." He turned back toward the spaceport, his gaze going out of over the concrete and flaring lights. "You need to give Joshua some wider avenues to explore, or he'll self-destruct. I am sure of it."

"I've OK'd the tech training beyond L-Group norms. Are you telling me this won't be enough to challenge him?"

"Yes. That's exactly what I am trying to tell you." Drew shoved his hands deep into his pockets. "He feels everything, Prime, in a way you and I will never fully understand. Right here, in his guts." He pulled one hand free and touched his stomach. "L-Group may have given him structure, but it will never accept him. He has no reason to live, no moorings, no ground. We," he emphasized the word, "must find one for him. Or in the end, there will be nothing I can do. You will lose him."

Prime drew a long breath. She could feel a feathery headache behind her eyes and it irritated her. *You know he is Illion's son. And what else do you know, Drew? Or what do you suspect?* "Suggestions?" she finally asked.

"Let him read outside of the Tech manuals. Let him explore music a bit, art..."

She immediately pictured James Illion, bent on the floor of his cell with tears streaming down her fade. She barely contained the shudder. "No. No music."

"Alright," he said with an admirable lack of curiosity. "But books..."

"Some. If they are approved by me." She shook her head a little, trying to dispel the picture of James from her mind. She rubbed at the corner of her right eye, and then beckoned with her head for him to continue down the hall with her.

He took up his position at her shoulder

again.

"What you want to do for Joshua is commendable but dangerous. Don't speak about these extracurricular forays to others. I'll do my best to keep one Administrator in particular, Thomas Muligan, off your back, but he dislikes the ARR program in the extreme and Joshua is a very visible reminder of that distaste." His shadow-presence at her shoulder forced her to turn her head a little as she spoke to him.

"I understand." He lengthened his stride a little, crept up beside her.

"There are people who want Joshua executed for the Lunar One accident, despite the lack of proof. Adam's actions actually garnered a fair amount of sympathy from the Administrator classes."

"Fueled no doubt by Thomas Muligan?"

"And by people within L-Group itself, Commander Tony for one. Why is that, do you think?" Andrea laced her hands behind her back as they walked along.

"Alec was his body-unit for a long time, then he broke it off. Perhaps there were lingering feelings there, and he wants to pin the blame on someone. Joshua is incredibly convenient in that regard."

"Maybe that had something to do with it, although it verges on the irregular. Soldiers are made to die, after all. Look into it. And watch over Joshua, Drew. I am putting a lot of faith in you."

"Why?" he asked quietly. The lines around his eyes softened as he looked at her. "Why the interest in this particular boy for all these years?"

For a moment, she wanted to confess everything to him, tell him that Joshua was as much her son as Illion's. But she clamped down on herself and merely shook her head. "I don't want to bore you with profit scales and internal development issues, Drew. He's important to me because he may indicate a line that will one day be useful to the Company. He's just part of my job."

"I understand," he replied formally. But his yellow-flecked gray eyes hinted otherwise.

Chapter 8

I suppose we all knew our jobs were shadow play. But showing up, looking at the data, making recommendations that nobody paid much attention to still ensured that food would make its way onto the table, and that the luxuries like actual bathwater would continue to flow. Married into the Core Families, I have always worn masks of one kind or another; it's not merely prudent to do so, it is the very stuff of life.

Matthew Dennon
Core Analyst assigned to
Company Central, Earth

New York Government Center
Family Housing Complex

Matthew Dennon slept with his head cushioned on his folded arms, one elbow splayed into the remains of a sandwich. His desk, never a neat expanse even on the best of days, groaned with the debris of a twenty-hour study stint. Within the confines of his still-active data reader, a digital hawk in flight turned and pirouetted through the air over his workstation.

Matthew's mouth, half opened in sleep, curved into a habitual near smile. Long lashes brushed against his cheeks and heavy auburn hair twined around his ears in waves that really wanted to be curls in spite of current fashion. His sweater, a soft fawn color, sagged comfortably on his frame.

The computer screen flickered and the hawk image froze with its wings extended, its eyes golden and the partially open beak the color of mellowed ivory. Matthew shifted, twitched and suddenly threw himself backward with a strangled cry.

He shuddered and gasped in his chair. Fingers gripped over the padded arms, he squinted into the shadows of the luxury apartment. The gentle arches of the hallway lit up and Lietta, his wife, shuffled out, blinking sleepily in her filmy nightgown. She put one hand against the wall, her head cocked a little to one side. "Matthew? You OK?" she asked.

He swallowed and shoved himself upright, peeled his hands off the arms of his chair and made a show of putting trying to organize the mess before him. "Yeah. Everything's OK." He smiled at her apologetically. "Go on back to bed, Lietta. I'm fine. Really."

She nodded once and left him alone without another comment.

He paused the frantic scrambling of his hands, his eyes resting on the spot she had so recently occupied.

The spot the Other in his mind had also so recently occupied.

He could still see the shadow image, the retinal after-burn of a man. He could still recall the shades of blond hair, gray eyes and a face filled with what Matthew took to be both concern and compassion. The figure was handsome; his cheeks lifted by an artist's thumbs from clay, and then backed smooth and stained ivory. A black uniform had fit tightly over a trained and honed body. He had felt a tug of desire, deep in his own gut. But then the man had spoken to him. "You're still missing it, Matthew. Keep looking. Don't give up. Or they all die."

The oh-so soft words had ripped him awake.

Matthew sank his head into his hands. A stack of ancient Company record-disks canted sideways and clattered over his wooden desktop. Of course the headache would come next, blinding and incapacitating. "Damn you, James Illion," he whispered. "These dreams...damn you!"

—

L-Group Medcenter
Company Central, Earth Complex

Joshua shuddered and tightened his grip on Drew's extended forearms. The commander smiled his encouragement and backed up a step, teasing Joshua to walk with him. They had been at it for over twenty minutes, criss-crossing the room in baby steps. He dug at the floor with his bare toes, as if he could soak the coolness into his sweating body. He wanted to free the strands of hair caught up in his mouth but he could only muster enough concentration to keep shoving his uncoordinated body forward, one shaking step at a time.

"There, you see? Four times across the room. You're improving faster than you realize." Drew stepped back again, opening up a potential chasm for Joshua to fall into.

He followed his commander, his lips pasted

tightly over his teeth. They struggled toward his bed, Drew with his short sliding steps backward, his eyes fixed on Joshua's, supporting him lightly but never dragging him.

Drew stopped, the bed frame curled into the back of his knee. Joshua leaned heavily on him at last as he pivoted around and nearly fell across the mattress. Drew's hands on his face were cool as they pushed Joshua's hair out of his face. "You should let me cut this for you."

"No." Joshua murmured. He threw one arm up alongside his head and turned his face into it. He remembered the grace he had once commanded, the unconscious ease he brought to any movement. Now all he felt was fatigue. His chest ached, from his breastbone out to the edges of his ribcage.

"Tomorrow, we do six passes. You watch. It won't take any more time." Drew patted him on the shoulder. "You're doing fine. It's all going to come back. Just be patient."

Joshua smiled grimly. "Tomorrow, Drew. Six passes," he agreed.

Chapter 9

The Core Families were all descendants of the
original founders of the star-spanning
enterprise now simply called The Company.
But they, as all society, had become
dependent upon the very biological products
they had created. Administrator units now
held all the positions of power within that
behemoth, and the Core simply assumed,
without looking too deeply, that they were
still in control. Oh, to be sure, the Company
kept them in high economic standards, but
only because they were so much easier to
manipulate that way.

A History of Old Earth
Raymond Pelle
Terrantata Cultural Repository

The Cello's Nest Café
Old New York City

Matthew poured the wine himself, his eyes intent on the silvery flood of liquid into the crystal. He handed it across the table to Lietta who took it without comment and sipped at its contents with a bland expression on her face.

He leaned back, surveying the wreckage of the meal: the bones on his plate, stark against the sky-blue porcelain; the half-radish tucked under the lip of his salad bowl like it could hide from the waiter's disapproving eyes. Lietta took another drink of wine and Matthew watched her eyes rove over the fake spray of flowers on her right, the vaguely gaudy chair he lounged in.

Her tight black dress hugged her slim body in all the right places, offering only a modest peek at the flesh of her breasts. She had twisted her hair up into a tight vertical wave at the back of her head, and the tension seemed all at odds with her obvious boredom.

"Why don't we ever sit near the windows, Matthew? I should think you would be used to this place by now."

"I'll never get used to heights, Lietta. It doesn't get better with time or exposure.

Probably why your father pays for this every month—he knows I can't stand being this high up." He picked up his wine glass, but mostly because he needed to do something with his hands. Only the finest café for Lietta, youngest daughter of one of the Core political patriarchs of the current Continental regime.

She turned her carefully made up eyes on him. "Aren't we a little bitter tonight!"

"Just tired," he replied. He finally took a swallow of the wine. It burned a little; he had never developed a taste for the stuff. He patted his lips with a napkin and looked at her cold, beautiful face. Yes, she really was *quite* beautiful he admitted. But it was a thing without pleasure to him.

"You're always tired. This Company research is pointless. It's wearing you out. I'll ask my father to reassign..."

"No," he cut her off angrily. "I don't want you to do that."

She pouted a bit, then, her finely drawn brows pulled low over her surgery-perfected nose. "You never seemed to mind my interference in the past. I hope you haven't forgotten who got you that original Company assignment in the first place. A lot of NCP

Govtechs wanted it, you know. Men and women who've been at this for years longer than you."

He stared out over the tables, over the shimmer of silverware and candles and drinks. The eyes of the tall windows, black beyond their red valances, dimly showed him his own haggard face, his rumbled shirt, his ill-chosen tie. He sighed, mildly surprised that it came out sounding a little more like a strangled whimper.

"Lietta, I had that dream again last night. It always seems so damn real. It's getting to the point where I don't want to sleep anymore."

Lietta watched him coldly. Finally, she set her glass down and shifted uncomfortably in her chair. "Now is not the time or place to talk about your hallucinations," she mouthed, with just enough breath he could hear the words.

When had the vague discomfort he had always experienced around her bloomed into something very close to disgust? Had it come on with his visions, or had it started a few years back, when he pushed the ring onto her finger and felt the Family's eyes fall on him, totally and forever. *They marry the ones that they can control, who won't threaten their power structure. By marrying you, they say you really are nothing, a*

tool, a plaything for bored children. But you
always eat, and you will always have a good job if
you want it. Fair trade, or so you thought.

He shoved his plate aside and leaned on the
table with his elbows. If she could have pushed
her seat back unobtrusively, she obviously would
have. She sat stiffly, her chin pulled in a little
and her eyes glittering dangerously.

"This is the perfect place to talk about it."
Matthew bit out each word, his voice rising a
little bit with each word.

"Fine."

"I think," Matthew said, modulating his voice
more for his own sake than hers, "that I'm
supposed to go out there. That something is
happening at Company Central that I can't see in
all this data. Something dark, and something
hidden. Something that could affect us all. I have
to get out there, talk with the biological products,
go deeper."

"Is that what the man in your dreams tells
you to do?" she asked. Her tone was faintly
mocking, her face pulled into the beginning of a
sneer.

"Yes," he said simply, sliding his elbows off
the table.

She licked her lips and tilted one shoulder a

little downward. It should have been provocative, the little wiggle there and in her hips, her tongue touching her painted lips. "You do *everything* he tells you?"

Matthew blinked. "What?"

"Does he tell you he wants to fuck you?"

He sat there, stunned, feeling the blood drain away from his face. He clamped down on the urge to glance around him, to see if anyone was following their interplay, was getting off on the way she simpered and hacked at him with her words.

"Oh, come on Matthew. You've always liked boys, well, men anyway. We've been married just long enough that you can't hide things like that from me. Wouldn't my daddy just love to hear that, hmmm? You're as cock-happy as a batch-bred L-Grouper."

"Shut up, Lietta. Now."

She plucked the napkin off her lap and tossed it on the table. "No. Not this time. Despite what you might think of my family and me, I loved you once, Matthew Dennon. Not just for the game of it, but for real. I wanted to touch you, to lick..."

"Shut up." But the words came out as a whisper.

How small he felt, his own anger turned against him, her own rage and grief so clear on her face. He wrinkled the tablecloth with his fingertips, pulling into little waves of cloth then smoothed it out without looking up.

And then something shifted, a coldness that seemed to settle into his belly. It emanated from her as well, like a closed door, like a locked window. And a deeper kind of tiredness washed over him, poking fingers in the back of his eyes.

"So that's all you have to say to me? Shut up? That's terribly unique," she murmured. She dropped onto her own elbows then and shook her head. "Why is it that we have stayed together for so long, Matthew? We don't love each other anymore. We were friends once, at least. I know that. But not now. Not even that."

He didn't look up at her.

"Most people who marry into the Core family circle try to at least fake it if they can't feel the love anymore. It's in their own best interests not be thrown back out with the masses again. But I don't think you're capable of that, are you? God knows I'm not." She seized the glass and threw the wine down her throat. "I hope you understand what you are doing, though. No parents of your own, too old to be considered pretty anymore, not much social capital, and no one to protect you if you make a bad call. You do realize that at least, yes?"

"I'm not an idiot, Lietta. Quit being so condescending. I'll manage."

She stood abruptly, her dress a rustle of silkiness against the table linen.

Matthew raised his eyes to her.

"I'll hold off on the divorce papers until I have transferred my personal holdings and had time to speak to my father in person. It's for your own protection. Divorced from the Core, men and women who do not have a family structure to avenge them sometimes have a habit of...disappearing. I don't want to give them a reason." For one moment, her brow wrinkled delicately over her nose and she seemed soft, almost vulnerable. "It's the only thing I can do for you."

"Thank you." He meant it because she did.

"And Matthew? Take that damn hawk sculpture you keep in the closet with you. It gives me the creeps.

"I will," he replied, a little listlessly.

She nodded then, a stiff thank-you, and then wove her way through the dining room towards the doors. They'd come in separate 'lectrics anyway, and that was the way they would leave.

—

Administrator Exercise Rooms
Company Central, Earth Complex

The upper level practice rooms, with their
padded floors and bronzed lighting sconces,
made Joshua feel distinctly self-conscious. He
worked to follow Drew's motions, his open hands
resting lightly on Drew's as they moved in a slow,
stately circle. He had discarded his soaked shirt
in one corner of the room. A pair of black tie-top
pants moved softly against his body; his uniform
trousers still sagged on his hips, no matter how
much he tightened the belt.

Up the commander's hand climbed and he
followed it with his left. "One hand, one mind,"
Drew reminded him again. Joshua tried to hang
onto the contact feathering between their open
palms. *I'm still trembling too much. Two months,
and shaking like a baby. When is this going to
fucking end?*

Drew abruptly jerked his hand away from
Joshua's and slapped him across his jaw, hard
enough to sting but not really enough to knock

his head away. Joshua drew himself up slowly, his hand going automatically to his cheek. He could feel the anger flash up inside of him.

"I couldn't have touched you if you were paying attention. I can see your gaze wandering. Focus!" Drew, dressed in his command uniform, cut a harsh shadow in the soft light of the practice room.

"Yes, Sir," he snapped back. He knew how insolent he sounded, but he couldn't help himself. The slap had more than stung his skin, it had hurt his pride.

Drew's hand flashed up again, but this time, Joshua knocked it away, and tried to drop into a defensive crouch, fingers curled into tight fists. But he couldn't maintain it. His legs shook violently, and if Drew had simply stepped into a punch, he would have sent Joshua to the floor. They both knew it.

Instead, Drew stepped back and bowed. A smile teased the edges of his lips. "Well, at least you're a little more focused now. Can we begin again?"

Joshua straightened, holding Drew's gaze. For a moment they stood together, still and silent. Then, he bowed back and opened his palms to his commander.

Chapter 10

I am acutely aware of how differently I have been wired. If I am reading the genetic tech manuals correctly, the human mind is capable of perceiving only one reality at a time. But I am aware that I see a layered world, filled with ghost images, voices that no one else hears, scents that come out of nowhere. Sometimes, in the night, I catch strains of music. And locked as I am in this body that has only a partial pallet of nerve impulses for my brain to interpret, who can blame me for trying to discern between this world and the one that haunts the corner of my eye? Who can blame me when I inflict pain on another-- pain I will never really comprehend-- if only to try to grab a life-line in a consensual reality?

Commander Tony 393
L-Group Archives

Administrator Exercise Rooms
Company Central, Earth Complex

Drew crossed his arms and leaned his shoulder against the training room wall. No L-Grouper had ever been allowed such luxury. But Joshua, who worked through his katas beneath the amber lights, would keep such secrets to himself. The room, some forty feet by forty feet, shone with the metallic patina of all the Administrator-class rooms, and made Drew feel as if he floated in a vast, if slightly yellowed, fish tank.

The lights played across Joshua's shoulders and drew smudged shadows around the clean lines of his mending body. The young man drew his hands closer before him, holding an invisible ball of energy. He shifted his hip, dropping one knee slightly and swayed his body to the left. His face, reflected in the mirrored surfaces was calm and focused. Drew could still make out a slight tremble in Joshua's thighs, but at least he could keep his feet now and shift his weight with control. The speed, the agility, would come with time.

And why does that body, that mind, not move me? Drew wondered to himself. Pairing off, command use of body units so encouraged by the

Company had never appealed to Drew. He liked the way Joshua moved, enjoyed the quick mind that seized upon any new idea it came across. Joshua ate up story and philosophy equally, his face flushed and his eyes shining. Drew had never seen an L-Grouper respond so fully—except himself. But beyond the bond of growing mutual respect and a sort of warm aesthetic appreciation for the real beauty Joshua embodied, he felt nothing. No passion. No need to possess the other. To demand sexual favors was his right, perhaps even his duty. But that desire simply did not exist.

And Drew certainly knew the difference between appreciation and real passion. He'd known it ever since he had been stationed on the agricultural planet named Rialga. He'd tasted it ever since he'd touched the small white hand of Krystine Malar, and had watched the Rialgan sunlight filter through her unforgettable red hair. James Ilion, a friend then, had laughed at his expression, and the memory still twisted in his gut.

"Does Prime know you like women, Drew?" James had asked it with a quick and friendly grin. "Hope there aren't too many others like you— might be bad for business. Of course, as far as

164

we're concerned here, that's the whole point of the ARR program, isn't it? To upset the status quo. We're going to be the dream catcher to their darkness and only light will stream through when we are done." Then came the friendly pat on the back, the dispelling of hurt. Illion knew how to do that, how to cut and anesthetize at the same time, in the same gesture.

The woman, Krystine, went to Drew with a smile and tucked her arm into his. "Don't let him bother you, Drew. You're both wonderful men. Whole. Complex. I like that." She smiled at James, her eyes gentle and warm. And in that instant, he knew how both lust and dismay felt, all the turns and alleyways it could force the mind into.

Maybe that was when he knew he had to hand James over to the Company--when he'd started to realize what James had and how that made him feel. He wanted that, wanted her, and if James' great vision played so well into that plan, then so be it.

James died in that cell, alone. Because of that moment's choice. But he would do it again, wouldn't he? Betray and rationalize it all for a chance with that lovely, red-haired woman.

Enough, Drew told himself. He pushed away from the wall and silently let himself out of the training room. Hands shoved deep in his uniform pants, he strolled the hall and kept pressing the memories back. Prime's new lights reinforced a sleepy sort of complacent luxury in the upper levels. The halls with their thick carpets and expensive walls were the leaves of the Company tree, the finery, the place where deals were made. But Drew knew the roots, the lower levels with their battered metal dividers, garish Company logos and gray carpets showed the true heart of the corporation—barren, sterile and cold. L-Group lived and worked in those roots. And still, he brought Joshua here to relearn the ancient katas and rebuild his battered body and mind amidst the leaves. Why?

At first, he had told himself that the young man needed to find his own space away from L-Group and its homogenizing environments. Joshua had to become an individual and fast. Tech graded L-Groupers above level 2 did not exist; from uniqueness to uniqueness, Joshua was going to be pushed. He so wanted the young man to see the differences, to feel the inequalities between him and others and recognize there the startling possibilities in himself-- possibilities James Illion had gifted him with from the beginning.

But now he couldn't be so sure of his motivations. It went deeper than merely challenging and protecting the young man. *I need him to be like me, don't I? I want him to have a chance to feel the burning ache of being an individual, the gut-wrenching birth of himself into a world that will never recognize it. I want someone to understand what I have come to understand, who will go beyond where I am now, who will look me in the eye and say, "I see it, all of it and I will help you forward." Like James Illion could do, so damn effortlessly. But it's not an easy route or a safe one. God, Illion! How did I become the caretaker of your son, your woman and all your damn dreams when really I hated you so much?*

He hesitated at the first intersection but his feet carried him on. He turned left and quickened his pace; his arms swing by his sides in sharp, military style. The doors of the corridor whipped past, doors into rooms he had never visited.

The hall, though, ended in a cap of double-doors, a rich chocolate colored wood with brass fittings. He pulled them aside, a hand gripped on each handle, stepping between the two. The narrow conference room blazed in sunlight.

Windows wrapped around three sides, feeding the light across the marble-topped table, the burgundy colored chairs. But beyond the windows, the blue sky drew him forward. A wisp of a cloud drifted low to the horizon, undulating with a wind Drew could not feel. He crossed swiftly to the window and pressed his hand against the glass. How he wanted to feel the heat from that sun. He leaned his head against the window, and then pressed his cheek up against it. Let his mind run wild like the first day he had stepped into this room alone. *Yes, let it come*, he thought.

The room seemed to shatter in a flash of brilliant shards that ripped through his flesh, his mind. He spread his fingers, and they sent runners of shadow and shafts of illumination out into the chaos. He threw back his head, and opened both arms, letting the light carve him up into sentient ribbons of flame. *The sun and stars run in my breath, my muscles are fibers of light...James! Do you still feel this where you have gone?* Now he could feel the wind, driving him apart and into all creation, a small glass dropped from a great height and shattered on shadows. But even the waves of light licking at the remains could not dispel him, all he had ever been and would always be. Consciousness in the glorious brilliant madness of it all. Even his tears traced mother-of-pearl reflections in space, then outside of space, outside of time. Finally, the darkness swept in, wrapped him around. *Let it go, Drew,* he thought. *Let it go and return.*

Drew dropped to his knees, and trembled with his hands braced against the floor. "Forgive me, James," he whispered. "Please, forgive me."

—

Highway A
Approach to Company Central, Earth
Complex

Matthew let the expensive hardcopy of the letter flop on his lap and tried to allow the motion of the cab work a little on his stiff muscles. But moments later, his eyes drifted back to the ugly little *san serif* words spelling out "divorce" and "homosexual behavior" and "psychotic episodes." His own signature, duly copied, scrawled across the bottom of the page next to Lietta's. *Truth hurts, Matthew. Truth really fucking hurts.* He glanced at the back of the driver's head. "How much further?"

169

The redhead shifted a bit as if he wanted his voice to carry, even though the plastic interior was designed to minimize road noise. The greenish dashboard lights illuminated his rather large nose. "You can see it over there."

Matthew craned his neck and looked between the shallow V of the seats. The entire skyline glowed with lights. "What part of it is Central?"

"You kidding?" the man chuckled. "All of it is Central, and most of it is underground."

"My God," Matthew murmured.

'Yeah, that's how most new NCP's react." The man shifted his hands on the steering wheel and slouched back into his seat. "They forget the place is the size of a city. Hear they run 'lectrics inside some the buildings, and I mean regular four-lane highways in there. Rumor is, they could close down and stay operational for years if they had to. It can become a regular fortress."

Matthew didn't comment. He pulled his eyes off Central and stared out the side window. The last glimmers of sunlight colored the blowing dust a rich shade of orange. *What is crawling around in my head? It's more than the divorce. Something is out there, something I need to find.* He folded the paper on his lap once. "How far out are we?" he asked the driver.

"Not that far. Ten miles give or take a handful."

"Stop the car."

The man craned his neck around. "What for? You sick or something?"

"I want to walk in," he found himself saying. "You can go ahead and make sure the bags get delivered to my new address. I should be listed in Central's registry by now. I'll pay for full fare of course."

"Government's picking up the tab on this one anyway, right? But look, this is crazy. Ten miles is a long way and the sun is just about down. It's gonna get real cold here in the desert."

"I have a coat," Matthew answered. "Please, pull over here."

The man shook his head and guided the 'lectric over to the side of the road. A bigger transport lumbered past them, rocking the lighter taxi. Matthew fished into his pocket and pulled out his ident strip.

The man took the gold card, turned it over, studying it. "Mid-level government man, huh? Kinda had you figured for one of the Core, with your leather carry cases and all. Hard to get those kind of amenities doing Mid-level work."

"I inherited them," he replied.

The driver ran the ident through his meter and handed it back to Matthew. He pulled one knee partially up on his seat and leaned an elbow on the back. "You have any idea how far ten miles really is? You're absolutely sure you want to walk all that way?"

"I'll be fine." Matthew opened the door, dragging his coat after him. It really was cold and the wind buffeted him. The divorce papers flapped in his fingers. He made a face, then wadded them up and crammed them into his pocket.

The front seat window rolled itself down. "What should I tell 'em, up at Central? I could get in trouble for this. Even if you are just a Mid-level."

Matthew chuckled but it sounded bitter, particularly to him. "Tell them I'm crazy. That usually covers all the bases." He fumbled with the buttons on his expensive coat.

"Yeah, right." The man laughed a little, but it broke off when Matthew simply stared at him pointedly. His natural flush deepened and then his eyes flicked aside. "OK. I'll tell them the truth."

"You do that."

The window rose smoothly back into place and the 'lectric whispered back out onto the highway. Matthew didn't bother to watch it for long. The road stretched out black and coarse in front of him, an unbroken line to the horizon-filling glow that was Central.

He pulled up his collar and started to walk. The dust stung his eyes and face, and he could even taste it when he swallowed. *This is the flavor of endings,* he told himself, *no nuclear blasts, no great plagues. Just potable water wicked out, and leaving the husk behind. All our reliance on the Ag planets, Company units overtaking human population here and on other worlds— just more drought of a different kind. Humankind mummified in the dryness of it all.*

He let himself fall into a rhythmic stride, and in that slip-step he began to hear the echoes of a voice. He stopped dead, his eyes searching the growing darkness. The wind wrapped his curly hair tight to the nape of his neck. It whispered softly, *"find him, Matthew."*

"Who's there?" he asked aloud. But nothing answered him. He started to walk again, his skin lifting into goose bumps of flesh.

Find him, Matthew.

He lengthened his stride, but the words

repeated over and over in his mind, in perfect cadence with his steps, even when he shifted into a jog.

Find. Him. Matthew.

He broke into an awkward run then, his breath harsh and pulse thundering in his neck. *Find. Find. Find. Find.* Matthew slammed himself to a stop, spinning to glare into the darkness around him. "Leave me alone!" he screamed. "I'm here aren't I? I'm doing what you want!"

Only the low and erratic breeze touched his face, full and pregnant, and breathing with presence. For a long moment, he stood there gulping air and trying to be more real, more solid, than the voices in his head. And when they did not come again, he turned and began the long walk to Company Central, making himself go slowly, his arms wrapped around his chest and his back hunched against the inconstant push of the wind.

Chapter 11

How do I measure creativity? It has been a mystery to me since my early training years. More and more, I would say it is that which makes the profit margins fat, further refines the genotemplates, and is always at the beck and call of logic. Otherwise, creativity is an anathema to stability, a quirky and barely harnessed remnant of an unpredictable past.

Administrator Thomas Mulligan
Company Central Archives,
Earth

Medcenter Private Quarters
Company Central, Earth Complex

Joshua sat on his bunk; one leg curled up beneath the other, and turned the book over in his hands. He loved the smell of the thing, the musky antiquity, the faint raised lettering on its spine. "I didn't think there were any of these left, outside of museums."

"Oh, they're still around. You just have to know where to look," Drew answered. He drifted over to the wall and twitched a new picture a little to the left. "Glad you finally finished this," he added.

Joshua smiled at him, enjoying the book in his hands, his own artwork on his walls. "Yeah, me too. The pattern was insistent."

"Circles inside of squares inside of circles..."

"...Etcetera," Joshua cut him off with another smile. "That's what I'm calling it, anyway." He dropped his gaze back to the book. "The Bhag-ha-vad..."

"Just call it the Gita. Easier."

"Alright. Gita it is. So what is it about?"

Drew didn't answer right away. He strolled across the room and seated himself at the foot of Joshua's bed. *He's usually so painfully present. But not today.* Drew opened his hand for the book and Joshua handed it to him. The commander ran this thumb over the spine and then fanned the pages, breathing in deeply. "It's about finding yourself between the armies of conflicting voices in your head, about choice and action in the world and the consequences of both. Read it and tell me what you think." And he passed it back to Joshua like a benediction.

"I will," Joshua promised him. He laid the book on the fold of his legs. His commander stared at the floor, his brow pulled down and his shoulders melting finally into a rounded softness. Joshua had rarely seen him like this, distracted, almost beaten. He reached out and lightly brushed Drew's sleeve with two fingertips. "Sir?"

"I'm alright," he answered immediately, with just a hint of embarrassment. "Changes are coming, fast and soon. That's all."

"Changes?"

Drew pulled his brows down and in. His lips started to part, then closed with a slow finality. In that instant, Joshua thought he might have seen something in those yellow-flecked eyes. But the commander silently shook his head, and shook off the question as well. "I won't be able to stay today, but I expect you will practice as usual."

"Three hours," Joshua said.

"Good. Your technique on the mat is getting better...and on the canvas." He gestured to Joshua's newest painting. "I'll see if I can smuggle in some more red. God knows you use a lot of it."

"Yes, Sir."

"So, are you the circles or the squares, do you think?"

The question, like all of Drew's questions of late, struck something deep inside of him. He glanced up at his work, remembering the red lines and black circles tracing themselves across the canvas, his hand a mere conduit for some thundering beat in his veins. "Both, I expect," he replied honestly.

Drew nodded, a small smile playing at the edges of his lips. "I'll check in with you tomorrow. Might be late, though." He stood then and without further goodbyes, walked from the room.

Joshua watched him go until the door clicked shut. "And you are the frame, Drew, holding me together. But you already know that, don't you?"

The silence of his room mocked him faintly as he turned his eyes to the book on his lap.

—

Tech Training Sector
Company Central, Earth Complex

Gripping the console frame, Joshua pulled himself beneath the simulated SR7 tightbeam unit. "The crossover connection is loose," he called out to the Tech proctoring his test. He pulled out a fuser, shifted it to fine beam with the edge of his thumb, and set to work on the repair.

"Good call." A hand tapped his ankle approvingly. "Takes most kids about an hour to catch this. Twelve minutes is damn fine work."

Joshua allowed himself a fleeting grin before he finished his work. He hadn't considered himself a kid for a long time. With a final thumb-rub over the cold patch, he scrambled awkwardly out from under the console. Propping his back against its metal frame, he allowed himself a short stretch and a groan. "Guess I understand why you guys are so small now."

The proctor, one of his lab instructors simply named Senior, snorted and clapped him on his shoulder. The man *was* small, only about five feet tall and slender like an old earth jockey. His bald head shone merrily under the lights. "Shipboard techs like me are smallish, but not those grade Sevens and Eights. They're bloody giants."

Joshua chuckled. "Eights work with the NCP populations as doctors. Maybe height makes them imposing or something, so regular folk don't try to push them around."

"Oh, maybe," Senior replied with a vague

wave of his hand. "Hadn't really thought much about the why of it. 'Course you, everything is always why, why, why isn't it?"

"Blame it on Commander Drew."

"Uh-huh." The bald man shook his head, clearly not wanting to know more. "Drew's a good sort," Senior went on. "Sure was right about your tech potential, which I never would have guessed. L-Groupers can be the worse students to train in even rudimentary skill sets. But you, you're as quick as any tech unit I've worked with. And I've worked with a lot of them."

"Thanks. I think."

Senior suddenly softened. "There's a lot of tech in you, you already get that. But there's more, isn't there? I could never talk to an L-Grouper like I do with you. You're really a different breed altogether, aren't you?"

Joshua winced at his words then tried to hide it behind a quick smile. "Sounds like you're hinting at a why there, Senior."

"And it gives me a headache, trust me." The tech extended his hand to Joshua. "Up with you, Tech Grade Four."

Joshua took his hand, but he didn't really need it. He was strong now, his movements unconsciously predictable.

"So, you going for a Grade Five pilot rating to complement this troop carrier wake-staff certification?"

"I don't think so," Joshua said.

"Well, your commander will be proud of you anyway."

"Yeah." Joshua answered. "I suppose so."

"You headed back to L-Group then, full time?" Senior didn't wait for Joshua's answer as he started to shut down the various power switches to the simulator.

Joshua turned to help him, flicking off a few power relays with a wave of his fingers. "I don't know what is next." He stared down at the darkened panel. "Would it sound crazy if I said I want to go back?"

"Yes," Senior pulled his tool belt off and slung it over one skinny arm.

"It'll be OK," Joshua murmured. He could almost believe his own words. "Part of me needs to go back. It's a kind of test."

The diminutive man shook his head. "Like when you ran the repairs in zero gee, with oxygen packs? Tests are one-time shots, not something you live day to day. You know, you really have the brains for a higher Tech grade, maybe clear up to seven. Maybe I could say something to

Drew..."

"No. That's not necessary, Senior. I'll be fine." Joshua unfastened his own tool harness and handed it formally to Senior. "Thank you, though. For everything."

The smaller tech took the belt slowly, a frown puckering little lines in his forehead. "You trying to prove something, Joshua?"

He stared down into Senior's earnest gaze. "That I'm not afraid of them," he replied at last.

And I'm not afraid of myself.

———

Muligan pressed the lock unit with a practiced hand, and then removed the outer covering. He glanced lazily up and then down the corridor. It remained empty. Shifting his root to the left side of his mouth, he typed in the over-ride numbers manually. The door slid obediently aside and he replaced the plastic cover with a snap. The Company AI could have issued the over-ride with a simple voice command, but that would have generated a traceable record and that might prove an annoyance later.

He moved cautiously into the room, his eyes straying across the neatly made bed before fixating on a collection of paintings hung on the white walls. He reached behind him without turning his head and closed the door. "What the hell?"

He drifted across the room, taking in the paint-stained easel in the corner, the book that dimpled the pillow of the bed, the sitting cushion that just protruded from beneath a plastic chair.

His eyes flicked back to the pictures and he chomped down hard on his root. Somewhere, deep in his chest, he fancied he could feel his heart rate pick up. He touched his own ribs with his fingertips and smiled around his drug stick. He'd almost forgotten what adrenalin could do.

He pulled his hand-pad out of one pocket and typed a quick note to Commander Tony, L-Group, to meet him in his office in half an hour then replaced the small piece of tech.

He left the pictures, and picked up a book that rested on Joshua's bed. He idly flipped through the pages. Arjuna. Krishna. Strange names to him. He dropped the book back with a negligent gesture of his hand. He'd check the title with the Company indexes later—the name of the book would stay in his mind like everything he had ever seen in his life, carefully filed away and ready to be retrieved as needed.

"So Drew, what are you doing to Andrea's little pet?" He walked back to the easel and picked up a tube of paint. Brilliant Red the container label read. The cap popped up easily and he sniffed the contents before carefully replacing it.

Yes, a meeting with Tony seemed very much in order.

—

Muligan poured the pale wine from the decanter, and then held the glass up to the light. He never really expected to see anything of note when he made such a gesture, but it seemed wonderfully ritualistic. Tony sat on the edge of his chair, his hands folded neatly in his lap. His cold eyes regarded Muligan with a mixture of distrust and impatience. But fear did not linger in those L-Group eyes, and that intrigued him.

"You like the apartment?" Muligan asked.

Tony's eye passed over the ornate woven wall hanging, the knobby carpet and glaring orangish furniture in a single economical sweep. "Colorful," he said at last. Those blue eyes came back to him then and waited.

"I like color," Muligan said affably. He sat down on his puffy couch and thrust his legs out over the carpet. The base of his wine glass balanced neatly on his blue silk shirt. OK, not real silk, he told himself. But a very fine facsimile. He let his pinky touch the soft fabric for a moment, and then narrowed his gaze on Tony's face. "Your information about Joshua 1011 was correct, but I wonder. Why did you feel it necessary to involve me in L-Group business?"

"Joshua is a danger."

"I've known that for years," Muligan said in a bored tone.

"And there have been rumors that you and Prime do not agree about the usefulness of this particular unit."

"Ah. Rumors make for dangerous toys, Tony," Muligan murmured. "Very dangerous indeed." He took a sip of wine. "But in this case, I see no harm in clarifying the rumors into fact. It comes down to this. I don't like the ARR program, or anything it has produced. I see a great danger in the basic unpredictability of the units created under the auspices of that experiment. Prime, however, seems fascinated with the very same danger. This has led to some tension between us, but I have no acceptable way to force her to see things my way."

"Do you want her forced, Muligan?"

He studied the pattern in the ceiling, the wild sweeping star pattern that spun out from center of the room to wash against the tops of the walls. "Perhaps."

"I may be in a position to help you, then." Tony spoke without urgency, his lips forming the words precisely and slowly.

Muligan took another sip of wine. "Go on."

"You realize that Joshua is a fully rated Tech Grade Four now, the highest anyone has ever been trained within L-Group. There is no need for him to go further, and you could suggest it is high time he is returned to his group. To me." Muligan watched Tony's face harden, and he found the transformation intriguing.

"That is a decision that is out of my hands, Commander." Muligan shrugged his shoulders a little, emphasizing his apparent powerlessness.

Tony's jaw tightened and Muligan imagined he was fighting with his legendary L-Group temper. "Use the information you garnered in his quarters to leverage Prime. Surely even she will see that he is becoming something that is not L-Group. Hell, he's not even a Tech. We don't have a category for him. That makes him dangerous unless I can contain him. Unless his batch can give him boundaries."

"I'm not sure that Andrea would be bothered at all by my findings. In fact, she may find them quite, well, *interesting*."

Tony knit his hands together, his fingers tight and white.

Muligan chuckled then. "Don't look so glum. I have been sparring with Prime for a great many years now. I simply need to know why you want him back if you see him as an outsider and a threat. Why you would chance him infecting your precious L-Group."

"Because I can do a favor for you, Muligan."

"Really."

Tony nodded. "I can kill him."

Muligan sat up and stretched a little. He placed the wine glass on table next to his elbow and patted his shirt pocket for a root. Empty. Ah, well, all things in time. He laced his fingers together as he leaned out over his knees. "How?"

"Perhaps the less..."

"Don't." Muligan warned him mildly.

"Adam will take care of him. A lover's feud, if you will. He has a nice record of instability and Joshua's death will be easy to pass off as an unfortunate incident, precipitated by their respective mental aberrations."

"Why would your man take this kind of a

fall? He will be executed as well. You do know that. One drugging might be overlooked, but a second attempt on Joshua's life? Well, Prime will get involved and it will be the end of Adam."

"I *own* him, Administrator. He is my body unit and he is L-Group and by God he will obey me."

Muligan could feel his body sliding toward needing his root, the sweat gathering on his lip, the dryness in his throat. But he couldn't resist one last question. "Were you the one who got Adam the drugs in his botched attempt to kill Joshua in the Arena?"

"You didn't need to ask me that," Tony replied coldly.

Muligan chuckled to himself, then rocked back and wiped his sweaty palms against his pants. "No, I suppose not. Proceed with my blessings, Tony. I will be sure to steer the blame from you in return. You are dismissed."

Tony rose to his feet, a powerful and startlingly malevolent presence in the garish apartment. Muligan looked up at the man, the perfect example of the soldier the Company marketed so successfully across the worlds. And this one in particular, without exactly the right kind of control, could only really be called a monster. How easily he talked of murder. Perhaps he would not shield Tony quite as well as he promised. Yes. That would be the better call. Wipe the board of the whole ugly mess once and for all.

Tony bowed formally to him and let himself out.

Muligan sat a few more moments in his chair. They were the conquerors of worlds, L-Group, and he was their master through and through because he was designed to be smarter, less bound by the nicety of rules and protocol. That is how it had always been and how it would always be to maintain order and symmetry. The Administrator classes ruled because it was in their DNA to do so. He stood to find a new package of root.

Chapter 12

I know I push the boundaries of Administrative discretion when it comes to my son. What I do not fully understand is why. Why is it so important to me that he continues to live? It's like falling in love with an office chair or holding a data chip to my heart like an infatuated teenager from those old historical romance novels. Disgusting. He is a product. I am a product. We are not allowed to even contemplate the chains of procreation. But still, I insist on calling him my son in my own head...and in my own heart.

Prime Andrea Annon

Company Central Archives,

Earth

Company Central, Earth Complex

Spaceport Grounds

Prime parked her 'lectric on the tarmac beside

the lumbering delivery transports and switched her lights off. She continued to grip the wheel though, her nails trying to bite into the soft, molded plastic. Such perfect nails, too, painted a soft mauve to match the silk scarf wound around her neck.

James Illion. He was so much on her mind that she felt pursued, driven out here under the sky to try to lose him in all the spaciousness. Or was it only a move to draw him closer somehow?

She opened the door and stepped out onto the pavement. Floodlights played over resting shuttles, their hulking metal shapes flashing with silvery panels and the dark Company logo. She shut the door, slamming it hard when the first gentle push didn't quite work. The wind lifted her loose hair and breathed against her neck. She pulled one particularly insistent tendril from her mouth and tucked it up behind her ear.

Where are all the stars you wrote about, James Illion? Littering the sky, salt crystals thrown over velvet, isn't that what you called them one time?

She looked up and could only see the monotone orange haze of lights. Like the pictures the music painted for him, she stood outside his senses and his vision. No stars here, only floodlights and shuttles and wind that flattened her skirt again her thighs.

If she could get beyond the lights here, she would be able to see them. But there was no place on Company grounds where they did not reach, those shimmering threads of brilliance rocking the night into a blurry haze.

And she had never, in her entire life, left the complex.

"Your son actually paints pictures, do you know that Illion? He's more like you each day, flickering just beyond my control. He's beginning to frighten me a little. Are you surprised to hear me say that? I restrict his reading, his access to music and art, and he still flowers in his Tech classes, seeing what even the Tech units themselves tend to miss." Andrea strolled across the pavement, her arms gripped around herself and she spoke to the wind.

"Drew, you, Joshua...you're all alike. Feeding off whatever it is that the ARR set loose in your mind. But no harm done, not yet. Drew has just been flicking the rust off him, clarifying him, but into what? That's the question, isn't it?"

"I watch him sleep sometimes, on the monitors and I wonder what you would think of him. He's glorious. And Drew never touched him, not once. I would know. But then, you probably know the Commander is not a poster child for the old Alexandrian model of sending lovers into battle together." She paused in one of the cast shadows of a shuttle. "I wish I could touch him just so I could touch you." And she did touch her own lips with one delicate pinky. She shuddered then, her eyes closed.

"I have to know, James, why you created this boy. Was it a stab at immortality? A dig at the Administrator class? I should destroy him, you know. I should have from the moment he showed up as an aberration. I wake up at night and run through all the why's that float around our son and nothing makes sense."

The words finally stopped in her, and she found herself walking almost in a daze back to her 'lectric. She opened the door, eased in, and sat staring into the orangish darkness. "I'm still missing something. Missing the logic of it." She raised her hands to the wheel. "But maybe there is no logic in it." She struck the wheel hard, feeling the sharp pain, echo deeply into her bones. "James! Help me you bastard! You need to give me a reason not to destroy my son or you need to help me let you both go!"

—

Joshua sat cross-legged on the floor mat.
Even with his eyes closed, he could mentally feel
his way around the little meditation room. A soft
breeze touched his cheek, whispering up from
the floor ventilation panel. He could hear his
own breath echoed in the canals of his ears, and
all around him, mirrors reflected and ingested his
image in equal measure, spinning it out smaller
and smaller as they shared it back and forth
between themselves into infinity.

The door at his back murmured aside. And
the almost silent step on the wood floor belonged
there as surely as the mirrors and canned air.

"Drew," Joshua greeted him softly. He
opened his eyes and turned toward the man who
stood just inside the room in a flood of corridor
light. The commander smiled, his light wrinkles
lifting to his yellow-flecked eyes.

"Tech Grade Four," the other responded.

Joshua returned his smile. "News travels
fast." He shifted over to make room for the other
man.

Drew folded himself onto the black mat with
a practiced grace. He sat straight, without strain,
his forearms resting in the crook of his hip.

"Senior said you declined pilot training. Any reason for that?"

"You're always subtle, aren't you?"

"It's a great failing of mine," the commander replied. "So where's your head, Josh? What are you thinking?"

Joshua glanced at him, again aware that the line of his shoulders, even when seated, was inches above his commander's. "I've been thinking that maybe I should use some of the self-control you've been teaching me. Maybe it's time to get back to L-Group where I belong. I'm not a tech, Drew. I'm a soldier. You know that. It's what I'm meant to do."

Drew shook his head. "You're more sure of that than I am, Joshua. But maybe that is how it should be. Near as I can tell, you're healed, you've leveled out the Tech training I ordered for you. And, finally, the matter has been taken out of both of our hands. Prime has asked that you be reassigned to your batch, effective immediately. I've cleared your apartment seals and had your paintings and books moved already." He smiled again, a pained and small thing. "I was worried about how you would react, but I can see you are, as always, a step ahead of where I think you should be."

Joshua glanced away then, not wanting to see the concern in his commander's eyes.

"And she wants to see you. Today."

Joshua snapped his gaze back. "Prime? Why?"

"I don't know," Drew said. "But you need to get your butt up to conference room A-11-14 when you're through with your work here."

"I'll go immediately, of course."

"No. Not immediately. Keep your calm." Drew looked him in the eye, fierce and protective. "She wants to meet the L-Grouper who managed a Level-Four Tech grade. But I feel like there is more to it. Be polite, but be cautious."

"I will."

"I really wanted you to get that pilot rating, but for the time being, that will have to wait." A kind of tension feathered across Drew's brow for a moment. A few months ago, Joshua would never have caught it, but now he did and it sent a little shiver of foreboding down his spine. Something was eating at Drew, something big, something he had pushed away again and again until the mental movement had become routine. But that something spilled out like a shadow over his lined face now.

"Are you alright, Commander?"

The man drew himself up a little straighter. "Tired, Joshua. Deep in the bones tired. But I'll be able to rest soon, I suspect." His eyes focused inward for just a moment, and then he shrugged the mood off. Drew rose to his feet, almost without any discernable effort, and laid a hand on Joshua's shoulder.

Joshua looked up at him. "Can I ask you something?"

"Of course." Drew responded without withdrawing his hand.

"Why me? Why have you taken all this time with me? Why all the training, the talks, the books? Not to be rude, Sir, but all of this isn't exactly your job. If you want something in return, if there is a... a *need* you have, I want..."

Drew ran a finger down Joshua's cheek, and touched his lips, silencing him. "In life, Joshua, there are certain debts that must be repaid if your soul will find rest. You are part of a debt I owe to a man I once knew."

"I don't understand." He wanted the hands to continue to touch his face, his lips, but they pulled away as always, chaste and final.

"You weren't meant to. But it is the only answer I can give you." Drew left him then, shutting the door softly behind him and leaving him to the room of mirrored eyes.

———

Joshua only took time to change into his dress uniform and pull his thick hair into a neat ponytail at the base of his neck. The conference room lay up near the Arena level, not far from the space where he and Drew had moved painfully from slow katas to the faster martial arts. The closed doors, with their brass knobs and elegant numbers, still made him a little cold inside, and he had to will warmth back into his fingertips.

A-11-14 finally loomed up, and he stopped there in front of the door, his hands tingling at his sides. She would be waiting just beyond, the Grand Master of the Company, Prime Andrea Annon, who he had only seen in vids and stills. *I am nervous, but I am not afraid of her.* The thought hit him hard, confused him with its strength and surety. He should have been scared—it was common knowledge that sometimes units reported to her and were subsequently decommissioned. But he felt more excited and intrigued than fearful. *Maybe because I have looked death straight in the face a few times*

now. And death is what others most fear in her.
Still, he smoothed a few stray hairs back from his
forehead before he knocked to meet his highest
commander.

She answered the door herself. He allowed
himself a moment to stare, his eyes going quickly
over her smooth, professional smile, the thick
brown hair that fell heavily on her shoulders, the
push of her small breasts against her black
sweater.

"1011. Come in, please." Gracefully she
stepped out of the doorframe to make way for
him.

Joshua eased himself into the room then
stopped. The glass wall in front of him revealed a
gray afternoon sky, heavy, monotonous but
wholly wondrous to him. He forgot about Prime,
the clouds capturing him. He could feel his heart
pound hard in his temples. He wanted to tear
the glass away, to try to touch the sky beyond.
Little hesitant flecks of moisture tapped at the
glass for a moment, then stopped. "Rain," he said
out loud. He felt dizzy, then, disoriented. *The
outside I have never seen before.* "My God."

"Your batch was designated urban and
colony-enclosure class and was not designed to
encounter outdoor fighting, correct?" Prime

stood close to his elbow. He could feel her presence but couldn't rip his eyes his eyes away from the sky. "Should I opaque the windows? Would that make you more comfortable?"

He caught the irritation just flavoring her voice. *I report and then stand here and ignore her. What the hell is happening to me?* He turned toward her, surprised by how tiny she really was. Her head barely came to the top of his shoulder, but she stared into his eyes without any sense of being at a disadvantage. "The shades would be a good idea. The view is...distracting," he answered her.

"Opaque conference room A-11-14." A bronze sheen ate up the gray sky, from the outer edges of the window into the center, until Joshua was left only with a brassy image of himself and Prime.

"Come. Sit with me."

He followed her to the two chairs she had pulled out at the end of a long table. One wall shimmered a little with a huge data screen, and a small bar filled the right wall, framed 'round with expensive wood paneling.

He sat down precisely and formally, his hands on his knees, his gaze locked on her face. Prime seated herself, crossing her legs and pulling a bit at the hemline of her skirt.

"What did you feel, when you looked outside just now, 1011?"

Joshua blinked, and then met her gaze more steadily. "I apologize..."

"That's not what I asked."

He cocked his head a little and measured her for a moment, trying to find the thread of her question. "Small. I felt small, looking out there"

She smiled at him, the expression softening the harsh narrowness of her face. "That wasn't so hard an admission to make, was it?"

"No, Prime." Her gaze on him remained intense, almost to the point of being intrusive. He found he did, indeed, want to look away from her, but he made himself hold her eyes.

Suddenly, Prime reached out and touched his hair. He froze beneath her hand, unsure of what she was doing. "I like your hair like this. When it's L-Group shorn, you look beaten somehow. This is better."

"My batch mates did not always agree." He could remember the laser cutter, hacking his hair too short and burning his scalp. The other, darker things they did, he pushed away. His big-jointed teenage body had not been strong enough to hold four boys off that time. They were faster, more powerful then. But not anymore.

She dropped her hand back to the chair arm. "I persuaded your commanders to let you keep your long hair once you could defend yourself well enough. It was a trophy for you, a mile-marker."

"Thank you."

She shrugged his words off. "I usually don't concern myself with L-Group internal affairs," she said. "But you are certainly different from other L-Groupers, Joshua. Different in ways that are not simply physical."

He flinched a little when she used his name, when her cool gaze hacked him, tried to see into him. But there was nothing he wanted to say in response to her.

"I've seen the art in your room, read some of the things you have read. The part of you that intrigues me is why you continue to see yourself as a part of L-Group at all. Drew knew you'd go back, even before I ordered it. So I want to know why."

"Where else would I go?" he found himself answering, his words clipped and controlled.

"Indeed," she answered, as if she had not heard the undertones of anger beneath his careful tone. But her eyes told him otherwise, narrowed as they were, her nostrils flaring.

"There are those who would prefer to have you decommissioned, you know."

"You mean killed," he returned softly.

"You aren't afraid of me at all, are you?"

He smiled then, appreciating the brief show of her ability to read people. "You are Prime, my first commander. I respect you and your decisions. That is more useful than fear."

She considered him a long moment, then laughed, a surprisingly bright sound. "Yes, much better, in fact." She shifted in her chair, and he felt her gaze travel his body, consuming him with her gaze. "Tell me about the artwork that Drew assigned to you."

Joshua felt his toes curl a little in his soft, black boots. "I know that artwork isn't exactly in the L-Group manuals, but Drew..."

"Stop trying to answer questions I have not posed!"

Her tone cut him, like a thin whip. Her face had gone hard again, harsh, narrow and demanding. He lifted his chin slightly. "What do you wish to know about the art?" He kept his voice calm and smoothed the muscles in his face.

She pulled her elbows up tight to her body and rested her hands on her lap. "What do you feel or hope to feel when you create something?"

Joshua felt a wave of helplessness wash through him. She looked so small, her arms clutched to her sides, her own chin up, but her head tilted a bit to the side. But he could also feel the power inside her, radiating from her, judging him against an unknown scorecard. "Prime...there are....there are no words to explain how it feels."

"Try harder."

He wanted to get up, to put his back to her. But her eyes held him, willing him to speak. "When the image comes, here, in my mind," he said haltingly as he touched his temple, "form takes shape on the canvas without thought. It is light, and color and all emotions there. All of them." He said helplessly.

"But the feeling? Anger, fear, calm, joy..."

"Yes. All of them and none by itself. Like paints all knocked together onto the floor."

She pursed her lips and he could see a kind of anxiousness rising in her eyes.

"I hurt with it sometimes, when the picture is good in my mind and only a shadow of it ends up on the canvas. I feel small...before myself. Before everything I can imagine but cannot reproduce." He glanced away, collecting himself.

Prime, when he looked back into the silence

between them, had also turned her gaze away toward the opaque windows. "Then you may have found what the NCP's and we have both lost, the drive to excellence, the spark, the true creative urge."

She turned back toward him, her movement economical and relaxed. "Do you know why you admire the authors and artists Drew has shared with you? Do you understand they were from a very different time than our own, before the famines and reliance on the new Ag planets? Before the water went bad, the rain you see undrinkable and deadly, the NCP genetic lines producing as many idiots and monsters as functional human beings? But because of what lies in you, perhaps all of that energy, that life, has not been lost and bred out of us. You are a gift to us."

He continued to watch her, his spine tightening. It was just another way to say he was different. Another push at his chest, separating him from the rest of humanity.

"I don't understand what you feel," she continued. "But the Ancients created out of that energy, those feelings. You could not know, but we are *dying*, Joshua. No new innovations, not for generations. Art as such is nonexistent really, writing reduced to the report or political tool." She dropped her voice. "I can't understand many of the old masters. No, not their words, those I can read easily enough, but their intent, their emotional state. I can analyze structure, see the logic, the rules, place it in time and space, but I can't touch it like you seem to do. My heart rate does not change; my eyes remain dry. They are words on a page, notes in space, color on white, no more, no less."

In that moment, he could feel a kind of sadness for her. She recognized the lack, but had nothing to fill it, that space in her heart. He started to say as much, but she shook her head as if reading his expression. "But you, you are in a dangerous position, Joshua because much of this world simply *cannot* understand you. There is no point of reference for others. We think. But you? You feel."

"I can't be that different," he protested quietly. "I see emotional responses in L-Group all the time."

"No. The processes from which those externalized responses are derived are not the same. You *create* out of your emotional base. L-Groupers react in another way entirely. If they see a picture you have created, they will respond to it intellectually and from that intellectual experience, get a hint of joy, anger, impatience, true. You, however, seem to experience the feeling first and create the picture *from* it, which then reinforces that state or you are forced by this same internal wiring to redo the picture. I could not do that because I cannot start from the same place you do. In combat, we do not want the line soldier to feel and act creatively out of that feeling. We want observation and response, fast, uncalculating and immediate. A-designates are a bit different, but not by much. Nor are the administrator class units very dissimilar. It's a pattern that works for us, or at least, it has in the past."

"For us?"

"For the Company I serve."

Joshua shook his head a little helplessly. He could almost taste where she was trying to lead him, but he found a little stubborn place in his heart, the place that clung to the belief he was not so very different on the inside from his batch-mates.

"You can see my problem perhaps. If L-Group asks you to kill, can you, without hesitation and soul searching? Can you ever be a soldier, wired as you are?"

"Yes." He responded immediately.

"I'm not so sure." She nearly whispered the word. "You may feel far too much to be a predictable unit."

"But couldn't it be equally possible that a good soldier will feel pleasure when he kills, that a strong emotion is useful in combat? Would that not trigger the response you seek?" He hated the words the moment they were out of his mouth, felt the wrongness of them, but of course could not draw them back.

"Actually," she nodded in complete agreement, "early Company models were developed exactly along that specific line of thought. But the units ultimately became addicted to the pleasure principle, killing to get their high, even killing each other. We have learned to walk a very fine line, creating warriors without a true passion for war. We want L-Group to be efficient, not passionate, when they do a job. Passion cannot be controlled, aimed, depended upon."

"Yes. I understand," he said. And he did.

"But that circles us back to you, Joshua. Because you have neither the stimulus-response shield of an L-Grouper, nor are you, I think, a passionate killer. So tell me, how will you survive it, both the combat and the isolation of your position?"

Her soft voice maddened him. She was flaying him open, effortlessly, dissecting him as easily as a pinioned rat.

"I will do my duty," he said at last. His heart ached in a way he had not felt for months.

"I'm not sure you or I will know that until a real test comes."

Joshua tried to hold her gaze, but it took knotting his jaw to do it.

"So L-Group commanders must ponder how you may react, something they never have to do with any of their other soldiers. And they don't *like* to ponder such things. There are those who simply cannot tolerate enigmas, Joshua. There are those who want you quietly removed. Or perhaps not so quietly. But you've already experienced that."

He nodded, the echo of the months of pain and uncoordinated muscles rising in his memory. He shoved them down.

"I *can* move you. I can have you trained into other areas, safer areas. But I have a vision for you, about you if you will. I want you to stay in L-Group for the time being. I want you honed and sharp as a sword. But keep your goddamn head down. Don't question orders. Stay awake. Survive. And find your edge, because you will need it. And one day, I may need it as well."

Questions burned in him, but also the need to withdraw, to process her shadowy hints and half-revelations. She seemed to read this in him easily and he knew before she gestured with her head toward the door that she would tell him no more. "Dismissed, 1011."

He stood, tipping his head toward her in a half-bow.

"Joshua."

He looked down at her, hesitating. She had to crane her neck to look up at him in turn, and the movement pulled the slender cords in her neck tight. "Be well. Be safe."

Again he bowed, a little more formally. But her words, spoken with a softness and longing he could not explain, brought a hot flush to his cheeks. "Be well, Prime," he returned and then made himself walk slowly and evenly from the room.

Chapter 13

Everything, even sex, is a contest among us.
It flows from simply following the orders that
our own DNA will not let us disobey. To yield
or force another to yield, to bear or glory in
the cold invasion of flesh into flesh, to emerge
triumphant or to hold our stoic lines in
perfect submission, such sexual experiences
are a kind of pleasurable warfare for us. But
affection, feelings, to be haunted by
memories of such things? It is not in our
nature.

L-Group Voices
Company Central Archives, Earth

L-Group Apartments
Company Central, Earth Complex

Joshua keyed the hand-pad lock to his apartment,
nearly drooping with fatigue. He'd been roused
from bed and thrust into a 2 AM battle strategy
test, forced to perform the mentally challenging

data simulations for over two hours. Admin did that sometime, researching off-hour performance ratings. The fact that he had been back in his batch for only a few months seemed to single him out for such things. This had been the fifth test he'd gone through in the last two weeks, and it was starting to wear thin. In an hour and a half, he'd be up again, working out by himself in the gym and then on to weapons check and maintenance detail for the rest of the day.

After that, maybe they would let him sleep. Maybe.

His door slid aside, but before he could ask for lights, a thin blue beam snapped out of the darkness and full into his chest. The crack ran through him like cold fire, jerking his nerve endings in a wild dance of shock. His legs gave out from under him and the floor rushed up, dizzying in the afterglow of the military stunner. He couldn't even catch himself and the impact snapped his teeth together hard. He didn't lose consciousness, not exactly, although as the lights came up he wasn't sure if he was seeing three men or just one. Blond hair, black uniforms all sloshed together and ran like a too-wet painting. Finally a low groan escaped his throat.

"Strip him."

That voice he knew, even through his confusion.

Adam. No. Not like this. But the words couldn't shake through his tight throat.

Hands were on him then, hands that ripped at his clothing, jerking him over and around, efficient, cold. He could feel the harsh nap of the carpet against his naked skin, fingernails scraping over his shoulders and back and legs as the fabric came away.

"Bed frame."

He tried to focus, to make his muscles move, but the stunner had been set high enough that nothing wanted to work. He was hauled to his feet, his arms dragged wide and wrists plastic-corded to the metal loft frame. He sagged his forehead against the cold support bar as the plastic bit in, cutting into his skin and holding him upright when his legs would not. The first echoes of cold wafted over his skin, the first echoes of truer sensation.

But he wasn't sure it was a good thing.

"Legs." Adam's voice stayed low, battle quiet and sure. Joshua felt something cold clamp around one ankle and then the other, shoving his legs wide at their base. Someone ran a hand up the back of his thigh to his buttocks and he tried to twitch away. He could barely lift his head off the bed-frame. One knee collapsed, chewing the plastic into his wrists so deeply that he felt the first warm flush of blood there. At last his vocal cords worked enough for him to let out a couple low, coughing words. "No, Commander. You don't have to..."

"No? Beat him."

He heard the belts slip from their keepers, L-Group belts with ridged and braided edges of faux leather over wire. Heard feet rustle against the low carpet, the shift of uniforms as arms drew back.

And then the belts exploded against his back, first one side, then the other, the strikes fast and hard and snapping in the silent apartment, wrapping his sides and ribs and back in tongues of fire. He gasped, writhing without coordination until his head fell away from the frame and he could see the ceiling and he was sure the plastic strips at his wrists would cut clean through.

He was not sure how long it went on, only that at some point he started screaming, the belts carving into him without pause and without mercy. And then it stopped, and he could hear two men leaving his apartment without a word.

His own little animal sounds of misery filled the corners of his quarters and he hated himself for it. He reached out finally with his fingers and was able to take some of his own weight off his wrists, but his legs continued to buckle and shake beneath him.

Fingers suddenly touched his raw skin, and traced the welts and bruised ribs. "Stop," he breathed through his swollen throat. "Stop. You're a command designated soldier. We don't have to do it this way. I know my duty. I know how to submit. Order me. It's your right."

Fingers freed his hair from the disheveled ponytail; fingers combed it out long and stinging into the welts on his back; fingers drew down the curve of his neck, along the top of his shoulder line, and husky breath now as Adam's lips kissed along one shaking arm.

But no answers.

Joshua felt Adam step back, heard the uniform come off the other man slowly, mechanically. "No. Adam. Cut me down. I can please you. Let me please you. But not like this. I know you don't want this. I know someone is *making* you do this." He shuddered the words out.

"Still no?" Adam's voice rasped. Hands,

then, ran down his sides, over the curving lines of his hips, then back up to his nipples with long, slow strokes. He could feel Adam press against him grinding into the fresh weals and cuts. Something went around his neck, a uniform belt, tightening against his windpipe and twisted, but not enough to totally cut off his air, not yet. And then, Adam was forcing his way into his stunner-slackened body, shoving him forward into his bonds, and he couldn't fight back as he was ripped open, the other man's breath now picking up, panting with excitement.

With victory.

He could feel one arm snake low around his belly, the other dragging down more tightly on the belt around his throat. The noose tightened, and he writhed, his body jerking as his oxygen was cut off millimeter by millimeter.

"I'll die for this, you know," Adam groaned into his ear. "But that's OK. We go together." He began to pump into Joshua brutally, and the belt choked his agony back into his throat and locked it away. "You're in me, my blood, my brain, my mouth. And you'll die with me in you. Together. Bonded. My nightmare and my obsession. My last orders, all tied up in you. And finally, I'll be free of all these damn walls."

Joshua could no longer follow Adam's voice as the other man lost himself in his actions, the brutal rape banging his body against his bed frame, the noose tightening bit by bit until all he wanted was to breathe in one last gulp of air. The air shimmered, light-shards that rang with agony, and then shadowed.

Did the door open? Did he really feel the impact as Adam was smashed away from him? Did he hear a high-pitched whine of a civi-class stunner in his small apartment? Or was his mind painting the last strokes of consciousness, fighting back the only way he could, in a kind of vicious and violent death wish aimed at Adam?

The noose around his neck suddenly loosened and he drew in his breath with a ragged gasp. With the air, the pain came back, hot and red. He could feel the plastic being cut, ripping out of his skin at his wrists. His legs gave out. Still hobbled, he fell nearly straight backwards, only to be caught awkwardly and half-dropped to the carpet. He cried out, his near-scream driving a spike into his own skull as his raw back hit someone's knee and the rough weave of the rug.

"Shussssssh. Got you. I got you." The voice was lightly accented, the tones strained as if the speaker was barely keeping his food down. He felt the man fumble with the manacles around his ankles. "I'll get help. Just stay with me."

Joshua thrashed out, his hands finally going around the other man's wrist. He blinked up into a face backlit with the long fluorescents, taking in an impression of curly reddish hair and hazel eyes, the aura of light settling around his shoulders like a cape.

"I'm Matthew. A friend."

He didn't let go of the man's wrist. "Not L-Group," he managed to grate out.

"No. NCP, mid-level government. God, you're a mess. Here, roll to your side. No, your right side, less damage there. Oh, God, your back..." Joshua let the man shift him and he had to let go of the other's wrist. He could see Adam now, crumpled and naked beneath the tattered remains of his art work. The canvases had been knifed into ribbons of color hanging in crooked frames. Moments later, he felt the familiar nap of his sleeping blanket fall over him and heard Matthew's fingers flying over a touch-pad. "I've made some friends over these last few months. I want to get you out of here, moved to someplace safer."

"Can't leave L-Group areas..." Joshua murmured. The pressure behind his eyes was blinding now, the after-affect of the military grade stunner.

"Bullshit. You as hell can't stay here," Matthew returned. He paused, reading his handpad display.

Joshua could hear the adrenaline now in the voice, and knew the NCP's whole body must be shaking with it. "Dead?"

"What?" Matthew asked, then immediately seemed to realize Joshua was asking about Adam. "No. Stunned. I'm not a murderer." An awkward pat on his shoulder sealed the statement. "Tech named Senior is on his way. Teacher friend of yours, maybe? He's become a good drinking buddy of mine. He's borrowing a med-tech uniform and transport. We'll body bag you and lift you out. I think we'll that blond guy sort himself out when he wakes up."

"Senior..." Joshua breathed and then coughed. He could taste blood in his mouth, maybe from when he had gone down the first time. His consciousness wavered, hiccupped, shuddering the whole room.

"Yeah, and I know a med-tech who can make a house call, hush-hush. Company doesn't make its Techs very good at poker, you know? So she owes me. Anyway, she'll get you patched up."

Joshua liked the sound of the other man's voice, the unusual accent, the rolling shape of his sentences. But the meaning, it wasn't making sense to him. He let his eyes close, oddly content with the weight of the man's hand resting on his shoulder, the thin gray blanket between their skins.

"Stay with me, Joshua. Stay..."

But he couldn't.

—

NCP Visitor's Quarters
Mid-level Access Area
Company Central, Earth Complex

Matthew lay back in his chair, his fingers interlaced over his scalp and his elbows thrust out to the side. He'd gone through months of obtuse digging, playing out lines of inquiry then zipping in for a quick grab on something small and meaningless if taken only by itself. There would be no trail of his work; the very randomness of it would hide what he had been searching for. He was good and he was beyond careful. The painstakingly gleaned data hung in mid-air over his workstation. Even now, he could scarcely believe it was so clear and real.

He gazed at one name in particular, and then waved the file open. Joshua 1011. Physical and intellectual deviation from L-Group norms. Emotional irregularities. Months of isolation from his batch. And years of physical abuse, from laser cutter burns to broken bones, from a deliberate drugging and now...

He glanced at the form sprawled on his narrow couch. Now, a brutal rape to add to the file. If he hadn't accessed the apartment number and code, if he hadn't been so damn excited that he couldn't wait for a more civilized time to actually *see* Joshua 1011, the man would have been dead. Senior had arrived a few minutes after 1011 had passed out. They'd stasis bagged him and hauled him out with a minimum amount of fuss. They both heard the alarms go off in the apartment area after they'd pulled the 'lectric into the connecting tunnel, but nothing shadowed them out of the L-Group wing.

The med-tech had met them at Matthew's own apartment, cleaned and fuse-stitched the kid back up as best as she could, and then scuttled away into the early morning bustle of the Company. He was shocked at how fast the bleeding seemed to stop, how quickly the bruises faded. Senior had stayed only long enough to be sure Joshua would make it, then melted away to return the equipment he'd borrowed before it was missed. He'd shrugged off Matthew's thank-you, his eyes sad and large in his round face.

Matthew directed his eyes back to the data. He recognized the odd genotype splices that indicated a possible connection with the old Company ARR program. He read the lab dates again, shaking his head. They had known, and known early, that this kid was going to be a massive aberration and they had let him develop anyway. Hell, they had even perversely kept him as part of his L-Group batch. It verged on criminal. The tech training was frankly interesting, as was the artwork snapshots included in his full file. Again and again, he could see Prime's hand moving through the life of the boy, shaping, creating boundaries, flying full in the face of protocol.

But why?

He'd unearthed a number of other ARR units that were still functional in L-Group and the various Tech services. He'd also found tales of insanity, homicidal actions, erratic and irrational behaviors that sometimes verged on the bizarre. He thought back to the L-Group apartment, the blond man raping and strangling the beaten Joshua, and he shuddered. He dearly wished he could forget the lists of decommissioned men and women he'd found, all of them dissected and studied and set aside in neat data tables at last, but uneasy in their digital graves. So many lives, twisted and hurting.

And nobody beyond the Company walls knew anything about it.

And finally, just three days ago, he'd found a name that had sent him into his tiny bedroom for an entire day, shaking and cold and sweating with memories and shock. James Illion, dead from an overdose of Cziana Root extract, or at least that is what the report stated. *His* James Illion, the bringer of misery and the bringer of dreams. And another link in the toxic ARR chain that rattled around his own ankle hell, around his blessed throat for that matter.

He stared at Joshua's lean face, now cleaned of blood. If the line of his nose were just a bit more hawk-like, his shoulders a bit more mature and broad, he would look exactly like that shadow from Matthew's past—black hair, rangy six foot three or four frame, it all fit. He felt the cold fear rise in his gut, but he pushed it back firmly this time. He couldn't fall apart now. *Could*

*this be James Illion's son? My God. Why wouldn't
the past just stay the fucking past?*

Off to the left of the couch, a small brown
lump stirred uncomfortably and half-extended its
wings. Seymour was not a real hawk, but the
artist who had made him had come awfully close
to a life-like representation. He fanned out his
tail beneath the perch, the wide, red-brown
bands glistening in the artificial light as he shook
his head restlessly. "Down," Matthew murmured,
afraid the bird might wake his illicit guest. He
wasn't quite ready for that, even though the
sedatives the med-tech had given to him had
stopped his own shaking for now. A sleeping son
of Illion he could handle; having to actually face
the man that might awaken the ghosts in him,
that was something he'd rather avoid, for another
hour or so anyway.

Then he heard the door to his apartment
open behind him.

Matthew spun out of his chair and full into a
tall blond man framed in his doorway. He was
about fifty, with yellow-flecked gray eyes. His
face was hard as he aimed the military grade
stunner directly at Matthew's chest. His eyes
flicked toward Joshua, sprawled on the couch,
and then back.

"Bedroom, Mr. Dennon." He gestured with his head, but the gun never wavered.

"Easy." Matthew's arms raised slowly, his palms open. *My God, I know him. From Rialga. He was with James there. What the fuck?* His mind scrambled for a name, and then he knew it. "Commander Drew, right? Look, Joshua is going to be OK. I was trying to help, and this seemed like the safest..."

Surprise flickered over the blond man's face; shadow-quick and gone. "Don't make me repeat myself," he said softly.

"Rialga. James Illion. Krystine. I remember you, don't you get it?" Matthew said, his words quick and urgent. But he started to ease himself toward the bedroom without turning his back on Drew. "I was younger then. We met in the city park and James gave me that damn flute. I'm Matthew, remember?"

"Matthew Dennon. *That* Matthew Dennon?" Drew's voice was suddenly strained. The gun really did move then, the muzzle dipping before bobbing back into line with his body.

"Yeah. That fucked-up-four-ways-to-hell Matthew Dennon. Can you put the gun down now, or are you still set on blowing me away in the bedroom of all places? I mean, I don't even

225

sleep in there." And he tried a little smile, to prove he was wholly in control of himself. *Which, of course, was a bald lie.*

Drew lowered the tip of his weapon, and then thumbed the safety back on. He nudged the door shut with his foot, and set the gun down by the wall, his eyes still on Matthew. "What are you doing here?" he asked, his eyes again going to Joshua.

Matthew read the concern there, almost like a father for his son, and allowed himself a little internal sigh of relief. "I've been doing a little oversight research."

Drew nodded for him to continue.

"And I sort of got interested in ARR stuff. Illion's research most recently, and the people he created. Like 1011 there."

Drew's eyes glinted for a moment. "You called them people, not units."

"It the shoe fits..."

"Pardon?"

"Ancient expression. Sorry." Matthew shifted, still feeling his heart hammering in his chest. But he was surprisingly calm, all things considered. *God bless sedatives.*

"Senior told me Joshua would be here."

Matthew gestured vaguely at the gun. "And

that meant you were gonna come and what? Blow me away with that and just take the kid? You couldn't just knock?"

Drew gave him a withering smile. "Yes, you've divined the general plan."

Matthew frowned. "It sucked."

Drew moved forward then, and Matthew gave way before him. The blond man knelt, his long fingers brushed over Joshua's cheek and then the angry collar of red on his neck. "How bad?"

"Bad." Matthew said. "Beaten, stunned, raped while he was being strangled. Sick stuff, Drew, for Company products to be inflicting on each other. Felt like I was in the middle of a bad alleyway scene. What's the story?"

Drew ignored him. He pulled back the blanket that covered Joshua and his face paled even more as he looked at the fading bruises and cuts. "Damn it, Joshua."

"It was hardly his fault," Matthew protested.

"I know," Drew answered. "It never is." He stood then, his hands resting on his narrow hips. "Damn it all." He turned toward Matthew. "Get packed."

"Pardon?"

"Get packed. One duffle, that's it. And clear

227

your research, all of it. You have five minutes."

"If you think I'm going to dump months of..."

Drew turned toward him slowly. "I think, if you want to live, you're going to do precisely what I tell you to do. In half an hour, maybe much less, I expect another L-Group commander will have traced the DNA remnants in Joshua's apartment and found your lodging number. When he comes through that door to finish what he started with Joshua, he'll probably leave you pasted all over the ceiling. He's already dead as far as he is concerned. Taking you out wouldn't matter to him in the least."

"If you know so much, arrest him!"

"I can't," Drew said. "Understand, Matthew, he's ARR and I need to preserve that bloodline as best as I can, just like I need to protect this young man." Something hungry and desperate flicked over the commander's face.

"Yeah, like you're doing such a fine job," Matthew growled back.

"You now have three minutes to get packed," Drew said, his face once again smoothing into a professional soldier's mask.

"Fine. But where are we going?"

"Terrantata, Mr. Dennon."

"As in the outer colony?" Matthew asked

incredulously.

"Batch 416 Urban and 414 Bush have been asked to seize and hold the colony mine until further notice. You both need to be on board that ship as well."

"Why?"

"Two minutes."

"God damn you." Matthew spun and began to delete his research. He had been so close to making sense of it all, the shadowy genetic templates, the selective culls, all of it. He felt sick as the data screen went blank.

He glanced back and saw Drew pulling Joshua's heavy body up onto his shoulder. "Second thought, forget your gear. We need to go now."

"I can..."

"Get the door. And the gun." Drew settled the dark young man in a classic fireman's carry. It took a moment for Matthew to process just how strong the commander was. Joshua hung limp on his shoulder, still drugged into oblivion. The white Tech pants hung just off his hipbones; little spots and strips of red bled through the fabric here and there.

"Now would be good, Mr. Dennon."

Seymour shifted restlessly on his perch,

opening his wings again. "Seymour. Shut down,"
Matthew sighed. And the bird sculpture did,
settling almost grumpily into a facsimile of sleep.
He went to the door then, stooping to pick up the
weapon propped on the wall. "You have a
transport?"

"Yes." Drew brushed past him, Joshua's
limbs swaying with his stride. "Keep up."

*Yeah, like I ever do with the ghosts from my
past*, Matthew thought in resignation.

Chapter 14

*I want to steal it back for all of us—full
sensations, full emotional responses, full
relational abilities. I want people to laugh
and cry and create things that are wholly
useless and will never make a profit. I want
women to cradle a child in their own bellies,
and know the face of their lover again. Yes, I
may be a romantic. I actually do regret the
horrible chaos that must come first. But
that's how all real life begins anyway. It is
inevitable.*

James Illion
Genotemplate Tech Grade 8
Historical Archives
Terrantata Colony

Troop Transport Vessel
Command Quarters

Drew fixed the last monitor tab on his chest, and

then twitched the t-shirt back in place. The soft blue walls of his shipboard office curved up and around him, the one tiny window to the outside already darkened with radiation shielding for the first of many long hops to Terrantata.

Commander Tony stood in stiff attention in front of his desk; his own shirt bulging a bit with leads and monitor patches.

"Are they all put to bed?" Drew asked finally.

"Yes, Sir," Tony answered him; his eyes cast straight ahead, his squared-off jaw hard. "Tech lines just came in, and have been put to cold sleep. All canisters functioning and course confirmed by the pilot. He just turned in, less than fifteen minutes ago. Just you and I now, aside from your designated wake staff team." Something crept into his voice, a low, oily loathing.

"You don't agree with my wake-staff selection?"

Tony shifted. "I am uncomfortable with it, yes."

"You can't kill him here, you know," Drew said quietly. "Not here or on Terrantata."

Tony's eyes widened a fraction.

"I got a message from Administrator Thomas Muligan that you were behind Joshua's *death*.

But off course, the boy didn't die, did he? So the warning was vaguely amusing. Must have pissed you off to no end, to fail *twice*." Drew seated himself in his workstation chair, but offered no such luxury to Tony. He knit his fingers together, elbows on his chair arms.

Tony had flushed a faint and blotchy red, but his eyes never wavered.

"What I can't figure out is why you didn't just do it yourself. I mean, *Adam*? A little perverse, don't you think, since they were lovers of a sort."

"Adam is my body unit."

"And Joshua is Adam's obsession. Has been for years, if you opened your eyes a bit. But then, there's the answer, right? That makes it all the more sweet to you, doesn't it? The thrill of commanding that much obedience, enough to make a man kill his own lover."

"You have no right to conjecture..."

"Shut up," Drew nearly whispered. "I just want to be very, very clear: If I didn't need you and Adam so goddamn much I'd be dumping you both in the shipboard incinerator just now."

Tony's face twitched with the verbal blow. "Joshua 1011 is a danger. He killed Alec and Michael in the Lunar One sim, and..."

"I know who killed Alec and Michael. Don't insult my intelligence."

The flush on Tony's face and neck faded before a wave of pale and sickly color.

"And you think that Joshua figured it out, too? Right?"

Tony stared stonily ahead, his hands knit in fists.

"Well, he didn't. So you can stand down from your manhunt, do you get me?"

"If you knew..."

"Not if. I know. But I can't throw you out like the trash you are, Tony. You have something I would very much like to preserve but my patience is at an end. You or Adam make one more move to harm Joshua 1011, and I will dig you both so deep into Terrantata's soil that the miners won't even be able to unearth you. Got me?"

"Yes, Sir."

"I mean it Tony. I am done with this behavior. Done." Drew stood then. "Get your butt into your sleep canister. Now."

"Yes, Sir."

Tony pivoted and stalked from the command office.

Drew stood by his desk, closed his eyes and

breathed slowly. It would be easy to change his mind, to set the canisters so neither Tony or Adam woke again. Accidents happened, after all, didn't they? He sighed his breath out. *No. I can't. And not just because L-Groupers don't kill other L-Groupers.*

So close now. So close. I just need to hold them together for a little longer. A little longer, and then I can finally rest.

—

Troop Transport
Wake-Staff Quarters

Joshua opened his eyes to blue metal. His whole body ached and for a moment, he nearly closed his eyes again, just wanting to sink back into that place where he didn't have to feel, didn't have to think. But he sensed another presence in the room, and he forced his head to the side, driven more by habit than anything as benign as curiosity.

The other man was asleep in the bunk across the room from him. One arm trailed out beneath the gray covers, and his face was relaxed, his lips parted over even teeth, and thick eyelashes

feathered over his cheeks. Curly reddish-brown
hair scrolled over the pillowcase. He was not an
imposing man, nor was he shipboard-tech small.
Joshua remembered a flash of him for a moment,
backlit and scared.

Scared for him. And disgusted by the scene
he'd stumbled into.

He did shut his eyes then, trying to hold
back the memory. But of course, it squeezed
around the edges of his mind, oozed out in
splotches of black and blond and red. Too much
red. He made himself sit up then, and swung his
legs out of the bunk. The floor was cold on his
bare feet. He touched the bloodstained med-tech
pants he wore and felt his stomach rise hot and
acidic into his throat. There was no holding it
back. He lunged then for the small sink between
the bunks and retched hard, his hands slipping
on the frigid metal. Again and again he tried to
throw up, but there was nothing in his stomach
but ropy fluid.

A hand fell on his back, and he swung
around viciously. He drove the other man back
with his shoulder, slamming him into the cabin
door. He drew back his other hand, ready to
strike, but stopped, shaking, dazed, his own
vomit still bitter in his mouth. The man tried to

shield his face, the gesture more a beaten hunker than any real defensive move. Joshua released him, stumbled back and sat hard on his bunk. "I'm sorry," he murmured. "Sorry. Just don't. Just don't touch me again."

The man nodded warily, not moving from the doorway. "Yeah, I get that now," he said. "I'm supposed to tell you I got meds for the nausea. Drew thought you might need them..." he broke off, sliding a step closer to his own bed, but his eyes never leaving Joshua.

"We're ship-board."

"Yeah. About one day out."

"Out to where?"

"Terrantata evidently. That's the sum total of what I know." The man eased himself onto his bunk. He pulled his legs up and pressed his spine back against the wall.

Stupid way to sit. Indefensible, unless he can kick like a mule. Joshua shook his head a little, willing the nausea down and back.

"Drew left you wake staff orders up on the command deck. Said you'd know your way around the ship."

"He's cold-sleeping?"

"Yeah, like everyone else on board as near as I can tell. I walked around a bit, but didn't touch anything. I could use some food, though. And clothes. And a shower."

"No showers," Joshua murmured. "Sonics. I'll show you later. You NCP?"

"Yeah. Midlevel government research. Matthew. Matthew Dennon," he offered.

"Joshua 1011, L-Group Batch 416."

"Yeah, I...I gathered as much," Matthew replied. Joshua felt like he might say more, but he didn't. And he didn't much care. The memories came again, hands now, the beating and Adam violating him. He put his hand against his mouth, barely containing the nausea again. He could feel the bruising within, gouges inside of him that would never go away. He was marked, branded, cast outside again. And this man had seen it happen. Had saved his life, yes, but had *seen* it all.

I'm L-Group. I cope. This has happened before. I stand up. I do my duty.

"At least you're awake. And moving like you just did, you can't be feeling quite as bad as you look. You boys heal damn fast. Lucky." Matthew offered the words quietly, and Joshua knew he was trying to help. He could see the other man rub unobtrusively at his chest where Joshua had slammed into him.

Heal so damn fast. No, not really. Not in my mind where all the shadows live. Now more shadows. God, I am going to be sick again. Joshua swallowed hard, holding it down with gritted teeth.

Matthew unfolded a little from his wall. "Let me get those meds."

Joshua snapped hand up, palm out, holding him pinioned there with his will. "I'll be fine. I'm not going to make the entire jump fazed out on anti-nausea meds. I'll cope." *I'll cope. I'll cope. Right.*

Matthew faded back against the wall again. "Suit yourself. Let me know if you change your mind."

"I'm fully aware of the location of med-tech supplies on board," Joshua returned. "I don't need or want your help."

"OK." There was no hint of irritation in Matthew's voice, which vaguely surprised him.

He knew he should get dressed, get to his orders. But Joshua could not make himself move. "You were in my apartment, when Adam..." he couldn't continue.

Matthew simply shrugged, his eyes calm and his face only a little flushed from Joshua's attack. No gloating, no apologies, no expectations in that movement. It said more than anything else Matthew might have offered him. Past was past, done was done, that's what his body said, clearly and confidently.

Joshua nodded and found he could get to his feet at last. The man looked up at him, his curly hair gently framing his face. His eyes were so different from L-Groupers, hazel, like trees and bark he'd seen in pictures, like a moody brown ocean shot through with lines of green and amber light.

Matthew flushed under Joshua's stare.

"Come with me. I'll show you the sonics and clothing stores and then we'll get my orders and get you fed at least. Sound OK?"

"Yeah. Sounds good." Matthew answered. No excitement there, just a calm and gentle expectation radiated from the man.

"Thank you," Joshua murmured then.

"What?"

"For saving my life," he said. He needed to hear the words himself, let them sink in. *Dancing with death again, he swung me around, but he let me go. How many more times until that skull leaned in with its blackened teeth and took him? He almost felt ready. Anytime now, I'll just put my hand out and...no.*

No.

He stood and keyed the door, assuming the NCP would follow him.

—

As the weeks passed, they fell into an odd sort of routine finally, Matthew hanging out on the shielded stardeck as Joshua ran through all of his checkpoints. The cavernous sleep deck was always a little weird, red-lighted canisters glowing in rows like illuminated coffins. Just inside the front door, Joshua could call up all the data for the entire deck. He'd scan through quickly and move on, every day monotonously the same.

Sometimes they talked, more about what life was like outside of Central than anything else, but mostly they shared a kind of companionable silence, drinking poor synthetic coffee and staring at the blue metal walls. At first, Joshua thought that perhaps the NCP knew him from somewhere. The glances he would occasionally catch were both intense and edged with something he couldn't quite place. Joshua could make no sense of it. Gradually, the looks stopped, or rather, he was aware they changed,

Matthew's eyes warmer and less searching.

Matthew had been disappointed to find there was no music, no entertainment programs, not even any electronic reading matter other than tech manuals loaded on board. Joshua set him up a little workstation, though, so he could write if he wished, and cajoled Matthew to join him on his morning jogs.

He was about three-quarters through his checklist, day 97, when Matthew's voice came out over the PA. "Joshua, can you come up to the star-deck?" He sounded hollow, even in shock. Joshua shut down the diagnostics center with a wave of his hand and made his way up the three levels.

"Matthew?" he asked as soon as the doors parted. His eyes swept the room, and at first, he couldn't see anyone. He stepped in, his chin snapping right then left, as he stalked further into the lounge. Finally, he caught a low, hunkered shape, right under the edge of the radiation shielded window. Matthew had crammed himself small and tight into the corner, and his whole body trembled.

Joshua went to him at once, but crouched a few feet away. "Matthew?" he asked more quietly.

The man turned his face toward Joshua and swallowed. He blinked and blinked again, as if clearing the after-burn of a bright flash of light. "You gotta put me in cold sleep," he said, his voice reedy and shaking. "We're in fucking space, do you know that?"

Joshua nodded, just once, very slowly.

Matthew went quiet, although he curled his fingers up through his hair and gripped his skull tight. "He wasn't supposed to find me here, not out here. I kept seeing him on Earth, over and over and I can't shake him even now. He was right there, corner of my eye, touching my shoulder...I just can't take it anymore."

"Who?" Joshua asked, carefully pitching his voice low.

"I don't know him," Matthew said. "I don't."

Joshua crept closer and when Matthew didn't shrink away from him, he settled down, crossed legged. "There's no one here, Matthew. Just us."

Matthew shook his head, his own arms wrapping him more tightly. "I'm sorry. I'm sorry. I'm just so tired of it. Over a year of it, and I can't figure out what he wants."

"What does he look like?" Joshua asked, keeping his voice steady.

"Damn L-Grouper. Blond, blue eyes, real

243

light frame, like a dancer. Got about 1000 of them in the cold sleep level, right? But not this guy. This guy has been hovering around me for over a year. 'Find it Matthew, you have to find it,' he keeps telling me." Matthew dropped his head to his knees. "Just put me to sleep. Please Joshua."

"I can't," Joshua murmured. "Not any more canisters; we're at full compliment." He was lying but Matthew had no need to know that.

"Then turn someone out early to keep you company. I am begging you here."

"No," he said. "We'll figure this out. I'll get you a sedative."

"I don't want a fucking sedative. I want this to stop! Goddamn Illion, giving us all visions and dreams. Your father was a monster, messing me up like this."

Joshua went very still then. "I don't have a father, Matthew."

"Yes, you do. James Illion, Tech Grade Eight."

"I was created in a canister, from a genetic template. You know that."

"Damn it, Joshua. Grade eights are *genetic* techs!" Matthew said. He lifted his head, his cheeks flushed a deep and angry red, his hazel eyes shaded nearly green. "He made you just as surely as he made me." He shook his head, at least half angry now, and only half frightened. "You're him, all over again, just as tall, same coloring, same eyes, same hair. You're his kid. And I'm his science experiment. ARR genes, Joshua. ARR genes in both of us. I've read your file. I've seen the template he used to make you."

Joshua sat in a stunned silence.

Matthew looked at him then, but Joshua couldn't lift his eyes off the metal floor. *A father? Who was a monster?* "But you're an NCP," he found his voice rough, and cleared it. "You met him, though. Where?"

Matthew straightened carefully, leaning his head back against the wall. "Rialga. I was like eight years old. Same place I met Commander Drew and a woman named Krystine Malar. They were together in the city park, and I...I liked how he played the flute. Brought me right to him, like he was some kind of fucking magic."

"Rialga," Joshua repeated. "The first of the ag-planets."

"My home for a while, before my parents got recalled to Earth." He gave me the flute and this little bottle of oil to use on it, see? And I was so excited; I wasn't watching the traffic outside the

245

park when I tried to cross to head home. Got hit, bad, and the oil... God, Joshua. Just put me the fuck to sleep."

Joshua gazed at Matthew, and saw the tears there, wet on his cheeks. He slid closer then, and tentatively reached out to touch the dampness. Matthew froze under his touch. "L-groupers don't cry," Joshua murmured. "I'm not sure they can." He rubbed the tear between his thumb and forefinger.

"Can you?"

"Cry? Oh, of course. But I don't. " Joshua eased himself back against the same wall, their shoulders almost touching. "The oil changed you somehow?" *If I can just keep him talking, he'll be ok. He has to be ok. I'm not trained for this, and if he's like Adam...*

Matthew nodded. "The oil? Yeah, you could say it changed me. I was sick a long time. He...James, he came to the apartment and took care of me for free. Mom and Dad, they were thrilled to have a Grade Eight watching over me, playing the damn flute for me until it called out the dreams like he knew it would."

"Dreams?"

"Hawks. Horses. Oceans. Fields of grain, red in the setting sun. Faces, sounds, smells, so much I didn't want to open my eyes sometimes. I wanted to *stay*, Joshua. It was so...beautiful and alive and fierce and...everything my own life wasn't, in that bed, in that apartment. And later, in the world. It's like I got a glimpse of what we have lost and it's ruined it all for me."

"What does a flute sound like?" Joshua asked quietly.

"You've got to be kidding me." Matthew finally grinned at him weakly.

"I've just never heard music," Joshua murmured. "I mean, I know there are things called instruments that make sounds that go together in certain mathematical ways, but..." he trailed off with a shake of his head. "I've never been outside metal walls. I saw the sky once, through glass. Lots of space, gray skies, rain. I didn't want to turn away from it."

Matthew shifted just a bit toward him. "You're kidding, right?"

"I'm urban trained. They want our heads, our thinking, our frames of reference to be a certain way."

"That's cruel," Matthew said at last.

"But efficient, I suppose," Joshua returned.

"How have you done it?" Matthew asked after a long silence.

"Done it?"

"Not gone crazy. Not killed yourself." Matthew whispered the last, and Joshua smiled, his lips tight over his teeth.

"Maybe because other people were trying too hard to do it for me."

"What?" Matthew choked.

"I want you to tell me about him, this man you are seeing. Every detail."

Matthew blinked, his fingers gathering the folded cloth of his trousers. "He's just, just L-Group, Josh. Cookie cutter perfect."

"You never asked his name, after all this time?"

"It doesn't work like that; it's all one-way communication." Matthew sighed. "Right down my throat, whether I want it or not."

"Think, Matthew. Anything."

Matthew leaned his head back against the wall again, his eyes on the ceiling. "The first time I saw him, he was different. Bloody, reaching for me. If that was him at all. If it wasn't a dream."

Joshua wanted to climb to his feet then, as if the cold shiver in his spine went straight to his legs and wanted to drive him away. But instead, he breathed in through his nose, forcing himself to release his clenched jaw. Finally, he reached out and touched Matthew on his shoulder. The other man jumped again. It wasn't a recoil, just the skittish action of a man on edge. Joshua looked into his hazel eyes, holding him the only way he knew how. "Dust on him. Like he'd been caught in a cave-in. The blood so red on his skin. If you looked close, you could see where it ridged up with the dirt, a thin brown line framing the brightness of it. Eyes looking through you, deep gray eyes, but one shot through with blood."

"Yes," Matthew whispered. "Yes, exactly. But how..."

"His name was Alec, Matthew. He was killed in an accident during a training run. Or at least, it was labeled an accident. Some people think I caused it, that I murdered other L-Groupers because I am different from them."

"A ghost? Matthew asked, his voice rising a little. "You think I'm seeing a fucking ghost?"

Joshua shrugged then, feeling the implausibility of it and yet, the cold certainty of it as well. "Do you think he was he like us?"

'What?" Matthew asked, his voice telling Joshua that he was still struggling with the revelation.

"ARR. Do you think, maybe, he was like us?"

"I don't know. Maybe. Without my data, I..."

he shook his head. "I just don't have that kind of Administrator recall. I'm sorry."

"It's OK."

Matthew shifted a little, laying his shoulder against the wall so he could face Joshua. And Joshua let the other man study him, keeping his head tipped toward the floor. He could feel the room change a little around them, feel Matthew relaxing just a bit.

"Still want to cold sleep on me?" Joshua asked, turning his head to cast a small smile at Matthew.

"I guess not. But I'm gonna shadow you on your rounds for the next few days, if that's good by you. I don't.... I don't want to be alone right now." Joshua watched Matthew swallow down his fear, but it still edged his eyes. His curling hair fell over his forehead, and waved up under his earlobes.

Before he quite understood what he was doing, Joshua leaned toward him, one hand going around the back of Matthew's neck. Matthew drew in a startled breath and Joshua almost released him with a pang of regret. But to his mild surprise, the NCP tipped forward to meet his lips shyly, his own hands coming up to rest on Joshua's shoulders in a not-quite embrace. His touch was so very gentle, tentative. And when Joshua pulled back finally, Matthew's cheeks were flushed, his lips reddened. He was altogether beautiful, Joshua decided.

"I have to finish my rounds. Come with me." He stood and offered his hand to Matthew. The other man looked at it for just a moment, and Joshua could see a rush of fear, amazement, and confusion playing through his eyes. He took Joshua's hand then, letting himself be pulled to his feet. "Why did you do that? I'm not, I mean, I'd always heard that L-Groupers only..." Matthew started to choke out.

Joshua pushed him back against the blue metal wall, this time asking with lips and tongue for Matthew's mouth to open to him. He pressed himself against Matthew, pinning him, and gradually Matthew softened into him, kissed him back full and almost desperately at last. And when they broke apart, Joshua smoothed the curls off his forehead. The motion felt a little awkward, but good. So damn good. "You said you didn't want to be alone. I don't want to be alone, either. Can that be enough of an answer for now?"

Matthew nodded his head then, his eyes wide and intense.

Chapter 15

Routines breed complacency. Standards narrow vision. Discipline can be that which binds you. Knowledge sometimes serves the ego rather than frees the mind. That's how some of the Ancient philosophers diminish my current work, dismissing me across the millennia. How I love to show them wrong, time and time again.

Administrator Thomas Muligan
Company Central
Earth Complex

Arena Level
Company Central, Earth Complex

Prime negotiated her way to her reserved seat, Muligan trailing in her wake. He watched the furtive stares, the slight, barely-lipped whispers. Andrea seemed to either be oblivious to the other Administrators, or maybe she simply had grown used to their measured consideration. Her light gauzy dress fluttered as she slipped into her chair and then frowned at him to do the same. Instead, he bit down on his cziana root and wandered over toward the glassed-in combat floor, his hands in his pockets.

He could see her reflected in the surface, her hair streaked with a little gray now, her eyes wreathed with a few fine wrinkles. Were they really sixty-six years, four months and three days old? It didn't seem quite possible. And probably another hundred or so years left, although their minds might begin to lag a bit before their bodies eventually gave in to time. Cziana root addiction would take him faster, but it had been a fair trade, this cozy blanket of calm, the quickness of his mind, the eidetic memory. It had all served him well.

"Muligan," she finally commanded, and he turned to her with his everyday smile on his lips.

"You're supposed to be relaxing," he said.

"Like you?"

"I'm relaxed."

"How many mid-level Admin class observers are here tonight?"

"Twenty-two," he said automatically.

She simply smiled at him, a little smugly.

"And that is *relaxed*? Sit down. Now."

He did, slouching next to her, his eyes missing nothing even as he nursed his boredom.

The chair arm beeped softly and a small data screen lit up. The first match would be a singles bout. Muligan glanced at the batch number. "I thought this group was routed to Terrantata," he murmured.

"Short fourteen members for various and unremarkable reasons," she replied.

The men entered the ring in silence and bowed to each other. The audience waited, hushed and expectant. As it should be, Muligan thought to himself. We are not barbarians after all.

Both men were L-Group through and through. Average height, slender to a fault, gray eyes—boring. But as he watched them take position, one man in particular drew his eye. The combatant was still, even though the other had begun to shift and move in his corner.

Muligan chomped down hard on his Root and tipped forward. Andrea leaned forward with him. "What's wrong?" she murmured.

Muligan held up his hand, his eyes shifting from one man to the other. Blue swept his staff in lazy arcs, passing it from hand to hand, wrists free and soft. He sank into a crouch, the predatory light beginning to play over his even features. Everything normal, his whole demeanor chiseled from the classic L-Group form.

The red player, though, stood lightly balanced and perfectly still. He seemed to watch his opponent with a kind of detachment. He waited, as the buzzer sounded, for the fight to be brought to him.

"Muligan?" Andrew whispered.

"Wait."

Blue leapt across the arena, his staff whirring. Red knocked it away, without even a slight change of expression, and rammed the butt of his weapon into Blue's stomach. The man nearly went to his knees. He staggered awkwardly back. Red let him go, quietly resuming his waiting stance.

Again Blue closed, more cautiously this time, and then sprang. Their staffs thudded together as they executed a lightning exchange that brought a soft sigh of excitement from the observation chairs. Blue managed to offset Red just a bit, and then brought home a vicious stab, bouncing the other man off the glass partition. Blue slashed in again with a snarl, but Red tucked and rolled, coming to his feet. He carefully shook his head, clearing the blow as he gave way to his adversary. Yet, through it all, he still seemed incredibly calm and focused.

"I've seen men fight like this before," Muligan muttered. His voice was nearly lost as the men collided again, their staffs blurring with their speed.

"I should hope so. You're about as addicted to the matches as you are to that Root in your mouth."

"Well, the one man I am thinking of wasn't what I would call a typical L-Grouper," he answered, with just a hint of amusement in his voice.

The crowd gasped as Red swept the feet out from under Blue and brought him crashing to the floor. With an almost casual efficiency, he tapped the man's head with his staff to prove he could have had his kill, then extended his hand and pulled Blue to his feet. The two separated, bowed formally, and walked from the arena. The observers muttered amongst themselves, tapping their handpads and settling their side bets.

"Spill it," Andrea said quietly.

"Adam, Tony, Drew, Joshua, and, ironically, James Illion when we finally cornered him on Rialga. They all fight like this. Calm. Efficient."

"ARR products," she said, nodding. "But Red—" she scanned her small data display. "Olan 416. He's L-Group normal across the board. Maybe training techniques..."

Muligan reached out and gripped her arm. She looked first at his fingers and slowly raised her gaze to his face. "We have to be sure, Andrea. You understand that, right?" He held her eyes, trying very hard to summon a kind of fierce resolve through his emotionally drugged haze.

She must have seen it. She brushed his hand off and nodded. She punched up Olan's tech templates, her lips thinning when she read the designer's name. *James Illion, Tech Grade Eight.* She stared at the name for a full minute. "Do whatever you have to do to that unit," she whispered. "Take it apart. Let me know what you find."

"I hope I don't find anything," he said. "Because if I do, we may have a huge quality control problem on our hands."

She didn't answer, but her eyes, going back to the empty arena, were large and dark in her skull.

—

Muligan leaned up against the doorframe, watching the burly med-tech secure Olan to the metal table. The soldier had been stripped, and his white skin shone dully under the operating theater lights. He turned his head toward Muligan, his gray eyes guarded in his nearly expressionless face. But he winced, just a slight crinkling of skin around his eyes, when the med-tech set a needle, drawing blood.

"You feel pain," Muligan noted, as much to himself as to the man on the exam table. He drew the cziana root out of his mouth for a moment.

Olan didn't answer, but he didn't look away either, and Muligan smiled a little. "I appreciate a challenge, you know."

Olan returned his grin then, but it was fierce, his teeth clenched. "Am I a challenge? Or are you just hovering because you like what you see, Administrator?" he asked.

"Priceless," Muligan answered, his smile widening. "Oppositional authority responses in an L-Grouper? However did you survive so long?"

"That's the operative word, isn't it?" Olan replied. "Survive. And is that what that root does for you, Administrator? Help you to *survive?"*

"Something like that," Muligan answered, replacing the root in his mouth with a flourish. "But you, you have nothing now. And you'll be less than nothing soon."

Olan shrugged against the plastic bindings that ran over his chest. "Not all endings are final. Maybe you're just setting me free, ever think of that?"

"I don't deal in metaphysics," Muligan murmured. He nodded at the med-tech who hovered at the table-edge. "Full workup. Then full autopsy. I want reports by tomorrow morning."

The man nodded, his round face flushed as he turned away to collect his tools.

Olan laughed then, nothing strained at all in the sound, it's bright tones echoed in the small medlab.

And to Muligan, standing stunned near the doorframe, it was one of the most awful noises he had ever heard.

—

Troop Carrier
En-route to Terrantata Colony

Matthew leaned closer to the displayed schematic he had cobbled together, and then studied the object in his hand. He activated the laser cutter with his thumb, and began to carefully punch another small hole in the metal tube. Little sparks jumped onto the floor, twitched and went out.

He paused suddenly and switched off the tool, placing it and the metal rod beside him on his bed. The silence just beyond his breath was too deep, too pregnant with something. He stood cautiously, ears straining to filter that quiet, and crept to the door panel ingress, pressing himself hard against the wall.

Abruptly, the panel hissed aside and the very tip of a stunner entered the room first, an evil little black nub against the blue of the walls. Without hesitation, Matthew leapt for the weapon. He attacked from underneath, forced the gun up and kicked around the doorframe savagely. His foot half-connected, but his assailant neatly snagged it and twisted before he could recoil. Matthew tried to shield his face as the floor rushed up at him. He felt the cold muzzle of the stunner dig into the back of his neck.

"Three points," Joshua said in a voice that shook with mirth.

Matthew rolled away from beneath the weapon's nose. "Not five points this time?"

"I didn't catch you in bed," Joshua answered with a grin. He held out his hand then, but Matthew swatted at it in mock anger.

"I thought the door panel sounded funny yesterday. No entry beep. I've sort of been waiting for you, thinking that just once..." Matthew sat up, rubbing a little at the memory of the gun at the nape of his neck. "Should have rigged one of those mobile repressor fields and scared the shit out of you."

"Why didn't you?" Joshua asked, still grinning down at him.

"Because I don't know enough about Tech stuff, aside from assembling a stunner in the dark, or the fine art of hot-wiring a door. You know, those important little things in the life of a wake staff NCP. Besides, I've been working on a personal project that's a bit more aesthetically pleasing." He shifted as if he was starting to climb to his feet, and then swiftly hooked one leg out, stiff and hard, catching Joshua just behind his knees, bringing him crashing to the deck beside him. He snatched at the weapon, but Joshua was faster, and he found himself staring at the barrel of the stunner again. He lay back with a dull thud. "Goddamn it! Joshua, one day..."

"I've been waiting," Joshua chuckled. "I think you're feeling faster simply because you're making me slower. Oh. Three more points. You cook dinner tonight." He grinned widely.

"Fuck you," Matthew replied, but there was no venom in it. He brought his hands up beneath his head as a cushion against the metal.

Joshua set the gun aside, both hands raised. "Truce?"

"Isn't that supposed to be my line?"

Joshua eased up and his quick eyes spied the metal tubing on Matthew's cot. He glanced back down at Matthew. "What is it?" he asked as he picked it up and turned it over in his long fingers.

Matthew, with a sigh, left the decking and came to his own feet. He hovered by Joshua's shoulder for a moment, liking the companionable warmth radiating from him. Hell, soaking in it, he admitted to himself. "Well, that depends on the workmanship, I suppose. I was just touching up that last hole. Sit."

Joshua handed him the tube and complied.

Matthew retrieved his cutter and took a seat beside Joshua, close enough that their knees brushed. "I thought I'd give this a try anyway. It'll probably sound terrible." He bent his head over the thin pipe, making slow punctures through the metal. He could feel Joshua watching with his usual silent intensity.

"A flute," Joshua guessed at last. "You're making a flute."

"We'll see," Matthew replied. He ran his finger over the hole, making sure it felt smooth. He turned it over in his hands. "Well, here goes. Might want to cover your ears." And he balanced the instrument carefully in his hands before raising it to his lips. His first blow brought nothing more than a hollow sound of air. He grimaced in a kind of apology, and then rolled the flute more carefully to his lip again. He closed his eyes and gently sighed his breath across the open hole. And the flute responded with a low, mellow note that hung like a benediction in the quiet cabin.

Beside him Joshua twitched, but he couldn't tell if it was in appreciation or distaste.

He ran a quick scale then, his fingers running over the holes before he pulled the instrument away from his lip. "Here, why don't you—"

Matthew didn't get his sentence out before Joshua hit the floor, and rolled to his back. His chin lifted, the cords in his neck straining. "Josh!" Matthew dropped the flute and fell beside the other man.

His lover shuddered and jerked, and then sighed, his eyes still open, but unseeing, his chest still. Matthew frantically knit his hands in the fabric of the Joshua's shirt and he shook him, hard. "Joshua!" Matthew dropped him back to the deck, his fingers scrambling for a pulse. "Don't you fucking do this to me!" He leaned in close with his ear, trying to catch any whisper of air.

Nothing.

"What do I do?" Matthew cried into his face.

Brown eyes blinked, slow and stupid. A moment later, Joshua gasped, then rolled to his side, coughing. Matthew held him as best as he could, shaking and sick to his stomach, his fingers still full of Joshua's uniform shirt.

Finally, Joshua quieted, and turned his face a little toward him. "What happened?" he muttered. "I heard the most beautiful..."

"You had fucking seizure, that's what happened. What the hell, Joshua?"

"I don't know...your flute, and then I saw a bird, I think. Red striped tail, talons. Flying."

"What?" Matthew knew his voice was too loud and he had to keep himself from shaking Joshua again.

"I saw a bird. And blue skies. And mountains." Joshua blinked quickly. He glanced down at the fabric knotted in Matthew's hands. "I'm OK."

Matthew rocked back, making his fingers let go of Joshua's shirt. "Fucking Illion," he muttered.

"I was there, really there," Joshua murmured, his voice slurred but full of wonder. He pushed himself slowly to sitting, and Matthew backed off to give him room and air, but he didn't want to move too far away. "Is that what you used to see, when James played for you?"

Matthew nodded, not quite trusting himself to speak.

"What a gift you've given me."

"It's a goddamn curse," Matthew replied, but quieter now. "Illion's own special brand."

Joshua looked at him then, and he found he had to struggle to hold those dark brown eyes. "No," the other man insisted. "No. It was..."

Matthew dropped his eyes away, trying to

shut him down and Joshua didn't finish his sentence.

He fiddled with the edge of his trousers, and jumped when Joshua covered his hand with his own. He wanted to resist the contact, but their fingers finally knit together. "I'm OK. Matthew. OK."

"Yeah, I can see that," he said. "You just scared me, that's all."

Joshua didn't let go of Matthew's hand. "Are there others like us, do you think? Who can experience things like this? Did Illion do this kind of work on other templates at the Company?"

Matthew groaned and let Joshua go. He climbed to his feet, scooped up the flute and cutter and replaced them high in the storage locker above his bed. He could feel Joshua's eyes on him.

"Matthew?"

He hovered there, one hand still on the locker frame. "They won't *let* people like you just *happen*, you know. The Administrators, the Core, none of them."

"I'm not sure they'll have a choice. It's part of us. It's..."

Matthew glared down at the dark young man

266

at his feet, silencing him. "You really don't get it, do you? They'll be terrified of us! Especially Prime and the Admin classes. Their whole social structure is based on status quo. They depend upon your *predictability*, Joshua. They've built an empire on it. God, I still haven't figured out why you are alive, after all these years. Must be a crack there, somewhere, but it's a damn small one.

So you don't let on about what just happened here. Not to anyone. I mean it." He could hear the fierce tones in his own voice. He sounded like an older or wiser brother getting ready to lecture a younger sibling. He flinched inside, waiting for Joshua to close down, to turn away.

But the other man simply looked at him thoughtfully, then nodded. The silence hung there for a while, and then Joshua shrugged. "OK."

"OK? Just OK?"

Joshua smiled a little as he came to his own feet. "We don't have to solve this right now. We share this thing, and that is enough to think about." And he reached out and freed Matthew's death-grip on the locker, his dark fingers knitting around Matthew's wrist as he tugged. Matthew let himself be led to the rumpled cot and gasped in surprise as Joshua fell back, pulling him down against his chest.

"Now?" Matthew half-growled. "You were flat on the floor like three minutes ago." Joshua reached up and kissed him hard. He could feel the lean body pressing against him, the hands already shoving at his clothes.

"Now."

Chapter 16

I let it happen. It wouldn't have taken much to push him away, put up walls, shut him down. My once-wife, Lietta, taught me how to do that, after all. But in the end, I couldn't. To finally gaze into the eyes of someone who felt the world like I did, who hungered to understand his own heart and mind, who loved so completely and generously, was a revelation and a gift. I know I am the older man. I know how I have compromised him, but he looks at me, his face flushed after making love, I would not trade this indiscretion for anything or anyone.

Matthew Dennon
Mid-Level Governmental Observer
Historical Archives
Terrantata Library System

Medlab Research Offices
Company Central, Earth Complex

Muligan seated himself on the cold plastic chair, the precisely ordered workstation between himself and the Med-tech. The man looked exhausted, his round face nearly gray beneath the florescent lights. He scratched a bit at his brittle, brown hair and gestured at the data display.

"I almost missed it," the man admitted to Muligan. "Called in a Grade Eight last night to make sure I was really seeing what I was seeing, if you know what I mean."

"Explain it to me," Muligan murmured.

"These protein sequences are being created because the subject contracted a virus, a virus that was designed to awaken specific parts of his template and that, in turn, led to actual physical changes in his brain and nervous system. I mean, the craftsmanship, the fit, it's..."

"Not natural, of course."

"No. No, of course not. This is incredible engineering. These lines," the tech gestured, "they stay dormant until switched on by the agent."

"Which was introduced to the unit how? Airborne?"

"God, no. Direct contact, saliva, semen, blood."

"And where did the virus originate in the first place?"

"It was designed, I assume."

"Designed?" Muligan asked, frowning. "But where did it *originate* from?"

The lab tech shifted a little, blinking his little bloodshot eyes. "Not sure. But my first guess, or rather the Tech Grade eight's first stab at this, suggests that some of our units may actually carry it in their own bodies. That's what I mean about the engineering here. This isn't something that was taught as standard fare in the Company genetic labs. This is huge, it's totally new— bodies that create a viral offshoot that can in turn switch on certain genes in the template...."

"Shut up," Muligan muttered.

The man looked a little hurt, but settled back into his chair and crossed his arms over his rounding belly.

Muligan tapped the end of his root against the tabletop for a moment, his eyes staring at the data screen but not really seeing it. "Can you design a test, a filter, we can run our people through? Something that will catch the viral agent?"

"Sure, but I'll need three, maybe four Grade Eights to be re-allocated..."

"You'll have them," Muligan answered. "I need the tests just as soon as they can be produced. You sleep here, you eat here, and work until it's done. Do you understand?"

"Sure, sure," the man said with a wave of his hand.

Muligan pointed the gray-blue root at the tech's chest. "And all the research stays in *this* lab or I will decommission you myself. Do I make myself clear?"

"Yes, Sir. Quite clear," the man said in a smaller voice.

His little grovel didn't really mollify Muligan at all.

—

Joshua sat on the edge of the bunk, watching Matthew sleep. His chest was naked under the low lights, and he couldn't quite stop his hand from stroking over the NCP's fine skin, the light dusting of reddish hair on his belly. Matthew stirred then, and blinked a slow smile up at him.

"I'm sorry," Joshua murmured. "I didn't mean to wake you."

"Hmm." Matthew stretched his arms up

overhead, one knee tenting the blanket. His lean muscles shifted beneath his skin, taut and decidedly erotic.

"You're doing that on purpose," Joshua chided him.

"Maybe," Matthew answered him, his voice still sleepy.

Joshua gently pulled the blanket down, exposing the other man inch by inch. Matthew didn't lower his arms from above his head, but a light flush crept over his cheeks. "You gonna make me freeze to death or what?"

Joshua lowered himself to the floor, his fingers still stroking over Matthew's skin. "We're only six days out, Matthew. Six days." He couldn't keep the little note of despair out of his voice.

Matthew rolled to his side and Joshua felt his fingertips feather over the edge of his face. He was always so gentle like that, slow, never in a hurry. He covered Matthew's hand with his own, turning to kiss the other man's palm.

"We'll be OK," Matthew murmured.

"I wish I was that sure," Joshua returned. He nudged Matthew over and slid in beside him, his own naked body pressing all along Matthew's. He could feel the agitation building in him as it had for the last few weeks. The truth was, neither of them knew what would happen when L-Group and the Tech units woke up. Six days might be all they had left, six precious days before rank and politics and duty split them apart. And that was something he couldn't quite look at, square and cold. Because Matthew was all he had. All he had ever had, his very own lover and friend, a man so much like himself.

Joshua felt Matthew's fingers run along his spine, then curve tentatively over his buttock. He shut his eyes, letting go into the caress. "It's OK, you know. If you want to take me. I won't break."

Matthew's hand froze against his skin, and Joshua sensed he was reliving the first time they had met. *Met? Now that's a nice euphemism.* "What you saw, Matthew, it probably shocked you more than it would have another L-Group, do you understand?"

Joshua kept his eyes shut, his own hand stroking the back of Matthew's ribs. "Adam was within his rights to beat me, to use me; well, at least up to the point he tried to choke me to death. The men of L-Group don't have a real concept of pain, you know, so how could they understand what I feel? Besides, things like that have happened to me before. Just L-Group, Matthew. Just the side NCP's don't get to see.

And you've got to let it go."

Matthew's hand withdrew, moved up to rest between Joshua's shoulder blades. "What do you mean, it happened before?"

"You read my files," Joshua said quietly. "I'm a soldier. I'm expected to cope with physical and psychological stressors of every stripe, so I do. We all do."

"God." Matthew drew him closer, rested his lips on Joshua's forehead without really kissing him. "I'm sorry," he breathed against his skin. "I wish I could take them down, Joshua. The Company, all of it..." he broke off, his chest heaving against Joshua's.

"Do you still want me?" Joshua asked quietly.

"Maybe you want me," Matthew suggested, his voice mixed with both huskiness and wariness.

"But you've never..."

"No. You're my first, in everything. But only six days, Joshua. I want you inside me. Marking me. So I know..."

"Know you're mine?"

"Yeah."

Joshua kissed him then, teasing his mouth open and going deeper. It had become so familiar, so intimate, these kisses in the red half-light of their quarters. He let his hand stroke lower, feathering over Matthew's lower back, then over his buttocks. He eased a finger gently into the space between the soft mounds. He could feel Matthew's skin shiver under his slow, soft touch as he probed and stroked.

He slid his hand over Matthew's hip, running over his swollen cock, over his sack. He went deeper, asking Matthew to open for him, to shift away a little, so his hand could reach his anus again, so he could stroke his lover without hurry and without urgency.

Matthew moaned into his mouth, his knees opening and Joshua rolled him onto his back, dropping down to lick and tease the little rim of flesh. He could feel Matthew shuddering beneath his tongue, could feel the sheets complain a little as Matthew knotted them in his hands.

Joshua spit into his hands then, slicking his own cock, before he leaned into Matthew, pressing, asking, his own body suddenly tense and trembling all over. He bit down on the urge to simply push in as he hitched Matthew's legs around his shoulders. "I do want you," he managed to say. "If you are sure. If you..."

"Stop talking," Matthew gasped.

He pushed in then, feeding himself in slowly, feeling Matthew's insides grip him. He stayed still, letting Matthew relax around him, even when everything in him wanted to drive forward and take him. *Take him. Claim him. Yes.*

Matthew panted, his face deeply flushed now and framed with his curls, his eyes wide and staring into Joshua's own. Joshua eased almost out, and then slid back in, controlling himself, but he wouldn't be able to for much longer. His own need was too great, too powerful to be reined in and safe.

Matthew. My Matthew. Mine. Fucking MINE. He could feel himself skating over Matthew's sweet spot, could feel the tension transform into ecstasy all around him, Matthew's arms rising so he could grip Joshua's shoulders, sinking his fingernails into flesh. The pain was sharp and sweet as nails broke skin, and he plunged in deeper with a growl, with desperation, with a hot possessiveness and Matthew bucked beneath him, slid with him, his mouth open now with his own cries.

He closed his hand over Matthew cock, squeezing and drawing, and moments later, they both jerked into their climax. Joshua dropped down, tearing into Matthew's lips with his own, consuming him, grasping him, gathering him to himself and feeling Matthew's quiet sobs as they both started to come down, prayed to drop down into a sleep that would let them forget those damn six days for a little while at least.

—

Office of Prime Andrea Annon
Company Central, Earth Complex

Prime sat still and rigid in her chair, her fingers gripped around its padded arms, and watched Muligan pace back and forth.

"I'm struggling with containment options," Muligan muttered. "The numbers are astonishing—fully eighty percent of Earth-based L-Group members are infected with the virus."

"And what percentage of triggers have you found?"

"Only one man who is planet-side, Andrea. But who knows how many off Earth? We found elements of the old ARR template in his workup, which suggests that at least some of the ARR units themselves are the triggers for virus production."

"So we eliminate every unit with ARR program genotypes and we can contain this," she said. She peeled her fingers from her chair arm. "But then, you'd like that, wouldn't you, Muligan?"

He stopped his pacing at once, the sickly gray root dangling from his lips. "You have got to be kidding me; you're going to make this *personal*? Now?"

"Someone with access to living emotion needs to think this through, not just you. There are interesting ramifications here..."

"Someone with emotion has mutated at least eighty percent of the last ten *years* of L-Group Batches!" He cut her off, ripping the spent cziana root from his mouth and stabbing it at her directly. "It's going to destroy us! Is that enough emotion for you?"

"Most units are functioning just fine in the field," she replied. "The virus itself isn't passed along without direct contact, correct? It has to be engineered within the host cells, if I understand the report correctly. It isn't mutating and with no triggers, no virus."

"Meaning?"

"Meaning," she sighed, "you finally win. We take all the ARR soldiers off the board."

"Techs, too."

"Yes," she answered a little impatiently.

"It has to be all of them, Andrea."

She sat very still for a time. "Please understand, Muligan. By taking them off the board, I mean isolation or embedded in NCP facilities without other units to interact with."

"That's not good enough!

"It will have to be."

He turned toward her then, his eyes a little crazed. She knew his cziana was out, had been out for the last hour, and this Muligan was the one that was perhaps a little closer to the truth of his being. His lips pulled back from his teeth, a kind of snarling smile. "He's not really your son, you know."

Andrea tipped her head toward him. "Excuse me?"

"I can read a genetic template, Goddamn it! You think he's your son because you share some interesting proteins? Please! You're no better than Illion, trying to preserve himself for what? So some other poor creature can suffer like he did? At least he had the sense to put himself down when offered the chance!"

She sat there, not varying her expression or gaze. *Let him hang himself*, she thought to herself. *Give him lots and lots of rope...this is delightful.*

"And Drew? You would really like him in your bed, wouldn't you? Is that why you won't terminate his ass as well?"

She smiled without showing her teeth, and still did not answer.

"They aren't family, they aren't pets, they're a real danger to this company, and hell, maybe all the worlds! Wake up, Andrea!"

She sort of liked him like this, waving his arms at her and yelling. It was exhilarating in its own way. "How effective, statistically, was the fighting style we observed last night?"

"What?"

"I'm asking you to access your cziana addicted lump of a brain."

Muligan's eyes dulled for a short moment, then snapped bright but more guarded. "83% win category when correlated with the soldiers we know to exhibit this particular..." he broke off, frowning.

"So," she took up smoothly, "it is an improvement over the standard style. Less waste of energy, more focus, and from what I saw, more mindful awareness of the battle arena. All this would be equally applicable in a real-life confrontation. Agreed?"

"Yes," he said sullenly. She let him stew for a moment before she posed her next question.

"How many new advances have we made in the labs over the last hundred years or so, Muligan? I mean, real break-through advances?"

"You know the answer to that," he said. "Our product lines are sound and functional. There has been no *need* to alter our production techniques or fiddle with the template lines."

"So we are, essentially, dead," she murmured. "Except for one or several rogue Techs who gave birth of this interesting virus, that, among other things, has spawned a creative new fighting style."

"What?"

"Dead, Muligan. Company products, NCP's, all of us. And if I widen my gaze, far beyond scientific breakthroughs, there has been so little energy and newness in all facets of life—from government to art and everything in between. And when an organism stops creatively reacting to its time and place, it *will* die. It's only a matter of time."

"We *saved* the human race," he whispered.

She sighed a little. "Did we?"

"Yes, goddamn it! No one *wanted* to be

soldiers, so we made them in our development centers! We crafted units who love to do what they do. No one wanted to commit to the long training programs in the advanced sciences, so we created units who thrive in those environments, who support the whole damn infrastructure now from genetics to medicine to ag techniques."

"But we never asked ourselves if the lack of soldiers meant we were moving beyond the need for violence. We never asked ourselves if the lack of science-based students was because there was a greater need for relational experiences in our populations, simplification instead of growing technological dependence. Maybe we saved a part of what it means to be human that *should* have been allowed to die. That should have been allowed to rot so it would feed something new."

"Conjecture," he retorted.

"Oh, certainly," she replied. "But it's a fascinating line of thought, isn't it?

"No," he said. "It's madness."

"I don't advocate a fast and unmediated rate of change, which *is* the danger here," Andrea said quietly. "If there is a way to slow the process, to create new ways to harness the ARR-generated virus, maybe we can honestly say one day that we saved the human race instead of damned it. So I want them isolated, but I don't want them dead. I want to see what they will do, but put limits on them."

"They'll crack up and take others with them," Muligan growled.

"Now that *is* conjecture," she returned.

He actually glared at her and it was all she could do not to smile. It would be cruel to bait him when he was like this, showing himself to her as he was, brittle, agitated and stuck in old ruts running through his brain.

"So what are you going to do about the troops bound for Terrantata?" he asked, his fingers driving into his pockets, probably so she wouldn't see them shaking.

"I'll have Joshua continue to cold sleep the ARR units until the occupation of the mining facilities has been accomplished, then bring them home and isolate them like I said. Orders will go out to the new designated commanders. They'll step up and in as they've been trained."

"You'll take Drew and other commanders off the board before a major operation?"

"You're the one telling me they are a danger, Muligan. You can't have it both ways."

"And what do you do with Joshua, then?"

"Order him to sleep."

Muligan smiled at her then, and she could feel her skin crawl as his eyes ate into her own. "And why do you think he'll do that?"

"He'll obey orders. He wants badly to be L-Group."

Muligan laughed then, shaking his head. "One moment, you play with the destiny of mankind like God, and the next you show just how fucking blind you can be."

She narrowed her eyes at him. "Be very, very careful, Muligan."

"He won't do it!" Muligan pronounced with a frightening certainty. "He loves Commander Drew like an old fashioned papa. You have let him develop a high level of individuality that will guarantee he will practice whatever kind of self-preservation he feels best, and he'll protect his own over and above any L-Group orders. It's a sure bet. He'll take one look at the continued cold sleep orders and ignore them. Worse, he'll connect the dots, notice who we are gunning for. And then what? I can't even predict his behavior. I should be able to but I can't!"

"What do you suggest then?" she asked, conceding his point she knew, but she couldn't help it. She felt so curious beneath her own irritation. She knew they *both* could be right, and when it came to unit management, this sort of scenario simply didn't happen. She always knew what certain orders would trigger, and so did he. In a sense, this was exactly what she had been craving for years. Yes. She craved it, this challenge, this interesting, messy and unpredictable dance of behaviors that sparked the energy arcing between herself and Muligan. She felt more alive than she had in years.

"I did some digging into that government observer Drew dragged along on this mission."

"And what does that have to do with our current situation?"

"He was Core, Andrea. Married into it, then divorced out of it."

"So?"

"What NCP in their right mind leaves that kind of stability and luxury?"

"I'm sure you'll enlighten me."

Muligan acted as if he didn't even catch the sarcasm. "Mood swings, visions, erratic and aggressive behavior. Sound familiar?"

Andrea blinked. "But in any mix of unaltered genes, you're bound to get..."

"No. I dug deeper and found out that one Matthew Dennon was struck by a transport on

Rialga and then went under the care of one James Illion who just *happened* to be on site that day."

Andrea stared at him then. Muligan did, she reflected for a bitter moment, have his uses. "So you might as well go on and speculate," she murmured.

"Illion wasn't just aiming his virus at Company product lines. He had a broader vision if you can call it that. Matthew Dennon who is on that ship, Matthew Dennon is ARR to his bones; I'd bet every last credit I'm due for the rest of my life on it. If you would like me to run probable liability factors if this ever leaks to the NCP's, then add up the Company product losses, you might, just *might*, begin to see the seriousness of what we are facing." He wiped at his forehead and then ran his hands along the edge of his trousers.

"You were going somewhere with all of this," Andrea said mildly, "besides your usual end-game speech."

He grimaced at her, visibly slumping. "I need cziana root. My head is exploding."

She gave him a thin smile of barely veiled triumph. "Go. Then get back up here and lets finish our discussion."

"Is that what we were having?" he muttered

as he left her office.

—

Muligan fed his ident scrambler in first to
the feed line, then pulled his chair a little closer
to his workstation. His root hung out off the
edge of his lips as he waved an old-fashioned
keyboard display onto his table. His two fingers
tapped across the letters and numbers, both fast,
and of course, unorthodox in style.

He looked again at the security feeds from
the ship. The stills showed the government man
and 1011 tangled together on the star deck, their
naked bodies gleaming under the inset lights
filling the 3D data screen. The blue background
suited neither of them, but then, their attention
wasn't on such details. His nose wrinkled a little
in distaste. How did they abide such raw
physicality? He found it disturbing, disgusting.

Andrea would not take action, not today and
not tonight. She really did see the disaster
brewing and was *choosing* not to interfere. Cold
sleep. Isolation. Muligan snorted in derision.
He'd isolated James Illion for four years and the
man was still fucking with him from the
basement incinerators.

As he saw it, he had two choices, both of

them rife with variations that had his head nearly splitting with the complexity of it all. The first was to simply blow the ship, self-destruct it with Prime's passcodes. But that was frankly wasteful, and, in the final analysis, neither clever nor particularly satisfying.

The other, though, the other would have so many delicious ramifications that he could hardly wait to see what might happen. She was the one who wanted to play with them, after all. So he'd give them a new game. His fingers hunted a little faster on the keyboard and then sent the tightbeam order to the communications relay. He eased back, pulling the root from his mouth and letting it dangle, two-fingered, limp-wristed. Now he could return to argue with Prime. Because the decision had already been made, he'd made it, and there was nothing in all the worlds she could do to stop it.

Even if she terminated him, which, well, she just might.

Playtime, indeed.

Chapter 17

We will always fall back on our genetic predispositions and our past experiences, on our natures and our biases. Without the very randomness built into life, we will run like those rodents from the ancient stories, tumbling off a cliff together.

James Illion,
Genotemplate Tech Grade Eight,
Historical Archives
Terrantata Resource Library

Troop Ship Outbound
Three days out from Terrantata Colony

Joshua turned the tightbeam monitor off, but it took two tries for him to hit the button with any kind of accuracy. He sat there a long time, his eyes not really seeing anything, his spine slumping forward. "Damn you," he finally whispered, and his voice bounced back at him in the tiny room.

A quiet scratching at the door pulled him around. For a moment, he wanted to ignore it, to continue huddling there, in the blue-lighted communications hub. But he found his feet and keyed the door. Matthew waited in the corridor, his shoulder leaning up against the metal wall, arms crossed over his chest. "So we're locking doors on each other now? What's up?"

"Standard procedure when accessing priority orders," Joshua said automatically. He brushed by Matthew, his eyes on the floor, his arms stiff at his sides.

"Whoa, there." Joshua could hear Matthew turn to follow him. But all he could do was walk straight ahead, put one foot in front of the other just so he wouldn't stumble.

He heard Matthew's steps quicken behind him. The other man's fingers brushed his shoulder. Before he could edit his motions, he spun, knocking Matthew viciously against the wall, his arm locked over the other man's throat.

Matthew's face reddened above the black uniformed arm, but he held Joshua's gaze with a hurt but simple trust. He flattened his hands against the wall and let himself hang in Joshua's punishing hold.

Joshua released him abruptly and stumbled across the hallway. He turned his back on Matthew and slammed his fist into the unyielding metal. And he kept slamming it until the skin over his knuckles split and he was dimly aware that he was leaving interesting red splotches on the baby blue paint. His knees collapsed and he slid his fingertips through his own blood as he dropped. He leaned his forehead against the wall, his teeth grinding tight, his eyes shut and hot behind their lids.

He twitched when he felt Matthew's hand on his shoulder again. "Don't," he whispered, but he didn't shrug the touch off. He could feel Matthew settle beside him, his hand gripped firmly at the base of his neck. It hurt more than his hand, the gesture of such a gentle touch in exchange for the violence he had erupted into. The blood continued to ooze from his knuckles and he could already feel the swelling set in.

Matthew shifted around, turning him off the wall and into his arms. For a long moment, he hung stiff and unresponsive in the embrace. Then slowly, he curved his arms around Matthew, holding, gripping so hard that he finally realized that he might be hurting the other man. He released his lover, grabbed Matthew's hand in a kind of apology, and held on. The bone ground a little and he winced; yes, he'd done more than merely split the skin this time.

"I have orders," Joshua said at last.

"Nothing good, I take it," Matthew murmured.

He didn't quite trust himself to speak more. The words seemed chained to the anger; when they rose, it rose, too, black and terrifying.

"Want to fuse that hand and clean this mess before you tell me?" Matthew suggested.

He couldn't even find the energy to shake his head. "I can't do it."

"Can't do what, Josh?"

"I have a choice to make," he said at last. "And it is impossible." He let go of Matthew's hand and stood on shaking legs. Matthew came up with him, his hands hovering to help, but there was no need. Somehow standing did feel better, though. He cradled his broken hand against his chest and finally looked into Matthew's face. "I have a list of men I am to deactivate before we reach Terrantata."

"Deactivate as in..."

"Kill," Joshua returned. "About twenty different men, more than a few commanders. Drew. Adam. Others I don't know as well from the other Batch."

"You won't do it," Matthew said at once.

"No," he answered just as quickly. "But then, supposedly, your ex-wife's family has issued a warrant for your arrest and termination because you may be carrying the same virus the men on the list have, or some such thing. Takes an NCP to bring justice against another NCP. If I don't do what they ask, *they* will make sure that every commander on this ship receives orders to terminate you."

"Shit," Matthew murmured with feeling. He seemed more amused than afraid. "Wait a minute. How did they know to use me as leverage against you like that?"

"Security feeds," Joshua answered.

"You mean every time we..."

Joshua shrugged. "Well, maybe not every time..."

Matthew shook his head, flushing but obviously trying to stay focused. "And if you *do* commit the murders? There's a payoff of some kind?"

"You live. *I* get to die."

"Excuse me?" Matthew asked sharply.

"They scrub the bit about you and pin the executions on me. The Company, L-Group, you—

clean bill of health all around. 'The aberration named Joshua 1011 simply acted out of its faulty genetic template' or something like that I am sure."

"But the message you have, wouldn't it implicate someone else?"

"It was an interesting piece of artistry. It co-opted codes from this ship so it would look like a fake, originating from here in a sloppy attempt to cover my murderous tracks. I'm only a Tech Grade Four after all. I'm not supposed to read Grade five and six coding. If I point to that message, to its orders, *it* will light the incinerator fires for me."

"But you can? Read that level of code, I mean?"

"I get bored easily and it has been a long trip," Joshua said and he was even able to give Matthew a small smile. It slipped when he noticed that Matthew's throat was already red and bruising.

Matthew seemed to read his look, and his hand went to his neck. "It's nothing."

"It's me," Joshua corrected him. "Ugly and brutal. I hurt the one man in the universe who I don't want to hurt. I'm broken, Matthew. Inside and out. And I don't know what to do. Not about this and not about us. I'm just broken."

"Broken," Matthew echoed immediately, his eyes going back to the communication's hub. "Does the ship need that thing to fly?"

Joshua followed his gaze, confused for a moment. "The tightbeam?"

"Yeah."

He ran the schematics quickly in his mind. "Not for this kind of run—no complex docking procedures, no..." he stopped and grinned in savage joy. "Take it out, message, transmitter and all. That's what you're thinking?"

Matthew nodded. "And maybe you and I need to find a way to stay on Terrantata when this is done. Get us officially killed or something. Nice climate, and it might have enough folks to fade into if you get my drift. I can do the basic accounting and data doctoring in our favor, and Tech grade fours, well, there's a lot of machinery in the mining complex, right? You'd learn fast. We could survive."

"I can't..." But he stopped, his hand throbbing against his chest. *I can*, the voice echoed back to him *if it means I stay with him*. It was a revelation, a breath of freedom, and he wasn't quite sure what to do with it.

Matthew nodded to him, as if seeing the

possibilities blooming there. "One step at a time. No killing anyone, especially me, is a good first step, I reckon. Can we see to that hand now? I'm getting a little nauseated looking at you."

"No. I need to rig an accident first. This will wait." He started to turn away, then reached out and touched Matthew's bruised throat with his good hand. He raised his eyes and the other man only smiled, his hazel eyes a little sad. "Feel like assisting me in this crime?" Joshua asked.

"Are you kidding?" Matthew returned. "After a day like this, I think I'll sort of enjoy wrecking things."

—

Today, they all awaken. Joshua pulled his black hair back and secured it at the base of his neck. He stood for a while before the mirror, studying his clean-shaven face and dark eyes. *They will all be there, all the men of my Batch, their first meal together, those who aren't still too cold sleep sick to come to the table. But not Matthew, not yet. Not ever if I have my way. I can't protect him from all of them, so I will have to hide him. Gods, Drew, why did you throw us together like this?*

And why did I do this to him?

He glanced at his bunkmate through the bathroom door. His lover still curled around Joshua's pillow, his lips parted slightly as he slept. He hadn't let Matthew leave the cabin for over forty hours, but he knew he couldn't cage him here forever. Terrantata would be looming up on the view screens in a few hours; the pilot was already shifting the vast troop carrier back into space normal. And then, they'd be parted, maybe forever. The thought stung enough that he had to grip the bathroom sink for a moment to steady himself.

Unless they could find a way to disappear.

Finally, he breathed again, the pads of his fingers aching where he had driven them into the unyielding metal.

He passed the bunk silently and let himself out into the hall.

The changes over the past two days had been startling. Men crowded the narrow hall to the mess, still mostly quiet and dragging a little with the effects of their long sleep. By this afternoon, though, they'd be running the halls, limbering up, their eyes bright and every sense alert. Most paid him no mind as he threaded between them, but some still summoned enough energy to glance at him with their cool gray eyes.

He collected his tray, asking for more food than usual so he could take enough of a meal back to Matthew. Most men wouldn't realize that he was even on board, and while he could pass as a Tech, Joshua knew that if the connection between he and Matthew were made, it might not go well for the NCP. His lips thinned at the thought of Matthew enduring the kind of abuse he had over the years. He could not let that happen.

He would not.

He seated himself near an exit, angling so there was a minimum chance of someone at his back. No one sat near him, although a few Techs from the training program at the Company nodded at him in recognition. He knew his black uniform unnerved them enough to steer them clear of him. And that was OK, too. Safer for them.

He ate quickly and then wrapped the silverware in his napkin, tucking it into his back pocket. A beep drew his attention to the huge data screens. He automatically lifted his eyes, quickly reading the assignments posted for his batch. The scroll dropped down, names, numbers, and duties. The last few were body

unit orders and he almost turned away before he
saw his name. *Joshua 1011 report to Commander
Tony after breakfast, command quarters A 04.*

He stared at it, until the moving lines of
script ate up his name. He stood, suddenly aware
of the silence in the room, the faces turned
toward him in speculation. And then he saw
Adam, his head bowed over his tray, lifting and
catching his eyes with something very much like
pity.

He would have preferred animosity or
distaste. Anything but the hint of sadness in the
gray eyes of his near commander.

Joshua scooped up the tray and walked
quickly out the exit.

The hall was emptier now, quiet enough that
he caught the sound of feet following him. He
turned, still holding the tray, and Adam pulled
up. The light shone in his blond hair, and his
skin, so very pale after his sleep, bloomed into
purplish patches under his eyes. The slender
man kept a careful distance between himself and
Joshua.

They looked at each other for a time, and
then Adam murmured, "Tony likes pain."

Joshua turned his back on the other man and
started walking again.

"He'll pull in your NCP, too. You know that."

Joshua stopped without turning.

"First time he's alone, or you're out in the field, he'll end Dennon if he can't end you. Just how he works. I thought you should know. I'm sorry, Joshua. But we never get to keep our toys very long, do we?"

Joshua started to turn back toward Adam, but the other man had already begun to move up the corridor in the opposite direction.

"Matthew is not a toy, Adam. And how do you know..."

"He's also not L-Group," Adam called back over his shoulder, cutting him off. "You fucked him and the moment you did that, you killed him."

Joshua clutched at his tray as two other L-Groupers passed Adam and looked at him intently. He spun then, his long legs driving him down the mostly empty hall to his cabin. He balanced the tray carefully, keyed his door, and slipped inside.

Matthew was dressed and sitting cross-legged on his made-up bunk. The flute lay by his right thigh. Joshua could feel his eyes roving over his face, and he knew Matthew could see the glints of fear and anger still there.

"Bad?"

"Bad enough," Joshua murmured. "I need to see Drew. I need to find a way to protect you."

"Joshua, I can take care of..."

"No!" He shouted, then immediately hated the whisper of surprise that ghosted over Matthew's face. "No," he said more quietly, "you can't take care of yourself here. You're the part of me that is vulnerable. Do you know that? You're the part they can beat and kill, even if they decide not to hurt me directly. Do you understand what I have done to you? I was so stupid, thinking this could go on." Joshua set the tray down beside Matthew, but when the man reached for him, he pulled back. The hurt on the NCP's face cut deep.

"I've been assigned to Tony for body unit detail," Joshua murmured. He moved back toward the door.

"And that means?" Matthew asked, his voice choked.

Joshua couldn't tell him the physically intimate services he would be expected to perform. "It means I have to give him all my attention."

Matthew came to his feet. "But..."

"I don't have a choice, Matthew," Joshua said

tiredly. "I'll find a way to get to Drew."

"I'll bloody get to Drew myself," Matthew growled.

"No!" Joshua faced Matthew, their eyes nearly the same level. *He's even more beautiful like this, flushed, his eyes wide and wild.* The thought cut him. *How do I let go of you now?* "You don't leave this cabin. You keep the door locked and only I come in and out, do you understand me?"

"I'm not going to stay locked up in here, Joshua."

For a moment longer, they contended, their shoulders rigid and their faces warped with anger and fear. Joshua finally looked down, and passed his hand over his forehead as if he could wipe the emotions away. "You're mine," he said softly. "You're mine and I won't lose you."

Matthew stared at him then, his hazel eyes brilliant green against the flush over his face.

"Please, Matthew. I'm begging you. Stay here. Stay safe. Can you do that for me?" He kept his voice low, opened his palms up, praying that Matthew would see that he was totally defenseless and totally vulnerable.

Matthew looked away, his eyes on his flute and food tray, but Joshua knew he wasn't seeing them. "Yeah," he said at last. "I can do that."

—

Tony was waiting in the hallway outside his
quarters. Joshua stood quietly while those cool
blue eyes traced over him. He fully expected his
commander to order him into his cabin but Drew
merely opened his hand to the hallway. "We
have a tightbeam malfunction. I want you to
look at it before I assign some other Techie to fix
it properly."

Joshua tipped his head but said nothing. He
could feel the sweat start, there in the palms of
his hands, but he forced himself to breathe. And
when Tony turned away, he followed just off the
blond's left shoulder. Tony was tall for an L-
Grouper, nearly as tall as Joshua himself, and he
moved with a characteristic warrior's
gracefulness. He'd never faced off with the
commander in the arena and felt a whisper of
misgiving in his chest. He pushed it down.

They took the lift to the top deck and were
soon both crowding into the tight
communication-hub room. Joshua watched Tony
key the lock, his fingers moving swiftly over the
number pad. He was acutely aware of the other

man's presence in the tiny room, his smell, and the punishing square features of his face.

"Go to it," Tony ordered. He leaned back against the door, crossing his arms over his chest.

"Yes, Sir," Joshua said quietly. He dropped to all fours and flipped on his back to scoot up under the first console. He would evaluate the room by the book, even though he knew perfectly well there would be no fixing this hub. He'd made sure of that, days ago.

Before he was ready to shift to the next station, he felt Tony's hand on his stomach. "Anything?" the man asked. His hand shifted lower, and beneath the console, Joshua shut his eyes, his breath held hot and anxious. He forced himself to swallow, to relax beneath the man's touch.

"The problem is a lot further up the pike, maybe as far as a radiation shield malfunction." It was a calculated risk, to jump that far up the checklist, but there were four more consoles here, four more times when he would be absolutely defenseless. He could feel Tony touch his cock now, groping his sack, and then the hand withdrew.

Joshua slid out from under the metal housing. Tony gave him almost no room to come to his feet, so he half-crawled a little away, and then eased himself up.

"So how do you run a check on the rad-shielding?" his commander asked softly.

"I can do it from the command center," Joshua murmured. He started to go around Tony, but the man stepped into his path.

"Why don't I believe you?" Tony murmured.

"I wouldn't know that, sir."

"Get on your knees."

Joshua froze and looked straight into the commander's eyes. He was not blinking, his pale face flushed in a look Joshua understood all to well. He'd seen it on Adam's face, too. His ears started ringing, and he felt as if time were slowing, just like in the arena. He stepped back, his weight balanced, his arms loose and waiting at his sides. He was L-Group. He was listed as Tony's body unit, but he couldn't make himself yield. All he could see, all he could smell in his mind was Matthew. His Matthew. His only lover, not this towering and gloating blond man in front of him.

He could not yield. He would not.

Tony smiled broadly, his eyes flickering, as if reading Joshua's mind. "I was so hoping for this. I was hoping I could catch you in some little error, but *this*? This is better. You're my body unit and when I say kneel, I mean KNEEL!" He stepped quickly into Joshua's space, his hands reaching to grasp his black uniform shirt.

Joshua knocked his arms away, backing up a step. "Sir, this is not the time..."

Tony lunged again, then spun, his foot coming up hard and fast toward Joshua's gut. He deflected the blow, but Tony recovered quickly, still smiling. "Alec told you everything didn't he?"

"What?" Joshua shook his head as he backed away, trying to open up more space between them.

"Lying there in the rubble, bleeding out, he told you about me, what I like to do to boys like him, told you all of it," Tony snarled. "And then, you don't have the common sense to die with that information, you piece of shit aberration."

"He didn't say anything! He opened his mouth and all that came out was blood!" Joshua shot back at him. Tony wavered. "But that blood, this is what it's all about, isn't it? His blood on your hands? And its been you all along, trying to put mine on Adam's. It won't work. Others will see through it. You won't ever come clean, Tony. It's all over you."

Tony pulled up, his eyes narrowing. His jaw

knotted and for a moment, Joshua was sure he was going to charge. Instead, he smiled, his lips twitching over his white teeth. "Good try, 1011. Make me lose it. Make me try to kill you so you can turn it around, try to take me down. Self-defense. You might be able to. But who will believe you? Drew can't protect you forever. There would be inquiries, tribunals. You'd burn in the end. The aberration. The freak." He stepped closer, and Joshua dropped back another step, feeling another console bump up against his legs.

"But how about this? You're on body unit detail. The whole mess saw it. I say kneel, you don't. So I throw your ass in the brig for disobeying orders and then what? I'm frustrated. I might have to go find a certain NCP to fill my bed for a bit, off record of course. Won't matter if he doesn't say yes. Won't matter if he ever makes it to my room, because I'll find a military-grade stunner on him and then *I'll* be fighting for *my* life, and if I break his neck, well, we're way out in space, and he's no one at all. And if you ever get out of the brig you come right back to me. And we dance again, until I get tired of you."

Joshua eyed the door. *Get out. Get to Drew.*

"Or, you can get on your damn knees and do

what I tell you to do. I live, Dennon lives, you live. Happy family all around." Tony actually took a step back, leaning one hip lazily on the console. "I used an command-designated code to lock that door. You won't get through it fast enough, understand?"

"What's wrong with you?" Joshua whispered. "What made you this way, Tony? You can see this is sick, right? Tell me something in you can see it."

Tony smiled, but showed no teeth at all. "Not a thing *wrong* with me. Highest command scores in years, sure to follow in Drew's footsteps when he is finally decommissioned. It's just a simple game I like to play, to feel what I am not allowed to feel. Passes the time. All the goddamn time before I go off and die for something I don't even understand or get a say in." He dropped his eyes away to the floor for a moment, and when he looked back up, there was a terrible craving there, something so hungry that Joshua could feel it in the room with them.

"Pain, Joshua. In that pain, there is something hot and alive and I can't feel it except when I see it in another. And then, oh, it's sublime."

Joshua reached back for the console behind

him, steadying himself, finding his balance.

"Used to do it to myself, hoping to feel something, but hell, I can't even show you the scars because we heal so fast. But not Alec. And not Adam, either, but he hides it well, doesn't he? They were a revelation, those boys. About how close pain is to lust. I watched the vid of Adam fucking you after he gave you that beating, do you know that? Over and over. Waiting for you to die, it was going to be exquisite, the capstone. But then you. Didn't. Die."

Joshua could hear his own breath, rasping in the tiny room. He realized then why Tony had brought him here. No surveillance in the communication hub. No one to hear them. All his life he had been cornered. But this? It was worse, being asked to step into it with his eyes open, submissive and beaten without even raising a hand to defend himself.

"But maybe you have other uses," Tony breathed. "Maybe I should be happy Adam couldn't seem to get a simple job done." He crossed his arms over his chest. "You do the math, Joshua. Smart Tech Four like you. What's a little bit of knee work, a little bending, if it means we all keep breathing in the sandbox?"

"Commander Drew…" Joshua breathed.

"Drew threatens and blows steam. Even if someone finds your dead body, what? Really, what? I get the brig or the airlock. But the thing is, *I don't care.* Don't you get it? I simply fucking don't care anymore. I'm not something to be shoved around a playing field. I want what I want, just that simple. So I take it when and how I can."

Joshua felt the edges of his ears burning.

"Like I said, you're good and locked in. You always were. You always will be."

Tony dropped his hand to his own crotch. "Doesn't have to be so bad, not this first time. It's your duty, 1011, to share with me whatever that NCP might have taught you. You do it, you go on and troubleshoot this damn communication hub. You come back to my cabin, and you do what I tell you, you pick up your duty roster and do it, too. All the same thing, doing your duty. Dennon goes on breathing. So do you. I've seen your tactical scores—you tell me, what choice do you have, really? Ah, but you? You won't do it willingly, will you? Because *you* can't. Because, in the end, your not L-Group."

Joshua looked away, his eyes hot. He couldn't even force himself to blink. *Do your duty, L-Grouper. Do your duty. But he's right. I can't. I can't.*

He found himself going to his knees anyway, his eyes nearly blind with rage and frustration. There was only one way out. He could feel his whole body shaking with it. Tony chuckled. "Well, maybe I was wrong about you." The commander sauntered over to stand above him, his hands starting to undo his belt.

Joshua erupted from the floor, his head slamming into Tony's chin, all his weight carrying the commander forward and down onto the metal floor. They hit with a hollow chime and Joshua's hands went around Tony's neck, jerking the man up and slamming him down three more times until the commander thrashed violently, fell to shivers and finally went limp under him.

Blue eyes opened and looked through him, blood trailing over his cheek, out of his nose, his mouth.

Joshua let out a low moan, and then scuttled back against the console frame. He knotted his fingers in his hair, gasping, struggling for even a hint of control. He knew without taking a pulse, without watching for the rise and fall of the black uniformed chest, that Tony was dead.

His first kill.

His first murder.

L-Groupers don't kill other L-Groupers.

And in the reddish light of the communication hub, Joshua watched in horror as another form slithered into the air, its uniform dusty and tattered, one eye nearly blood red. Joshua pressed himself further back, his muscles warped and tight around his bones. His lungs breathed in dusty fire. "Alec," he choked out. "Alec."

The ghost-image knelt, his fingers feathering over Tony's face. "Sleep now. Sleep," he murmured. There was the softest hint of regret there, and endings. He raised his eyes to Joshua then. "You and Dennon are still missing it, the end game. Find it. Or they all die, Joshua. All of them, across all the worlds."

And then Alec was gone, leaving him locked in the closet-sized room with a corpse.

Chapter 18

The Company had tried, on quite a few occasions, to market L-Groupers as single bodyguard products. It never worked well. The soldiers' entire early lives were spent as part of a group; they took their behavioral cues from the mirroring selves around them. Cut off from their batch, they often sickened, their mental and physical acuity ratings dropping off rapidly. But it was a small and specialized arena, the bodyguard business, and so no Administrator ever bothered to pursue changes in the basic genotemplate. It was simply easier to replace each unit as it failed rather than develop a whole new line of soldier.

Company Observer Notes
Historical Archives
Terrantata Research Library

Company Troop Carrier
Outbound to Terrantata Colony

Matthew paced back and forth, scratching at his curling hair every now and again as if that might free up a spare inch of breathing room. He'd never liked tight spaces and the past two days locked in the sleeping cabin was beginning to drive him right up the proverbial wall.

The sound of the door opening wheeled him around, his heart thudding with anticipation. Joshua would be there, they'd talk, they'd...

The man was not Joshua.

Drew stood in the doorframe, his face knit and serious. Without preamble, he pinioned Matthew with his sharp eyes. "Did Joshua report to Tony?" he asked.

"Yeah," Matthew returned cautiously.

Drew cursed under his breath as he stepped inside the cabin. The door slid shut behind him. "What the fuck did you two think you were doing?"

Matthew stared at him until those cold gray eyes made him look away. He felt like a teenager for a moment, caught in a compromising situation. Or like a little boy, sick in his single bed. He made himself raise his eyes again, forced his arms to his sides, even though he wanted to cross them over his chest. "I don't know," Matthew said at last.

"You don't know," Drew echoed. He sighed and sat down on the end of Joshua's bunk. He closed his eyes a moment, and Matthew could see him summoning...what? Courage? Calm?

"Why are you here, Drew?"

The powerful blond man knit his fingers between his open knees. "Do you understand what a body unit is, Mr. Dennon?" he asked quietly.

"A valet, I assume. Follow Tony around with a clipboard and help him button his shirt when he needs his ego stroked?"

Drew smiled grimly. "Not precisely."

"Enlighten me then," Matthew murmured.

"L-Group is based on the same basic army model used by Alexander."

"Alexander as in the Great? What does that have to do..."? Matthew began to ask.

"His lines often held against superior forces because he paired lovers together. They were not just fighting just for him, they were fighting *for* each other."

Matthew frowned. "Then body units..."

"The term body unit generally refers to a

long-term relationship between two men. Most of our soldiers pair off naturally, but A-designates get to handpick their mates. And they can order them to fulfill their needs."

"Mates." Matthew repeated the word, feeling the pulse begin to pound in his neck.

"You begin to understand."

"But..." Matthew cut himself off.

"Do you love him?" Drew asked.

"I don't...Joshua, you mean?" Matthew finally stuttered out.

"I have to deliver certain men to Terrantata in one piece. Joshua is one of those men, maybe *the* most important man, and Tony threatens my ability to do what must be done. I can't countermand his selection of Joshua, despite the fact that he has put two previous body units away. It would draw too much attention. I hoped to catch Joshua here, and speak to you both, but..."

Matthew frowned. "Two previous lovers?"

Drew smiled grimly. "A man named Alec who was killed not so very long ago, and Adam, who you are more familiar with."

"Alec was Tony's body unit?"

Drew looked at him curiously. "You know that name."

Matthew looked down at the floor. "Yeah, you might say that."

"Explain."

"I...I'm not sure I can explain it even to myself," Matthew murmured. "I see him, or maybe it's his...well...his ghost." He said the last in a rush, as if letting it spill out into the air would make it more acceptable.

"Really?" Drew asked quietly, considering him a moment, but not sounding particularly shocked. "Illion?" he asked at last.

"Probably. Yeah." Matthew shrugged his shoulders, and felt acutely just how tight his whole back had become. "I seem to get visions now and again. They are, well, disturbing."

"I can imagine," Drew replied. He let a silence hang between them for a moment again.

"So." Matthew swallowed hard, his cheeks tight. He could barely get the words past his lips. "You came here to tell me I've just lost Joshua, is that it?"

"Not precisely. I am hoping that you will do something for him, something I cannot do by myself."

"Anything."

"I want you to buy him out, private contract, full ownership."

Matthew stared at the commander. "Buy him?"

"You're NCP. You were part of the Core family. I took the liberty of checking your account; you have enough saved up for his down payment in any case. The rest can be siphoned off your regular pay period deposits, if I understand the accounting ledger."

"I can't buy him," Matthew said, shaking his head. "That's, that's..."

"He's a Company product. Of course you can buy him. It's the sole reason for our existence, units to be bought and sold. Generally, it's planetary governments footing the bill for entire batches, but occasionally single sales happen. Not often, mind you. L-Groupers are designed to work in groups, but there are a few precedents."

"But how do I look him in his eye, how do I..."

"Mr. Dennon, I frankly don't care. I *do* care about getting this young man to Terrantata, preferably in one piece."

"Why?" Matthew exploded. "Why the fuck is he so important to you? And what does that colony have to do with any of this?"

Drew smiled at him sadly. "More James

Illion. That's all I can say."

He contended a moment with Drew's gray eyes, then slumped. "It's all you have to say," Matthew responded, the anger wicking away as fast as it had come. "If I buy him, then I can set him free, too?"

"There's no legal provision for that," Drew said quietly. "That's why I asked if you love him. Because he'll be yours, bound to you. You've heard of a slaver implant?"

"Yeah. Small charge in the brain, and if the owned individual wanders too far away from a set parameter, boom. No more unit."

"Keeps Techs from being taken as off-site corporate hostages. But it is also installed in proprietary units, to keep them from running away. Regulations. Joshua will be linked to you permanently; otherwise the Company will not allow a sale. Seems a few generations back, some well-meaning NCP's tried to buy and release Company products. It didn't go well."

Matthew shook his head. "God, Drew. Do you know what you are asking of him, of me? How will we ever be able to be together, both of us knowing I *own* him?"

"He's been owned his whole life, Matthew," Drew answered quietly. "And I suspect you have as well. You were Core, after all, married into it. You did what they wanted, when they wanted."

"Yeah," Matthew replied. "And you can see how well that went."

"You never loved your wife, did you?"

"She was a friend once."

"Not the same, though."

"No." Matthew shook his head again, then leaned forward and covered his face with his hands. He sat like that for a time, his mind totally numb, his fingers pressing the growing headache away. "Yeah, OK. Draw up the legal works, clean out my account. Get him the fuck away from Tony. The rest, well... the rest will play itself out." He kept massaging his temples, his eyes closed.

"He's a good man, Matthew. He can't help who created him."

"I know."

—

Joshua finally stumbled out into the hallway, his fingers red and broken from where he had pried open the door keypad and rerouted the wiring to allow him to pass. He wanted to go to Matthew, to Drew, to an airlock—whatever came first didn't seem to matter much. He also wanted to fall down, into a dark corner somewhere. His skin crawled and he was sure Alec was following him, watching him, with that one awful red eye. Making sure he lived to find what? More insanity?

He made himself go forward for a few steps, then stopped. Two gray-clad techs had to cut off their conversation and separate to get around him.

"Yeah, here's the communications hub that threw its security alarm."

Joshua turned drunkenly, watched them key the door, and disappear inside.

And watched them fall over each other to get back out.

They'd obviously found Tony's body; their faces were ashen. They gestured wildly at him, at the room.

"There's a dead L-Grouper in there!"

"I know," Joshua replied. His eyes felt dry; it was hard to blink. "I'll get someone. Stay here. Don't let anyone else in." His voice was barely a whisper. He turned and started down the hall again; his body stiff and his gait more a shuffle than a stride.

Drew's office door loomed up quite before he knew where he really was. He waved his hand over the pass-pad, and it opened for him. He stood in the doorway, shivering. Two faces lifted in surprise. Matthew was hovering over Drew's shoulder, looking at a data display. "Joshua?"

"Tell Prime I can kill. She'll be happy, I suppose. For all the good it will do." He put his hand out to the wall, but even it seemed to shift and move under his hand.

Matthew nearly climbed over the desk to get to him, but he warded the other man off. "Don't." He couldn't look into those hazel eyes.

Drew hadn't moved. "Mr. Dennon, give him some room," he said quietly.

Matthew hung in space like a rag doll, hands open and empty. "Joshua?"

He shook his head, waving his hand vaguely at Matthew.

"Report, 1011," Drew murmured.

"I killed him. He was..." Joshua broke off, his eyes coming to rest on the edge of Drew's desk. "I killed him. He's in the communication hub, this level. He's dead."

L-Groupers don't kill other L-Groupers. But then, what am I after all?

"Oh, damn," Matthew murmured. "Tony? Or Adam?"

"Tony. I'm turning myself in.

323

Regulations...regulations say..." he cut off, rapidly blinking in the blue metal office.

"Joshua, can you understand me?" Drew asked quietly. He still hadn't moved from behind the workstation.

"Sir," Joshua responded automatically. He kept his eyes on the battered metal desk. Interesting, the scratches there, the flecks of blue paint. He could lose himself in it, the etches like a script, like art, like...

"He tried to kill you first."

"No, sir," he whispered. "He wanted me to kneel, to..."

"NO!" Drew snapped. He came to his feet then, sliding around the desk to stand near Matthew. "He wanted you dead and he's tried before. You did what you had to do."

Joshua shook his head. Shook it slowly back and forth and couldn't seem to stop it's pendulum movements. "No. I was assigned...body unit detail...I couldn't kneel...there was no...I killed him. I'm not..."

"Joshua!" Drew snapped. The commander moved forward fast then, shaking off Matthew's sudden grab at his elbow. Drew slammed him back against the closed door, and he bounced hard off the surface and then let himself hang in that grasp, his eyes still looking at the scratched and dented desk. "You had no choice, do you understand?" Drew growled into his face. He shook him. "Do you understand?"

Joshua opened his mouth, but nothing came out. Only slowly did he bring his gaze to Drew's fierce gray eyes.

"Say it. You had no choice."

No choice.

"He would have hurt Matthew. He would have..."

"Yes, he would have," Drew said simply. The grip on his shirt loosened a little. He stepped back, and he let Drew pull him forward step by step until he was forced down in one battered metal chair by the desk. Matthew pivoted with them, Joshua sensing more than seeing the movement. He looked down into his hands as Drew released him, studying the torn fingernails, the blood. His blood. Or was it? He couldn't quite remember.

Drew knelt beside him. "Damn it, Joshua," he said. "I mean it. No choice."

He blinked then, his gaze going to Matthew, then back to Drew. He nodded, a little more in control, the room widening, his vision broadening to something almost like normal.

"Mr. Dennon, stay here with him. I'll get this cleaned up. Don't leave this room."

"He never listens," Joshua murmured. "Damn NCP. What do they know about orders? What do they know...?"

"He'll damn well listen to me, Joshua. Tell him, Mr. Dennon."

"Yes, Sir, I will," Matthew said, his voice strained.

Joshua closed his eyes. *That was good enough. Matthew would listen to Drew. Of course he would. Everyone did. I killed him, Drew. Killed him, couldn't kneel, couldn't let him do that to me. Couldn't.... I couldn't be L-Group, not even for you. What am I, then? What?*

He heard Drew leave the office. Heard Matthew breathing too quickly, heard the other man come across the office and drop so easily at his knees. He could feel the warmth radiating off him, his breath smelling of coffee and sour with fear. But he couldn't reach out. His hands lay bleeding a little in his lap. He could see the edges of Matthew's curly hair just beyond his fingers, beyond those killer hands.

What am I?

He dimly felt Matthew place his hand on his knee. Perfectly trimmed nails, perfectly turned joints. He gazed at it, the delicate veins, pulsing subtly with life. He let his eyes ride up the arm, up Matthew's neck to his face, to his eyes. Hazel eyes, wide and frightened and full of questions. "I'm here. Right here with you, Josh. It's going to be OK."

For the first time in years, he felt a tightening in his throat, a wrinkling in his nose. And then, the single soft trace of cold dampness on his cheek, rolling along the edge of his nose, over his lips, plunging freefall, into the darkness of his uniform.

—

Drew crouched on his heels and surveyed the body in the communication hub. Tony's belt was undone, his zipper partway down. Even without Joshua's admission, it wouldn't have taken much of an imagination to see what had happened. He closed the soft eyelids over the staring blue eyes, resting his hand briefly on Tony's chest.

He might be able to get some good samples, certainly blood, chemical analysis, maybe get the techs on Terrantata a little closer to eradicating the damn aggressive tendencies Illion's work spawned as an after-affect of his genetic tinkering. He pulled his small touchpad out of his back pocket, and called for a med team to collect the body, run the tests he needed, then incinerate the remains. He shifted and straightened out Tony's clothing, tightened the belt, zipped his fly shut. He felt remarkably emotionless about the whole affair.

But Joshua? He straightened, his hands on his hips. The boy's reaction had been a little startling. He'd sort of expected a kind of bravado, or a cool indifference, even from Illion's son. Both were typical L-Group behaviors, supported and encouraged through their years of training. But shock? It wasn't useful, that was for damn certain. Had he *wanted* Joshua to kneel up to Tony and be the good soldier? He considered himself a moment, then shook his head for the empty room. No. It had to go down this way. Joshua had bonded with the NCP, bonded more strongly than any ordinary L-Grouper, but then, that should have been no surprise. He knew that would probably happen when he threw them together on wake staff.

In fact, he'd been counting on it, hadn't he?

Illion had warned him of such things as this; after all, the unpredictability in emotionally charged situations was the byproduct of both the virus and the ARR program. And he had seen the effects in himself, after he'd fallen quite madly in love with Krystine Malar on Rialga. Madly. Yes, the perfect word. He'd felt more than a little insane all those years ago and was still ashamed where that craziness had led him.

But this particular mess would work out well in the end. Dennon and Joshua would be bound together and therefore he'd have a leash on both of them to a certain degree. And Joshua would, in the end, be able to get to Prime and the Company directly, a simple bodyguard now, privately owned, the weapon they would not see coming until it was far too late.

The work was still unfurling, orderly and irrevocably.

Chapter 19

I knew James would never come back from Earth, even though Krystine never really gave up hope. Techs who try to run are decommissioned or at the very least, given slaver implants to keep them at heel. I never imagined they would lock him away in a cell for the rest of his life. I'm glad I never went and saw him—despite how much I loved his woman, I couldn't have let him rot in there if I ever got a look at those eyes of his. But of course, in my imagination, they haunt me anyway.

Commander Drew
Historical Archives
Terrantata Research Library

Troop Carrier, Terrantata Orbit

Matthew guided Joshua down the narrow passage to the med-center, Drew walking just ahead of them. Joshua was moving smoothly again; he'd lost that glazed and unblinking look that had chilled Matthew's guts. He would have preferred to wait a few days before fulfilling all the binding parts of the contract he'd bought, but Drew had insisted that there was no time now. Terrantata was spinning below them, and they'd be making planet fall in a couple of hours. He wanted Joshua's paperwork and proprietary implant through and done, so he wouldn't have to go in with the troops but could be rerouted with Matthew to the colony's city center. And Matthew had grudgingly agreed that sounded like the best idea.

Now all that was left was explaining the whole thing to Joshua.

And he had no idea how to do that, especially not the part where they would need to put a small bomb in his brain. *Until death do you part.* Part of him wanted to laugh shrilly at that unsolicited thought, but the part of him that felt sick about what he was about to condone won out.

How in the hell did I end up owning him when all I ever wanted was for him to be free?

They passed through the med-center doors, the cramped but efficient space wrapping around them in the ever-present baby-blue color. The Tech looked up and nodded, pointing to one little open niche. A black exam chair waited, the brilliant light bar posed over the headrest like a sword.

"This is a waste of time. I'm fine," Joshua murmured.

Drew merely pointed to the chair. "Sit."

Matthew was mildly amazed how pliable Joshua was around the commander, like a small boy with his father. The tall dark man seated himself, a little frown puckering his brow. The Tech elbowed in and began to loop the arm and leg restraints over Joshua.

"Are these necessary?" Joshua murmured. He'd cast his voice to the Tech, but also to Drew. And the gaze he flicked toward Matthew was wary and a little embarrassed.

"Afraid so, Joshua." Drew stepped up and rested and his hand on the young man's shoulder. "Do you know what a proprietary implant is?"

"It's a device used when a solitary L-Grouper has been sold into..." Joshua cut off, his lips closing tight around his lips. He looked up into Drew's face and Matthew found he had to force himself to stay, to watch his lover wrestle with the words that did not need to be voiced. He knew very well he was being tethered to someone and the confusion and distaste was written all over his face.

"Who? Where?" Joshua demanded.

"I bought your contract," Matthew blurted out. There, the words were free now, as cold and straightforward as the med-center itself. He felt a moment of nausea; he couldn't make himself move closer, hated standing this far away. Joshua's eyes batted quickly between the two men.

"You? Why?"

Matthew swallowed, and when he could see Drew was about to answer, he put out his hand to the commander's elbow. "Can you give us a minute?" It was hard to feel Joshua's eyes fall solely on him then.

The Tech slipped a needle into Joshua's arm, and Matthew saw the little wince, the rapid flutter of eyelashes against Joshua's bronze skin. Matthew stood silently until the man left them in the little alcove and drifted over to finish preparing his instruments.

"Matthew?" Joshua asked.

"It was to keep you safe. To get you away from Tony."

"Short term contract or..."

"Life," Matthew said. He looked down at Joshua's chest, rising and falling. "I'm sorry. Drew asked me to do it, and it made sense to me."

"I see," Joshua said.

"I wanted to turn you free, but..."

"That's not allowed. I know. Matthew, it's OK." Joshua seemed to drop more deeply back into the exam chair. "Sedatives are working pretty well," he murmured. Matthew looked at him, then, the half-opened eyes, the way the muscles of his face were relaxing. "And I had the gall to call you mine. Just the other way around now. So it's OK. I sure will be easy to get rid of, though, if you change your mind. You're gonna have to watch that temper."

Matthew finally allowed himself to move closer, and lay his hand on Joshua's chest. "I won't want to get rid of you. Ever. I'm sure."

"You think so now. But you need to remember something. The only constant," Joshua slurred out, smiling a little into Matthew's face, "is change." His eyes closed.

The tech shooed Matthew out of the little space, lighting the anti-bacterial filters and pulling the darker blue curtain over the entryway.

"He took it well?" Drew asked from near the

door.

"Sedatives. He'd probably take anything well right now," Matthew said, trying to make his voice light. It didn't quite work.

Drew rewarded his effort with a tight little smile of his own. "When he comes out, I'm placing orders routing you both to the city hub. I've arranged for an acquaintance of mine, Kayla, to conduct you to the science center there. Nicest rooms in the colony. Once the changeover in the mines is rostered and secured, I'll come and find you. Some other L-Groupers will be with you, Adam being one of them. It would be wise for you both to take your meals in your own room once you're planet-side. Rest. I'll check in when I can."

"I never did get out of Joshua why we're on Terrantata in the first place."

"You might call it civil unrest right on cue," Drew answered.

"What?" Matthew frowned, cocking his head.

Drew seemed genuinely amused. "Never mind. I'll explain everything in a few days. I have to go now. Joshua will know how to get to the correct transport."

Matthew nodded and watched the

commander slip from the med-center. He turned, wanting to peek in on the procedure, and knowing full well he shouldn't. His stomach didn't always behave around the sight of blood. Finally, with a sigh, he dropped himself into one of the two waiting room chairs, his hands crossed over his belly, his chin sagging toward his chest. It was good to shut his eyes for a few moments, but he couldn't call it rest.

A short time later, he jerked his head up at the sound of the med-tech running the blue curtain away. Joshua was still asleep, his head tipped to the side and his face so very young. Matthew usually treasured these times, the years dropping from him when his eyes were closed and he seemed so at peace.

Today, it made him feel old.

He hopped to his feet, and made his way over to the Tech. "Everything OK? You weren't in there long."

"Everything is just fine, Mr. Dennon. The tech clutched two big tubes of blood and Matthew frowned.

"What in the hell is all that for?"

"Standard procedure for verification of purchase," the Tech replied. "He'll be awake in a moment. I'll clear him and you two can get on with your day. Congratulations on a fine purchase." Something in the man's face hinted at other than professional small talk.

Matthew wanted to hit him. Badly.

Instead, he let the comment slide, and sat on the thin edge of the exam chair, one hand on Joshua's thigh. He watched life come back slowly, awareness twitching dark eyelids, little jerks playing through in his fingers, lips opening a bit.

The tech came back on cue, tapping quickly on his palm-pad. "Have you owned an L-Group bodyguard before?" he asked.

"No," Matthew answered, and he had to grind his teeth in order to keep it that short.

"It's not a long leash, you know." The tech looked up and had the audacity to grin.

"Pardon?" Matthew tried to make the word cold and edged.

The tech flushed a little. "Quarter mile is all the room the two of you are allowed."

"What?" Matthew snarled. He stood up, eyeballing the tech with clenched fists. "Wait just one minute. Drew..."

"Specified, very clearly, the parameters for the implant."

Matthew ground his teeth.

"The PI reads for your specific energy and DNA signature, and if you are not within the boundary set, it will turn this unit off. Ensures full compliance with the new owner, you understand. If you are undergoing any genetic interventions, you will need to notify hospital staff so that the new information can be downloaded to the implant. Failure ratings on this model are very low, but sudden onset migraine headaches, lack of coordination or changes in behavior should be reported at once."

"So it can be taken out?" Matthew asked.

"No," the Tech said, as if surprised by the question.

"Then why give me the warning label?"

"So you can arrange to have a backup unit in place should this one fail."

"Die, you mean."

"Yes, well, *fail* is the terminology we prefer to use," the tech murmured. He reached into his pocket and withdrew a thin black pen. "Where do you want your mark? It should be visible so officials on any planet will know not to separate the two of you beyond the prescribed settings."

"How big does this mark need to be?"

"Up to you. The implant carries an alert beacon for close medical scanners, too, but some kind of visual is always the best bet on these outer colonies."

"I don't want to mark him," Matthew snapped.

"It's for his safety as well as yours. And it is part of regulations."

Matthew glared at him. "And if he is at the end of his leash, will *he* at least have some kind of warning?"

"Oh, yes. Bloody nose, difficulty breathing, or any of the other disturbances I listed for you. It will be rather pronounced, I assure you, but should abate quickly when you're back within range."

"God, you're a cold bastard. Remind me never to get sick around you."

The tech actually laughed as if he couldn't hear the suppressed rage in Matthew's voice. Then again, maybe he couldn't, Matthew thought bitterly. The man ran his hand pad over Joshua's forehead, then down over his heart. "Looks like everything is functioning well. Just as soon as you decide on his mark and he can walk, you're welcome to leave. Be sure to brief him on his leash-radius. Unless you want to keep it a secret, as a way out of your purchase agreement." Again, the smirk quirked up around the Tech's eyes.

"Get the fuck out of here," Matthew whispered. His fingers ached from clenching them so hard.

"No need…"

"NOW!" Matthew roared.

The Tech sniffed in disdain and muttered something about NCP's as he passed. Matthew almost turned with him, his shoulders rising toward his ears and his breath hot and angry.

"Matthew."

He turned back to Joshua, to the dark open eyes that aged him ten years. "Let it go."

"That asshole…"

"Let it go," Joshua repeated.

"They want me to put a mark on you. You can't be more than a ¼ mile away from me or you die. Damn it! I'm so sorry, Josh." Matthew wanted to tear at his own hair in frustration.

"Stop it," Joshua murmured again. "Easier for me to keep you safe this way." And he actually smiled up into Matthew's face.

"You're still drugged, you stupid L-Grouper," but he said it with affection, knowing Joshua would hear it in his voice.

"And you're acting like a bratty command-designate who didn't get his way. Temper tantrums from an NCP? Really?"

Matthew felt himself deflate a little more and he tried to shake a something like normalcy back into his head. "So, what mark do you want?"

"Oh," Joshua said, a little resignation flavoring his voice at last. "It doesn't matter."

"You're the one who has to wear it," Matthew shot back.

Joshua smiled and Matthew could tell he was running ideas as quickly as his still-fuzzy brain could process. "A feather, then. Little. Off the edge of my left eye?"

"How about on your hand?" Matthew asked. He hated the thought of a permanent mark on the face he knew so well, a constant reminder that Joshua by his side was no longer a matter of simple lust or even choice for that matter.

"Hands get lost sometimes," Joshua returned. There was no humor in his voice.

"I hate L-Groupers," Matthew muttered.

"Not all of them, I hope."

"No. Not all of them," he answered. "I think we're ready," he called to the Tech.

Matthew explained the mark they wanted and the Tech frowned. "Pretty irregular. Usually it's a couple of numbers from the owner's access ident or initials."

"No," Matthew said. He reached out and

grabbed the little tattoo pen. "Give me that."

"You don't know how..."

"I know how to draw a damn sight better than you."

"See?" Joshua smiled up at him. "Still learning things about each other."

"Shut up. I just want to get out of here." Matthew bent, one hand resting on Joshua's forehead to help him hold steady. In just a few strokes, he penned a delicate feather with a curling tip running off the edge of Joshua's eyelid, snapped the cap back on the instrument and slammed into the tech's open palm. "Are we done here?"

The tech nodded once and turned on his heel.

"Asshole," Matthew breathed.

"You're more combative than I realized. Maybe you should be the L-Grouper," Joshua said. He shook his wrists meaningfully. "Get these cuffs off me."

"It's just been a really long day already," Matthew returned. "And three days locked in my cabin, well..."

"Cuffs, Matthew."

"Hold on." Matthew threw the buckles, moving around the chair. "Stand up slow, or you might be on the floor."

"I said I'm fine," Joshua replied. He swung his long legs out to the floor and stood. Matthew wanted to support him, to at least grip his arm, but he pulled back a little, letting Joshua find his own feet.

"We have to report to some city center transport. Drew said you'd know how to access your orders. We're scheduled to meet someone named Kayla. And there are others being routed there too. Adam, being one of them."

Joshua looked at him thoughtfully and nodded.

"That's all you've got, a nod?"

"It was all that was required." He smiled at Matthew then, but the faint glaze of sadness and worry was back on Joshua's face, the inked feather crinkling at the edge of his eye like a deep wrinkle. "I'm OK," he repeated. "And I want to get the hell off this ship."

—

Joshua twitched on the shoulder harness, gesturing what part went where for Matthew. He couldn't bring himself to talk, not since they had left the med center. As the sedative wore off, the memories came back, sharp and clear and terrible. The feather ink at his left eye burned and itched, as did the small incision high inside his sinus cavity. *These things pass,* he told himself. *But the memories?*

No.

He and Matthew stood out in the sea of blond heads, their seats facing the other row that ran the length of the side of the shuttle. As he started to study each man in front and beside him, his stomach went cold. He looked down at the floor, closing his eyes for a moment and wishing he wasn't right. But he knew he was.

All the men settling in, shrugging on their harnesses, were on the list of those he had been asked, no nearly *forced*, to terminate. He felt something big moving just beyond his reach, his understanding. He jumped when Matthew's hand fell on his knee. "You OK?"

"Stop asking me that," he murmured, shifting his leg to dislodge Matthew's hand.

He could feel the mild hurt radiating off Matthew, but it didn't shift his own heavier sensation. Alec kept insisting they were missing something, something right in front of them. It was here, breathing all around them, and he couldn't grasp it. These were ARR or virus positive units. They were all being routed to the City Center. The Company had wanted them dead. What did that all add up to, aside from what the Administrators would call a quality control issue?

He lifted his head, tipping it toward Matthew. "I'm sorry. It's not safe here."

He watched Matthew's eyes go unerringly to Adam. The commander was frankly staring at them, his jaw working under his pale skin.

"Matthew," Joshua breathed in exasperation.

"Sorry." The man sat back deeper into his seat, and closed his eyes. Joshua glanced at him, feeling a kind of tenderness mixing with fear and rage, hope and confusion. Like one of his paintings, everything, every emotion was in play when he looked at his lover.

His owner.

He pressed away from that thought, dropping his eyes to the metal at his own feet again. The craft shuddered as it lifted off the troop ship floor and then smoothed out. He'd simulated a drop like this hundreds of times, in full battle armor, and knew every little shake of the craft by heart.

He opened his empty hands, frowning, and then glanced up at the bulkhead storage lockers above the long row of seats. Strange to make a drop unarmed. Maybe the weapons were stored until touch down. He wanted to lean next to his neighbor, Timothy, and ask what their orders were, but the man's rigid face and straight-ahead staring eyes dissuaded him.

Anyway, it was none of his business anymore.

The truth was he didn't know where he fit. He wasn't L-Group, not part of these men sitting in their silent and perfect rows. He was technically a bodyguard now, weeded out and sold as a single unit. It should feel like freedom, he told himself. It should feel fucking amazing. He would be able to paint, to stay with Matthew, to experience music, hell, embrace a whole life. It's what he *should* want, wasn't it? The way out that even Drew had never been able to promise him. Then why the pain, so deep in his belly? Why the feeling like the ground on which he had always stood, the desert of loneliness and abuse, was lifting up and up, like something with a mouthful of teeth underneath would consume him, leaving his bones to rot under the hot sun?

Adam leaned a little forward in his harness. Joshua noticed the empty seat next to him. Was it saved for Tony? Most likely. He swallowed down a wave anxiety.

"We're reporting unarmed to the civilian center," Adam cast his voice loud. "Seems real weapons might make the population nervous. Once there, we'll be assigned barracks and regulation clothing to support the local government should the unrest now regionally located in the mine and some of the ag centers grow. You'll each be taking command of twenty locals, orders funneled through myself from the governing representative. We'll be issued Civi stunners only, nothing lethal or heavy. Can't kill off the workers after all. Congrats on getting a cushy assignment," he grinned. A few of the other soldiers chuckled.

Adam's eyes shifted to Joshua and a number of other men turned their heads with his gaze.

"NCP just wants a full-time fuck-buddy who will never leave him. Good riddance," Timothy murmured.

Joshua looked down resolutely but he could still sense Matthew tense beside him. To his relief the NCP in question didn't move, didn't even open his eyes.

"Yeah, nobody else would want him," another man murmured.

"Except Tony," another voice returned. "Did

you see in mess? Body unit detail? More like
bloody unit detail. Man goes through body units
like a pimp slaver. Where the hell is the
commander anyway?"

"Can it," Adam growled, his voice shaking
with the beginnings of an embarrassed fury.
Joshua barely kept himself from looking full into
Adam's face. *If you look at him, he will know.
Keep your eyes down. A few more minutes and
you're free of all of it.* He forced his fingers to
open over his kneecaps, breathed his face into
calm lines. *Nothing can happen here. And once
we're on the ground, it won't matter anymore.*

"Like you're not sitting right here. Assholes."
Matthew spoke so softly that Joshua had to strain
to hear him. He hadn't moved, hadn't opened his
eyes, but Joshua could feel him, sitting there
strong and still beside him.

Joshua shook his head, hoping the
movement alone would dissuade Matthew from
making more observations, even quiet ones.

The landing was smooth as such things go,
and the gull wing door panels lifted up and away.
The men threw off their harnesses, heading to
their assigned exits with purpose. Matthew was a
little slower, fighting with the buckles. When he
finally got free and stood, he gently brushed up

against Timothy who was just moving past him.

Joshua saw the punch coming, from the first flicker of the Timothy's uniform. He jerked Matthew back, swung him around, knocking the blow aside. Hands came out from other soldiers, driving Timothy forward into line with good-natured laughter. Joshua sat and tugged Matthew down with him. "Wait. I can't get your front *and* back here. We'll go last. We're not part of the formation, anyway. Not anymore."

Matthew merely nodded, his lips straight and pale over his teeth.

When the last L-Grouper stepped through their appropriate door, Joshua gestured Matthew up. He went first though, feeling Matthew's rising agitation in the very cadence of his step.

The landing bay was fully enclosed, the huge doors overhead retracted against the daily rains of Terrantata. He found he was a little disappointed in the drab metal, the scorched and smelly landing area. It already looked so used, so established. Three other ground-to-space shuttles shared the sprawling bay. Huge bolted sets of doors led out on each of the four sides of the enclosure. Stacks of boxes lined the walls, their stasis lights shimmering. Ag containers bound back for Earth soon, he reasoned.

He and Matthew stood slightly behind and to the side of the L-Group formation. Twenty men created two lines, hands held open-palmed behind their backs, their legs parted and balanced. Adam stood before them, his fine features harsh and bony under the artificial lights. But as Joshua watched him, Adam tipped his head up, as if breathing in the great open space of the landing pad. The look on his face smoothed to a moment of peace, and Joshua looked away, embarrassed to have seen so human, so poignant, an expression on his ex-commander's face.

Three NCP's moved toward them then, and Joshua watched them with a vague interest. Two women and one man approached Adam, speaking quickly and quietly. Adam nodded once and gestured to Joshua and Matthew. Moments later, he turned the group and headed off toward the nearest doors with his men.

One of the women, her hair dark and cut in a bob, stepped toward Joshua and Matthew. He waited for her to come to them, his own hands folded behind his back, his spine erect. "Stand in front of me," Joshua murmured. "Just a bit to my right."

Matthew complied without arguing. The

woman seemed to see the careful arrangement, the tactical lines Joshua used. She shorted her pace, and then extended her hand palm up. "Matthew Dennon and Joshua 1011?" she asked softly. Her voice was rich, much deeper than Joshua would have expected. Her brown eyes flicked from one man to the other.

"Yes," Matthew answered for them.

"I'm Kayla. Commander Drew asked that I meet up with you and direct you to your quarters."

Matthew extended his hand and she took it with a polite smile. But Joshua could feel her eyes on him, measuring him even as she opened her other hand toward the doors. "Please, I think you'll find the accommodations quite pleasant after being ship-bound for so many months."

"I'm sure we will," Matthew said agreeably.

Matthew walked with Kayla, but Joshua trailed a couple of steps behind.

"You were raised on this colony?" Matthew asked her.

"Oh, yes, been here my whole life. This business with the mines is very sad, particularly the need to tap outside intervention." Kayla swept one side of her short hair behind her ear. "How did you come to be on a troop transport?"

"Oversight," he said with a bureaucrat's weary sigh. "The Core has to keep an eye on Company performance, they're so invested in the damn thing."

"Understandable," Kayla returned politely. She glanced over her shoulder at Joshua, but he did not meet her eye. "And is it customary to travel with a body-guard?"

"This *is* a war zone," Matthew said with a slight tip of his head.

"Well, not here you know," Kayla laughed softly. "So where did you pick him up?"

"Why don't you ask him?" Matthew said, a little warning note coming into his voice.

Joshua could see Kayla's shoulder flinch a little under her red sweater. "I'm sorry," she said, again glancing over her shoulder. "Forgive me. I don't know the conversation protocol to use with L-Group body guards."

"Does he look like L-Group?" Matthew muttered.

Joshua frowned in irritation.

"Not really," she murmured. "You're indentured? I noticed your ident tattoo by your eye."

"If you've been briefed by Drew, you know what and who I am," Joshua said. Her intimation that he was an NCP slave irked him, even as he recognized why she would have made such a jump.

She pulled up then. "We really are getting off on the wrong foot here I see. Please, gentlemen, I sit in a lab most days and talk to computers and analyzers. It was not my intention to be rude." There was a kind of professional earnestness on her face.

Matthew intervened, a kind of matching socially correct expression on his face. "We've been alone for a very long time, Kayla, in a rather hostile environment. It was not our intent to be rude, either."

She smiled, a little tightly. "Yes," she said directly to Joshua. "Drew did brief me about some things but neglected a lot of details." She seemed to take the time to study his face then, and he saw a kind of recognition there, something she quickly masked. Matthew had seemed to relax a little, but Joshua could not let go of how she looked at him, through him, as if data played over his chest and memories of him or something like him ran in the folds of her brain.

She turned then and walked a little faster through the windowless tunnel. Step by step,

353

Joshua could feel the ground sloping down and away from the landing bay. After about a quarter of a mile, they stepped through another set of doors and into brilliance.

Joshua halted, his gaze going up the sixty or so feet of glass, the gray clouds pressing through fingers of brilliant green tree fronds. A wind stirred the trees, and then, a flash of red and green feathers shot over the clear roofline. The clouds broke a little, and a shaft of light speared through the glass, glancing off the polished stone walkway. He had an impression of running water somewhere, vines rippling up the columns that supported the ceiling, doors leading out of this central dome, but it all swung by in a crazy blur of color and sensation.

He stumbled backwards, into the enclosed hall with its familiar metal walls and cement floor. He was on his knees before he quite realized it, his hands gripped over his head, every nerve screaming, leaping. He toppled over, but felt Matthew's hands catching him. Dimly, he heard Matthew screaming for Kayla to shut the door, that he couldn't process that much space and light and sound. He heard the doors jerk shut, but it was too late. His mind danced with the light, the greenery, that wild bird in flight. He pinched his eyes shut, his hands over his ears, his knees curling toward his belly.

"Joshua? Joshua?" Matthew voice tried to cut through, but his mind turned it into wind, into rain, into the sound of air passing over feathers. And then, something in him turned inward, where it all spun together like music, like art, like space.

Chapter 20

It is a fine line I must tread with my fellow Administrators. I need to let them weigh in, push me a little, challenge me occasionally. But there are some behaviors I cannot allow, no matter what kind of affection I sometimes feel for my own batch mates. I cannot work as a solitary—it's not how I was designed to function. But I am the last discerning vote in how the Company is run, and I take such a role very seriously indeed.

Prime Andrea Annon
Company Central Archives
Earth Complex

Company Central
Earth Complex

Prime stood in the prison block hall, her arms clenched around her belly. She had put on a heavy sweater, but she was still cold here. Muligan mirrored her stance on the other side of the cell barrier, his jaw set and stubborn. But he was actively sweating, his eyes bloodshot and his whole body trembling and jerking.

"The troop ship never got your message," she said. "I have received confirmation from Drew that they've made planet fall and everything is progressing as anticipated."

"As anticipated," Muligan echoed her. He laughed then, and started pacing behind the reinforced clear plastic. "They got the message, oh yes. They got it. Don't you see? It confirms everything I've been trying to tell you!"

"The tightbeam was out of commission, Muligan. Loose rad shield fried an entire length of the hub, according to Drew. You don't repair things like that overnight."

"You are so goddamn blind," he screamed at her, then spun away, crouched, stood and crouched again, deep into his knees. She almost softened then, seeing him in so much pain.

"Why did you do it?" she asked, purposefully gentling her voice.

"Go away!"

"You know you don't move on Company-level decisions without orders from me."

"Knew and didn't give a fuck, because you can't see it. *I can*. It's all going to come down,

Andrea."

"See what, Muligan? When you're all hopped up on cziana root, how am I to trust anything you *think* you see without any real proof? You've ranted for days now. If you survive this, once you're clean we can..."

Muligan crashed into the barrier between them, his fists knotted. "Kill me," he screamed. "Just kill me, if that's what you're going to do anyway. Please, Andrea. Please, you have to stop this," he said again, his voice dropping into something like a plea.

Andrea moved closer, opened her hand over the cold surface of the low-security holding cell. "No. No, I can't do that."

"You can order anything you want, you bitch!" he hissed, turning away. He threw himself onto his cot, jerking and trembling and cursing slow and steady under his breath. "This isn't about me getting clean, it's about punishing me because I took initiative, isn't it? Isn't it!"

"I don't believe in waste," she returned, her voice pitched low and logical. "And you had this coming. You don't ever do an end run around me, Muligan. Spar with me, challenge me, yes. That is your function. But go behind my back and order the death of over twenty company products? That's going too far. Get clean, I'll see if I can let you out of here. Med-tech services will come over in a few minutes and give you something so you can sleep through the worst of it. Don't fight it or I'll have them cuff you to the bed."

"Fuck you," he returned.

"Nice," she replied, turning on her heel.

It had shaken her, when she had seen a copy of the message coughed up during a routine data dump. Something in him must have really wanted her to find it, she mused as she walked up the nearly empty cellblock. Some part of his mind had hoped she would discover the message, of that she was sure, although she couldn't tell if it indiscretion was born of a perverse sense of a challenge or simple insanity.

Or was it a small glimmer of guilt, of humanity, peeking from beneath the cziana root and acerbic mind? Hoping she would see him, and stop him? She rubbed her arms as she walked. Technically, she supposed she should have decommissioned him as soon as she had seen the message. But there was an itch in her own mind, of something big and not quite visible, and that had stayed her hand. That, and he was a fixture in her life, and she couldn't quite put him away.

Sometimes, she called such things affection, but it went deeper than that.

She shuddered, thinking of how close he had come to effectively ordering the death of Drew among others. That bothered her, too, the thought of her senior L-Grouper drifting in open space forever or fried in the ship incinerators. Part of her turned to analyze the reaction, part of her just wanted to push it away. *And Joshua?* her mind demanded.

She had pulled the security pics from the troop carrier taken and routinely filed before the tightbeam crashed. Had seen him making love to the NCP, mostly tender and gentle scenes, very unlike the L-Group couplings she occasionally reviewed. She could feel Drew's hand in it, putting the two men together for the long flight, both so alone and vulnerable. He had wanted them to bond, she was sure of it, even though the why of it still escaped her.

There had been all too many *why's* floating around over the years, that she was sure of.

No matter she mused. Terrantata would be forced back into order, and in a year or so, most of the group would cycle back to Earth Complex. Then, they could pick up the testing of the ARR and viral-infected units and chart the intriguing changes made to their DNA. Find something of use in the tinkering perhaps. She'd already decided to shift Joshua to the pilot school and then see just how far up the Tech ranks he would climb. And after that? She had played with Administrator training for him. What a wonder he could be, trained in all three of the main product lines, spanning them and maybe seeing beyond them? She smiled slightly. Maybe she would even let him keep Dennon, depending upon their relationship. Good to have a fulcrum with her son to lever him into what would only, ever, be for his own good.

She pushed the elevator button for the upper floors, and leaned back against the shining metal wall. She hoped Muligan would live through his withdrawal symptoms. She felt he would see reason then, see what she was aiming for. If he couldn't, then perhaps she really would have to decommission him. She frowned, shoving that thought away as well. There would be time to make such decisions later.

—

Matthew paced, his hands on his hips, his

right knee aching a little in the slightly heavier Terrantata gravity. Two green uniformed EM techs had taken Joshua away to the colony lab center after he had collapsed. Matthew had frantically told them they could only have quarter mile between them, and they'd grudgingly brought him in tow. Kayla went with them as well, but he didn't like the look on her face. It was reminiscent of a scientist looking at a new species of fauna.

He'd scarcely glanced out the windows at the tropical riot just beyond, and then they'd whisked Joshua away deeper into the med center and Kayla had drawn him into a small waiting room. A tank of strange six-legged pastel creatures floated at one end of the area, their eye stalks tracking him back and forth. He decided he hated the green and burgundy chairs, as well as the comfortable carpet he strode back and forth upon. And he hated those little alien eyes that never blinked or looked away.

He rubbed at his arm, where she had immunized him against the more nasty local bugs. It still stung, and that only added to his irritation.

"Has he ever reacted like this to spatial stimuli in the past?" Kayla asked. She'd been firing questions like that for the last fifteen minutes. He'd had quite enough, so he stopped then and glared at her. "You need to take me to him."

"Really Mr. Dennon, your property is quite safe with..."

"Don't call him that," Matthew snapped.

"I can't help him if you won't work with me," she said quietly. "And I'm sorry for my slip. Drew explained it was more like a marriage between you two. I wish you two weren't bonded in this way, but I can't alter that."

Matthew stopped cold "What do you mean you wish we weren't in a relationship? What does that have to do with anything?"

"He's the catalyst we've been waiting for. Over twenty-five years, we've waited for Illion to finish what he started. Joshua has an enormous roll to play and you tagging along with him is rather inconvenient if not dangerous for us."

He frowned and moved closer to the seated woman. "Illion? You mean James Illion? What's he got to do with all of this?"

"That's really all I can tell you, Matthew. All of us know pieces of it, nobody has the whole picture, except for Drew now." She re-crossed her legs, leaning comfortably on one chair arm.

"I'm not a Tech Eight after all, just a Six, and NCP at that."

"Then maybe you can tell me what the hell a catalyst is. And why Drew was so keen for me to buy Joshua's contract if it is such an *inconvenience*." He forced himself to sit beside her, even though his legs went on twitching and he couldn't stop his toe from dancing against the floor in agitation.

"I can't read Drew's mind and I can't tell you any more than I have," she responded. For a moment, he thought he saw a quick whisper of pity on her face, and that chilled him.

The intercom beeped politely and Kayla raised her head. "Yes?"

"A few stray bodies coming in from the mine. You're needed for sample analysis before disposal."

"Understood," she said, rising.

"People you know?" he asked, forcing himself to draw on his usual politeness.

"No, actually. Our personnel were all clear. The mine blew with all of the L-Group soldiers inside. Right on schedule actually." She actually looked away toward the exotic fish tank, and this time the pity was very evident on her face.

Right on schedule actually. Matthew found

he had somehow gotten to his feet and wasn't quite sure when it had happened. She had already started to turn to the door, but he grabbed her elbow, jerking her around. Her hair had feathered over her face and one flustered hand quickly smoothed it away. "Mr. Dennon, you don't want to spend your time on Terrantata under arrest, do you?" She looked pointedly where his hand mashed her sweater.

"What's going on here?" he demanded. He wanted badly to shake her.

"Life. Evolution. Product enhancement. Still doesn't mean anything to you, does it?" she said. She shrugged him off, and then gestured with her head. "I'll take you to Joshua's room and order some food for you. Then I need to get to the lab. I'll come by later and we can resume our chat. Perhaps Joshua will even be awake by then, and if not, I'll try to hit him with some stims and get him conscious. I suspect you'll both have a visitor in a while."

He let her get all the way to the door. She turned and raised a single eyebrow, waiting but not gracefully. And then he shoved himself forward, his stomach clenching beneath his ribs.

—

Joshua awoke to the feel of Matthew's hand in his own, the sound of Matthew's breath slow and even beside him. For one moment, he was sure he was on the ship again, but then his eyes began to focus on the mellow green walls, the small bathroom off to his left, and the faintly undulating energy screen between the room and the hallway beyond.

Matthew seemed to sense the change in him, and immediately released his hand. "Josh?" he asked quietly.

"Hey, Matthew." Joshua rolled toward him gingerly, his head aching.

"You seized again. You're in the med-lab." Matthew knit his fingers together, as if he wasn't quite sure what to do with his hands now that Joshua was awake. And he let the other man keep his distance, watching the flush bring out the green in Matthew's eyes.

"Too much, too fast I suppose," Joshua said, his eyes never leaving Matthew's face. "Like the flute, but on stims. What else happened? You're on edge."

"It can wait."

"We seem," Joshua said giving Matthew his

best dry smile, "to have some time."

Matthew squirmed under his gaze, small lines puckering up between his eyebrows. Finally, he shook his head. "They're all dead, Josh. All the L-Group and techs routed to the mines. All gone."

Joshua wanted to close his eyes then. Maybe the darkness inside was the kinder place to be, where reality didn't intrude only to crumble again and again beneath his feet. "The whole batch? And Drew?"

"Drew's fine. Command position was outside the main mining area. But from what I understand, the miners brought the mountain down on top of them all."

"Why?" Joshua asked. "Why would they do that?"

"It's a rebellion, Josh. But it's a whole lot bigger than just that mine. Beyond that, I have no idea."

Joshua shoved himself up to sitting, wincing as his headache bloomed again, hot and pressing behind his eyes. "You know more?"

"Only that Kayla is keen to activate you in some way. She called you a catalyst. And she was rather piqued that I couldn't be separated from you."

"I don't like this. We need to leave," Joshua murmured. He swung his legs out of the bed, his eyes scanning for his clothes.

"I'll find them." Matthew jumped to his feet, and began pressing open the pressure latches on the nearest cabinets.

Joshua padded over to the door, and tentatively reached out his hand. The energy field tickled, but didn't shock and he realized it was probably a bacteria and viral scrub curtain. In any case, it wasn't a barrier they couldn't pass through.

"Found them," Matthew called behind him. Joshua turned back, to see Matthew clutching the clothes to his chest, his eyes tinged with longing.

"Not the time," Joshua said quietly, even as the gaze warmed him.

"I know," Matthew replied, extending the uniform to him. "Get dressed before I try to change your mind."

Joshua snorted and reached for his clothes. As he stepped into his trousers, he glanced up into the corners of the room, but didn't see any surveillance equipment. It didn't mean it wasn't there. "We need to avoid areas where there are...distractions. Outside windows. That big open space we came through."

"I don't know if that will be possible, Josh."

"Then, I'll close my eyes and you can lead me past. Whatever it takes."

"And if you fall down on me again?"

"Hit me before I do. Hard. Preferably in the gut." He began to buckle his belt.

"Right. Because I'm so good at knocking you around all of a sudden."

"I seem to recall a nice little store of aggression in there somewhere," Joshua returned. There was no real heat in their exchange, just a kind of verbal anxiety, passing between them.

"Stop," Matthew said, and the tone in his voice changed.

Joshua froze.

"Turn toward the bed."

"Matthew..."

"Oh, good lord. Matthew grasped his shoulders, physically turning him. Joshua could feel the pads of his fingers touching someplace tender on his neck, near his shoulder line.

"You look bruised here. And there's something under the skin. Small, but I can feel it. Here." Matthew guided his hand so he could touch it himself. It felt like a little cylinder, no longer than the edge of his nail and thin like a snipped piece of yarn.

"What do you think?" Matthew asked.

Joshua let his hand fall away from the object under his skin. "Tracker? Another proprietary implant? Monitor? I have no idea."

"Wonderful. I knew I shouldn't have let that bitch Kayla separate us."

"How long?" Joshua asked, ignoring Matthew's more colorful use of language as he always did.

"Hour or so," Matthew answered.

Joshua nodded and reached for his shirt, shrugging it into place, smoothing it down over his chest. "It doesn't change anything. We're going."

"Where?" Matthew asked, a little exasperation in his voice.

"Back to the shuttle. Back to the ship."

"Can you fly it? The shuttle I mean."

"Not officially. But I am reasonably sure they largely fly themselves. There will be a logic to it."

"I'm not so sure I want..." Matthew suddenly stopped, his eyes moving toward the door. And the look of shocked recognition on his face drove Joshua around as well.

The woman standing just past the bacterial field stared at him, her green eyes wide, gray-streak red hair matching just a hint of her flush.

She was perhaps in her fifties, rounded with maturity but not fat. "James," she whispered.

Joshua drew back from her, the name driving him like a prod.

"Krystine," Matthew interjected. "It's been a long time."

The woman's eyes shifted then, a little frown puckering the edges of her obvious shock. "Matthew Dennon?"

"Yes."

"Oh," she said, her voice suddenly small. "Then this must be Joshua. Illion's son," she said, her eyes going back to him. Her lips parted as if she might say more. He could see her swallow, tipping her head a little toward her chest. "Forgive me. You startled me. You look very much like your...your father."

"We know what it is like to see ghosts," Matthew said, his voice pitched low.

"We all do, Matthew," she replied. Joshua noticed her soft Rialgan accent, recognizing it from Matthew's own rolled r's and soft lift and heartbeat hold of the l's. "I came as fast as I could. I had to meet him before it all began."

Joshua shifted, nervous, as she stepped more deeply into the room. Her proximity unsettled him, and he was more than a little happy when she stopped herself, as if reading his discomfort.

"L-Groupers don't mix with women much, do they?" Krystine asked.

"Some," Joshua said.

She looked at Matthew as if for some kind of support. "What procedures have they done to either of you?"

Matthew shook his head. "We were separated for over an hour. We found a little implant at the base of his neck, but..."

Krystine's lips went tight, and her eyelids feathered down. One hand came to her mouth and then she dropped it away, straightened as before an adversary. "It's starting, then."

"What's starting?" Matthew demanded.

Joshua found he could only stand and watch her, watch his lover.

Krystine shook her head. "What Illion began all those years ago. You know his work, Matthew."

Matthew nodded slowly. "Enough of it first hand."

"The pieces fit together, you see, ARR templates generating a virus that in turn alters other templates, until all our genetic bases begin to shift, dominoes on a micro-scale before they fall on the macro level."

"Are you a grade eight?" Joshua asked. He was a little surprised how quietly he spoke to her.

"No. I'm an artist, actually. I lived with a Grade Eight for nearly six years, though. Your father. He walked me through it, his vision I mean. I didn't agree with it all, but James was hard to push off the track once his nose was down and set. And then the Company caught up with him. But I see it didn't alter the trajectory of his work. You're here, like he said you would be. Right *when* he said you would be."

Joshua felt the familiar negation rise in his throat. *I don't have a father.* But he didn't give it voice. "His work?"

"We need to get out of here," Matthew interjected. "And Joshua can't quite process your great outdoors yet. Suggestions?" Joshua glanced hard at him, a little irritated to have the conversation shift. At the same time, he knew Matthew was right. They had to move.

"Get out to where?" she asked, her hands open around her. "This City Center is it, other than the now collapsed mine. Some outlying ag communities, but you two would stand out in a hurry. Our total population here is just something over 10,000 now—everyone knows everyone, pretty much, at least by sight if not name."

"So we really are prisoners," Matthew said.

"Guests," Joshua answered for Krystine. "Guests with leashes. We could walk out the door, but go where?"

Krystine looked pained for a moment. "I came because I knew you would be here, James' last work, his son. I had to see you, to really believe he is...he is not coming back. But I'm not going to try to stand in the way of his vision, not anymore. The fact you are here, this place, this time, is like a miracle. I can't fight it anymore."

"Fight what?" Joshua asked. He couldn't keep his voice from shading cold.

"I can't tell you that," she said.

"If it's such a miracle, the telling won't affect it, right?" Matthew must have heard the note in his voice this time because he turned toward him, frowning. Joshua ignored him.

"Krystine, surely there's a place we can go, where we can process what's happening to us. Just for a while. I think," Matthew said, "you and James both owe me that much."

"He gave you a gift," she said, but her eyes were unhappy, the brows pulled down sharply over her nose.

"He nearly killed me," Matthew shot back at

her. Joshua could hear how hard it was for him to stay calm. Any reference to the past seemed to do that to him, rub at him in all his raw places.

"You saw all of it," he reminded her. "The months of illness, the raging, the fevers. And a gift? The visions and what I saw in them? I've stayed one little prayer ahead of an overdose my whole life. Because I don't fit anywhere, with anyone. If I had been on that troop transport alone, or with one of those bloody Company L-Groupers, we wouldn't be having this conversation. Illion nearly killed me, and his son might have saved me for the time being, but the moment he's gone, so am I. It's that tenuous for me, this life, this *gift*."

Joshua swallowed hard, waiting, watching.

Krystine nodded, accepting Matthew's words. "The first steps into a new world are like that, Matthew. Lonely. Frightening. But you're still here, and you'll always be here, until time takes you of its' own accord. But not me. I couldn't take those steps with James, and I can't take them with you. I wasn't strong enough then. I'm still not."

Joshua tipped his head to the side. "Strong enough for what?"

Krystine's eyes sheened over a moment, and

Joshua realized she was on the verge of tears. He saw the emotions flicker across her face—relief, pain, joy, and finally a deep and abiding sense of acceptance. He wanted to step forward then, if only to offer her support, but he couldn't force his own legs to move. "I don't carry any ARR template artifacts and my body won't accept the changes the virus James designed will want to make," she said simply. She blinked, a dusting of emotional reds shifting over her cheeks. "There, I've said too much now."

"Mother." They all turned toward the voice. Kayla stood in the door, her eyes hard and lips in a tight line. She clutched a touchpad to her chest "Come out. Now."

"It's begun, hasn't it Kayla?" Krystine said. Her voice was hollow now, a ghost of itself.

"You're making this harder on them both. On you. Come out, and I'll walk you back to the studio. It's where you want to be, right?"

Krystine turned obediently toward her daughter and passed back through the bacteria and viral screen. Matthew turned with her, his strides fast and long. But the moment his fingers touched the sanitizing screen, he jerked back with a startled cry. Joshua was at his side in a moment, and more carefully reached out to touch the energy field. It snapped sharply now, nipping at his fingertips and he could feel the echoes of that small bite clear to his elbow.

Kayla and Krystine, their images warped by the field, paused only a moment. Krystine tipped her head, and he could feel her eyes devouring his face as if she would never see him again. The look alone made him back up a step, his hand on Matthew's elbow. "Let them go.

"Like we have a choice."

"There's always choices."

"That doesn't sound precisely like L-Group," Matthew grunted.

"Because it's not."

Chapter 21

Perhaps we have all become a little cavalier about death. But remember, that which dies makes new life possible. You have only to walk through a contained hot-house, seeing how decay leaps up newly green in some little flower or bit of moss. If we look beyond the end of an individual, do we not also see the continuance of many species feeding on that corpse?

James Illion
Genotemplate Tech Grade Eight
Historical Archives
Terrantata Research Library

Terrantata Mining Compound

Drew gazed at the panel of tracker spots on his mine schematic. The last one had taken nearly six hours to fade into an inactive red. He could have left long before now, but something in him rooted him there, watching until that last life faded away.

He waved the display closed, and hands shoved deeply into his pockets, he strolled out of the command shuttle. Night was beginning to fall, deepening the shadows around the rocks and debris, the sunset lighting the sky in fingers of greens, pinks and darker purples.

The heavier gravity made him tired in his bones. He feet seemed to spread too deeply on the damp gravel, his shoulders pressed toward his pelvic girdle like some giant had put a hand on each shoulder. It choked his breath, not badly, but enough. In time, he would get used to it, be stronger for it.

In time.

The miners gave him room, flowing around his shuttle as they made their way to their own transports. He stood watch over the rubble that had once been an entrance into the Astazia ore mine. It was more of a grave than most L-Groupers ever got. They were a necessary sacrifice; he knew that, in his head. The heart, well, he'd learn to carry it. Like he always did.

It was his grave as well, he supposed, as the shadows ran further and deeper toward his feet. There was no turning around now, no second-guessing the choices he had made for the last thirty years. Tiny steps, dance steps, with James and Krystine, Prime and Muligan, Tony and Joshua. Whirl around, and on the last pass, the gun came out, the trigger pulled. His hand would always and forever be on that weapon. He was a commander; blame and praise were always his lot.

He accepted that.

Finally he turned to follow the last drift of mine personnel. He heard the shuttle door shutting softly behind him, as its proximity sensors read his personal location. If he had his way, they would never have to reopen. The jungle would claim the craft; run green leaves and roots through its circuitry until it was pulled down in humus and tree branches and fungus.

At the mine transport door, he turned to look one last time where he had allowed two L-Group batches and more than a handful of Tech personnel to be crushed in the mine collapse. And then he turned resolutely away, nodding to his new acquaintances as they gave him space to sit with them on the narrow benches lining the huge old 'lectric.

One more trigger to pull, then it would be largely beyond his scope, and into the lap of whatever Commander played on the intergalactic scale, beyond the reach of the Company and NCPs alike. He looked forward to turning over the responsibility into those not so human hands.

—

Kayla turned on Krystine the moment they were clear of the medlab. "What were you doing?" She reached out and jerked the other woman to a stop, dragging her over close to one wall. "Mother?"

Krystine smiled sadly. "You would have to ask that, wouldn't you?"

"What is that supposed to mean?" Kayla hissed.

Krystine blinked, letting a couple of techs drift past them in the tight hallway. "Your father is the good little soldier, always and will be to the end," she whispered. "And you're just like him. You can't see it in yourself, but I do. You dye your hair to hide it, wear contacts, clutch your touchpad over your heart so you think nobody sees, but it's right there. L-Group. Doing what you're told, no matter how much I've tried to tell you this isn't right, what you are doing to that young man isn't right."

"So you march right in there and try to expose yourself like that? If you're so damn sure it's not right, what were you doing in there, with him? *Trying* to get infected?" Kayla hissed back.

"Trying to say goodbye to the only man I really loved."

Kayla jerked as if slapped. "That's not fair. You loved my father."

"No. I leaned on him," Krystine replied, her eyes dropping to the floor tiles. "Clung to him because I wasn't strong enough to stand by myself, not after they took James away."

Kayla moved closer, her voice dropping and angry. "He's here, right now, on Terrantata. Are you going to look into his face and tell him that?" she demanded.

"Oh, my little girl. He already knows." Krystine shook off her daughter's hand on her arm and started up the hallway.

"He's not reactive yet," Kayla said more loudly to her back. "Not until he gets back to Earth. You wasted your time."

Krystine paused, and half-turned. "No, Kayla. I had to see James in him, and think I did. It wasn't a waste. I'll walk myself home. I know you have work you think you have to do." And she left her daughter standing alone in the corridor.

—

Joshua crouched by the commode, his fingers cramping and knotting as he tried to work in the awkward position. He leaned his head against the metal cabinet and let it take a little pressure off his bent knees. The surgical fuser he was trying to significantly upgrade twisted in his sweaty hands, complaining in the only way it could. Matthew stood just to the left of the room's entry door, watchful still, but beginning to fidget. He wished he could trade places with the other man. If someone entered the room, he figured Matthew had a fair chance of taking one person down. Two or more? No contest, even with med-lab staff.

Finally the last few bits fell into place, and he turned his makeshift weapon over in his hands. He would have preferred to simply rewire the door from the inside, but it, too, had been shielded and had snapped him back the moment he tried to touch it. This makeshift weapon would be good for two, maybe three shots. He would have to make them count.

Aiming the fine wand of the fuser was the real problem and given enough time and materials, he probably could have rectified that somewhat. But he had neither. He was only grimly amused they had locked him in a medical room with enough raw materials to cobble something together at all in the one space where the surveillance eyes should not reach.

He pressed the toilet's clean button and slipped out of the bathroom, the fuser tucked in the back of his trousers and nodded to Matthew.

What now? Matthew mouthed, his lips and facial expression exaggerated.

Joshua gestured to him with his head. *We wait,* his own lips mimed back. He sat on the edge of the bed, watching Matthew walk over to perch next to him. The other man slid closer, so their knees brushed.

He could feel all the questions welling up in his partner, and was relieved when Matthew seemed to cork them down and leaned into what comforting contact he could find. The warmth, the shift of the other man so close to him made him want more, but he pushed the need down, his eyes on the faintly distorted open doorway.

His eyes caught movement as a person finally came through the door. He leapt to his feet, his makeshift weapon snapping out. Matthew fell in just behind his shoulder.

Commander Drew immediately stopped and opened his palms forward, his chin tucked and his eyes too bright. "You going to shoot me, Joshua?" he asked quietly. He stood very still, the perfect target.

Joshua lowered the weapon, even though he could hear the change in Matthew's breathing, the warning, the disappointment catching there. "Commander. Forgive me, I wasn't expecting you."

"The door shield keeps most folks out," Drew replied quietly. "Protection. You understand."

"Keeps us *in*, too," Matthew ground out, moving up closer to Joshua's left shoulder. "Mind explaining that and why we might need protecting? Because Kayla laid down a whole minefield of innuendos, and I didn't like any of them."

"Matthew," Joshua chided him in a quiet voice.

"I know it's been confusing," Drew said. He dropped his hands and Joshua could see the fatigue and something very much like resignation on his commander's face. "Do you trust me?" he asked Joshua, almost out of nowhere.

"Of course," Joshua answered, but frowned in some deep part of his mind.

"I'd like to open this door for you. I'd like you to come out to the common room and talk with me. Both of you, actually. It's dark outside; Kayla told me your nervous system was a little shocked by the flora here."

"A little," Joshua answered. He swallowed, trying to read his commander's face. "We heard what happened in the mine."

Drew closed his mouth, his eyebrows pressed down over his eyes for a moment. "Tragedy," he agreed.

"And the rest of the men who came in on the shuttle to the city center?" Matthew asked.

Drew sighed. "I'd really rather we sit down and talk, not stand here like this is a face-off."

Joshua glanced at Matthew, nodding, and stuffed the weapon back into place. "We'd like that, too."

"Speak for yourself," Matthew whispered.

Joshua knew he was still angry with Drew for setting the proprietary leash so tight. And if he looked closely within, so was he. But they both needed answers and Drew was offering them. He didn't like the little tickle in his mind, the tightness in his gut, though. He'd never felt on edge around Drew, but tonight, something was off, wrong. *He's lost two batches today, and a*

*fortune in techs. He should feel different to me, be
on edge, angry, frustrated.*

But Joshua suddenly understood why he felt
so much unease. Because Drew wasn't upset; he
just seemed tired, resigned. But beaten, cheated?
No, not at all.

Drew reached up and touched a small pass
tab at his collar and the shield door fell away. He
stepped aside, gesturing the men forward.
"Please, gentlemen."

Chapter 22

Have you ever built a structure out of damp peas and toothpicks? My mother loved such things, and together, we constructed rickety towers that stood as tall as I. Of course, I was only five, so my memory of that time makes everything larger. Always, her own art lifted my eyes up—she designed simulations of birds that actually flew, so lifelike that once I had seen a Terrantata Red Floater come and perform a mating dance for one of her creations. She might deny it, but I think that was why she loved James Illion ,whose eyes were always gazing up and forward at things the rest of us would never quite reach with our fragile human wings.

Kayla Malar
Tech Grade Six
Terrantata Colony Historical Archives

Terrantata Commons Dome

By night, the common room was lighted with
little strings of pinpoint illumination, catching
the domesticated vines and rivulets of the faux
stream that gurgled and splashed along the edge
of the soaring dome. Joshua kept his eyes down,
going so far as actually shielding his gaze with
the edge of one hand. But enough got through
that he shivered now and again, with something
very much like pleasure and a little like fear.

Occasionally, Matthew's hand brushed him,
a subtle asking if he was OK. But he had no clear
answers to pass back.

Drew led them to a little table, and Joshua
realized it was a massive chunk of tree trunk, and
three small benches of the same wood that served
as seats. He touched the tabletop reverently.
The material felt warm beneath his fingers,
almost alive, the shivery circles of growth
radiating out from a deep brown center.

"Sit," Drew commanded. He heard it clearly,
but it took Matthew's hand on his sleeve to
finally wake him up enough to drop down one of
the benches.

Joshua lifted his eyes from the table, but it
took an effort. He wanted to let his gaze roam to

the green things around them, ached to dip his hand in the water just off to the left. But at least his mind didn't recoil, or try to sink back within him. "Why isn't this affecting you?" he asked his commander.

"More experience. Cross training in bush when I was a little older than you. And I was stationed on Rialga for quite a while. It's all terraced Ag fields and windbreak tree lines there, but it was enough exposure that I can function without the linear referents you are used to. You'll be OK, in time. Your nervous system will catch up quickly." Drew sat almost formally, his spine long, his hands in his lap.

Joshua felt Matthew's hand on his leg, under the fantastic table. It grounded him a little, and he covered the hand with his own, squeezed, and released it.

"I have an assignment for you," the commander said quietly and without preface.

Matthew shifted then, and Joshua could hear his partner's feet settle hard on the damp floor. "He's not yours to command anymore, Drew. He belongs...he's a free man." Matthew corrected himself, his voice low and cold.

"I didn't say I was ordering you," Drew said to Joshua, rather than Matthew. "It's your choice, of course."

Matthew started to stand, but Joshua reached out, pulling him gently back to the table. "I'm listening."

Joshua looked into Matthew's face for just a moment, trying to tell him with a look that he had to give this to Drew, he had to at least offer his commander this much respect and attention. Matthew settled himself, his lips hard over his teeth and his eyes shading green with the light and background colors.

"James Illion and a handful of other ARR techs began something on Rialga when I was stationed there. Something extraordinary, something that would heal the human race and set it free again. Everyone. All of them. He called it a dream catcher, a kind of viral spider web that would sift out the bad dream humanity has made for itself, let a clean, new image through."

"You can't couch this in pretty images, Drew. Your talking about genotemplate tampering. If you haven't noticed, there are a few design flaws out there," Matthew growled. "You know that. You've seen it in Adam, in Tony..."

"Sometimes individuals have show troubling behaviors," Drew said with a sigh and an abbreviated nod. "But that's because you're only seeing little packages of data, little pixels of something meant to be three dimensional and complete. L-Group is all about aggression, passion, focus. You're right-- that doesn't make a complete human being." He leaned forward, and like Joshua, could not seem to keep his hand from brushing reverently over the wood surface before him. "Illion was building a new template, piece by piece, something that would rush over and past the Company's rewiring. Something that would sweep the wobbly NCPs off the table, too. Just like the mine here, but with hope, with the possibility of new beginnings. A reset if you like, on the crumbling human genetic code and the travesty the Company has made of it."

"Everyone changed somehow," Joshua murmured. "A return to an older, more complex template."

"Oh," Matthew breathed. He shook his head savagely. "Not everyone, I bet. And not as easily as he'd like you to believe."

"I didn't say easily. Evolution seldom is."

"You watched me sweat and scream through that reset for close to a year," Matthew snapped. "I was a freaking bug on the microscope. I almost died."

"But you didn't," Drew said.

"I had a fucking Grade Eight at my bedside! Are you seriously talking about changing the genetic coding on Earth and all the Ag planets and colonies? Who's gonna stand by all those beds, Drew? Who?"

"The strong ones will survive. And you suffered an overdose, many times the effect of what James wanted for you."

"That's cold," Matthew forced the words out.

Joshua reached over and wrapped his fingers around the base of Matthew's neck. "Let him finish," he murmured.

"You can fill me in on the details," Matthew snapped back at him. He violently shrugged off Joshua's hand. "Come find me when you're through—God knows I won't be that far away, right?" He jerked himself off the bench and strode off, his back stiff and angry.

Joshua let him go, watched his lover's fists snap down at empty air as he continued to snarl to himself, his strides hard and fast.

"Is he always like that?" Drew asked.

"No." Joshua said, forcing his eyes back to Drew. "That's the first time I've seen him quite like this. But we've been through a lot the last few days." He reached up and touched the implant near his neck. "Do you know about this thing they put in me?"

Drew nodded. "Yes. It was the final information package. Your personal genetic template has the information to link the data we've collected over thirty years. This last ARR batch, Adam, Tony, the others, all added in and fed into you."

Joshua let his hand slide away from his neck. "Into me?"

"It had to be that way."

Joshua stared at him. "What are you trying to tell me, Drew?"

Drew scraped at the wood with the edge of one groomed nail. He seemed, having come this far, to be at a loss for words. Finally, he nodded again, as if reaching an agreement with himself. "You're a trigger, a carrier for a virus that can go airborne. That will begin to modify the existing genetic codes present in NCPs and Company products."

"And was Matthew right? How many won't survive those modifications?"

"Joshua..."

"How many?"

"Most of the NCPs won't make it. Might be a few immune; there's always that chance I suppose. All the Company products that weren't protected either by first-level ARR manipulations or the virus that came out of them. Probably in the range of 70 percent of the total population will go down and stay down I should think."

Joshua sat stunned, the greenery and wood forgotten. "70 percent?" He whispered. "Drew...the suffering you are talking about...the societal collapse..."

"Yes. Horrific. But there is no other way," Drew replied. His fingers traced one circle of growth rings in front of him.

"All of this for what? To create a new kind of human?"

The commander blinked, shifted on his bench. "No. An old one. Spread out on the different planets, so many experiential opportunities for humans to find their way forward again. Broadcast the seeds far and wide. It's what your father and others began." Drew shook his head one more time, as if dispelling memories he could not quite meet straight on.

"I don't have a..."

"I made sure James," Drew interrupted him, "ended up back at Central, made sure I would be routed back to Earth with him a little later. He had to be there, had to *die* there so they'd lose the trail. It was the only way to finish his work, even if he couldn't or wouldn't see it. And please understand me, it had to be convincing—no warning him, no giving him time for goodbyes to the woman he claimed to love. They needed to see him fight back, the Admin on Rialga and Earth. And I knew it had to be me, because it would be too easy for someone else to just kill him, there in the field, before he built his capstone, before he created you." Joshua met Drew's eyes as he looked into his face. "He was my friend, Josh. I believed in his work, enough to sacrifice my best friend to his own vision. Do you understand?"

"No," Joshua murmured. His hand strayed again to his implant. "What is this thing doing to me?"

"The same thing you did to that medical fuser," Drew said, his eyes on the wood. "Changing some things, preparing you internally." Joshua felt the chill in Drew's words, felt the emptiness around them shuddering with what he was not saying.

"If I dig it out?"

"You can if you want. It's already done its job, and your body will just absorb the casing in a day or so anyway. Dig away if it makes you feel better. The next step is to trigger what's in you.

You'll survive it, you know the whole collapse. You'll be a leader, when it all settles down, when people need you."

Joshua let his hand drop to the tabletop. "What makes you think I would want to survive this? All the months of caring for me, saving me, the time you spent with me. It was about this. Not...not about me at all. It was all about James Illion and this vision you two share."

"I can't separate the two like that," Drew said.

"Really," Joshua murmured.

"Please understand, Joshua. We're saving the human race in the long haul. Together, saving it, like your father envisioned. No more sending test-tube men to die in stupid wars we don't need any more. Refocusing on real and meaningful relationships, arts, creativity that will flow from the inventiveness born of pure survival. No more powerful Core families, no more Company, just humankind, rebuilding, rethinking, resetting themselves. Have you ever known me to make a move that wasn't logical, wasn't fully thought out?"

"Do you feel, Drew?" Joshua asked.

"Feel what?" he frowned.

"Pain. Sorrow. Fear."

"Some," he said. "I'm ARR. But not like you, not so fully I think. But yes, I feel."

"There is no way you could have thought this through, not all the way. Not through the eyes of children without parents, through the hunger and bloodshed and raw suffering that you will cause in the name of redefining humanity. Did you ever think this is how we are *supposed* to be - - Company, Core, Ag planets and even the damn planetary drought? Did you ever consider that my father and you will be jerking us backwards into history, into the ugly rawness of what humans can also be?"

"I don't believe that. We feel, we create, and the survivors, they'll take it further, they'll be alive again, in a way they aren't now."

"What right do you have to make that call for everyone?"

"What right did the Company have to create Techs and Soldiers, twisting the human template into something essentially alien?" Drew shot back. He thumped his fist on the table. "Damn it Joshua! Can't you see the potential in yourself? James gave that to you! He wants to give it to us all."

"James gave me a life of misery, a nervous system that could barely cope with its time and place in history, a physical form that has made me feel like a freak for my entire life. That's been his legacy as I have experienced it."

"Yes, you're different, but it's good..."

"No, Drew! NO! It was capricious and cruel. Do you know what I would have given to be blond and gray eyed and feel cold instead of pain, and laugh, and hell, even *fuck* with others like me? Anything! I would have given anything!"

Drew set back from the table, his lashes batting quick and hard against his cheeks, his jaw bunched. He swallowed, and Joshua watched his eyes following the path Matthew had taken when he had stormed away. "And now?" Drew asked, his voice surprisingly calm, even as his body spoke otherwise. "Because you phrased that in the past tense. He loves you, right now, present tense, that NCP of yours. That wouldn't have happened to a cookie-cutter L-Grouper. Not ever, because they *can't* love like that. Everything he has awakened in you, would you give that up, too, to be like your batch? Because James gave that to you, too."

Joshua sat very still.

"This isn't about right or wrong, history, or any of that, not really. You asked me if I could feel, Joshua, and that's the whole point of this.

Yes, I can feel and I can love. God knows I even love you in my own way. Yes, I have been lonely and angry for a long time at my own differences. But unlike you, I believe *that* is what makes me alive, the rage and the tenderness, the fury and the softness, the interplay of it all. It's messy and smelly and terrible, but it's *alive*. L-Group doesn't have that. Techs don't have that. NCP's hell, they're the most empty of us all sometimes."

"It's not right," Joshua murmured again. He sat for a moment, shaking his head back and forth. At last, he stood slowly, and gazed down at his once-commander. "Drew, I understand what you are saying. I do. But this isn't the way, making the choice for everyone." He swallowed hard. "I can't be your weapon here. I won't. I can't be the *thing* that restores a humanity that doesn't exist anymore, and maybe shouldn't exist again. Love isn't enough. Not for me, not for this."

Drew started to open his mouth, but he was cut off by a startled shout, the sound bounced off the glass dome, masking its direction. The cry came again, more a scream, shuddering off the glass walls and ceilings. "Who..."

"Matthew!" Joshua spun and raced out into the open crossroads at the center of the commons. He jerked his neck around, one way and then the other, before finally spotting a group of men hauling another between toward the spaceport entrance. Their captive was kicking and struggling, and he could see the flash of hands and feet subduing him. He broke into a run, fists clenched, legs pumping. He could hear Drew behind him, but he outdistanced the commander, reaching back to snag the modified medical fuser out of the back of his trousers as he sprinted over the stone pathway.

For one moment, he caught the flash of Matthew's auburn hair, and then his partner was wrenched into the passageway. Two L-Groupers turned back toward Joshua, long, ugly bush blades in their hands. They raced forward, their teeth bared.

Joshua dropped to his knee and fired. The first shot went wide and he quickly compensated for the shift and fired again. One L-Grouper went down, a neat hole in his throat. He snapped his aim to the other man and pulled the trigger.

Nothing happened.

The man was on him then, his blade fisted and ready. Joshua caught the leading edge on the heaviest part of the fuser, turned the blade away and shoved forward, taking the man to the ground. The blade flew free as the man hit the paving stones, and Joshua followed through hard, smashing the fuser into his face. The L-Grouper twisted, tossing him hard to his shoulder, and instead of following through, scrambled hand and knee for the knife.

Joshua dug in, rushed forward, his hands going around the other man's neck and jaw as his fingers strained to touch the handle of the blade. He twisted hard and the man went limp.

"Down!" Drew yelled. This commander ploughed into him, knocking him flat. A thrown knife skittered over them both, hit and clanged off the stones.

"Get the fuck off me!" Joshua threw Drew off, leaping to his feet and whirled toward the door. For one moment, he felt the commander's hand on his ankle, and he kicked back savagely, feeling his boot connect with something. The fingers fell away.

He raced forward then, and bounced off the narrow corridor wall to halt himself. He caught just a glimpse of Matthew and two other men disappearing around the soft curve of the hall. Righting himself, he plunged on. A ragged scream then another bounded off the metal walls and hard floor.

He skittered around the turn of the hall and froze. Matthew was sagging face first into the wall on his knees, his hands skewered overhead by a knife driven through both of his wrists and into the metal wall. Two L-Groupers crouched in front of him, their hands bloody, but much more cautious and balanced than the last two. They came forward as one, flanking him, pacing, mouths closed and nostrils flaring.

Joshua clenched his fists, measuring the distance. Two opponents, limited space, no more time. He crouched, then exploded straight down the middle, spinning at the last moment, and slammed one man back against the wall. Using him as a moving anchor, he kicked out hard with both feet at the other. The three of them went down together, the man behind them making a harsh smacking sound against the wall, the other momentarily stunned but already clawing to his feet.

Joshua rolled sideways, scrambled to hands and knees and threw himself at the blade that had been run through his lover's wrists. He ripped it free and spun, driving the blade sharply up as the other L-Grouper fell on him. The weight smashed him back against Matthew and wall and he felt the hot rush of blood over his hands as the knife went home.

But the blond soldier merely grunted, and his hands snapped around Joshua's throat. He bore down, and Joshua could feel the handle of the weapon digging into his own belly. He was aware of Matthew's limp body under him. Blood dripped from the wounded man's mouth, framing each white tooth as he ground down on Joshua's throat. Joshua fingers finally released the knife, but the weight of the other man pinned his arms. He writhed, trying to break free, but the other's grip was too sure.

Then he could see fingers knitting into his assailant's blond hair. The man's head was jerked savagely back and a knife flashed over the windpipe. Blood spurted, hot and sickening and Joshua was finally able to throw himself to the side, kicking at the floor with the edges of his boots, flipping himself over to cover Matthew body with his own.

He panted there, for one breath, two, then swung around. Adam stood over him, the blade in his hand shining red beneath the long light cylinders. His once-commander took two quick steps back, his hands partially open, but didn't drop the blade. "Is he alive?" Adam asked.

Joshua could only blink in shock.

"Your NCP. Is he alive?"

Joshua reached numbly for Matthew, his eyes still on Adam. He was loath to shift his focus, his heart leaping in his chest and his breath harsh and gasping in the small corridor. But the hot blood beneath his fingers won and he pushed himself around. He grabbed both of Matthew's wrists where the knife had gone through. The other man's face was bruised and bloody, his eyelids only half-closed, his lip split and ragged. "He'll bleed out. Help me."

Adam was by him in moments, ripping his shirt from his own back, field stripping it in long lines of cloth. He shoved some of the fabric into Joshua's hands and they each took a wrist, binding the wounds tight. "Med-Center." Joshua panted. "Now."

"No. Stasis containers in the main hold. Twenty steps that way. That'll stabilize him."

"Just his wrists..."

"No," Adam grunted. He raised one pure red palm, before grabbing another handful of his shirt and stuffing it under Matthew. "I think he took a puncture wound in the side. Feels deep."

"The Med-Center..."

"He dies! And then you will too, you idiot. Proprietary bomb in your head is going to go off

405

the moment his heart stops for more than a couple minutes."

"How did you..."

"Damn it, listen to me. His heart is going to stop! Help me!"

They lifted Matthew between them, half-running in jerky and wobbling strides down the hall and out into the bay. They eased Matthew down, and then turned to one of the big ag containers waiting for produce. Adam leaped up and pulled the heavy metal square over on its side. "Get him in! NOW! Better hope that PI in your brain can tell the difference between true death and stasis!"

They dragged Matthew in, his body leaving thin trail of blood behind. "He's not breathing," Joshua cried.

Adam heaved Matthew forward the last few inches. "Look out!"

Joshua lurched back as Adam shoved him clear and slammed the container shut, his fingers dancing over the stasis pad. A baleful little green light flicked on finally and the two men could only stand there, gasping and bloody as the produce stasis box hummed to life.

Joshua wobbled and then let his knees go, sliding down the edge of the container, his hand splayed over the surface. Adam stood over him, his hands on his hips, his bare chest heaving and shining with sweat and blood. "We need to get off this rock," Adam growled.

He stalked away a few feet, and Joshua numbly watched him turning his head, looking at the various shuttles.

"We need to get a med tech here. We need..." Joshua began.

Adam rounded on him, fierce. "They killed my men! In the med-lab! Gave them something and they just fell over! First twelve went down and I mean now! The rest of us broke free and when we surprised your damn NCP, there was no way I was letting him bring it down on us."

Joshua shook his head helplessly. "No. Your men were ARR. They were saved. Drew saved them! They weren't supposed to..."

"I don't care what was *supposed* to happen!" Adam growled. "Get on your goddamn feet and help me find some antigravs so we can move your owner. We're leaving. Now."

"I can't fly any of these..."

"Snap out of it Joshua! Ag shuttles, all automated. We say go, they go."

"To an ag ship? Then where? Those things aren't set up for crews! You don't even know if there is oxygen anywhere on board!"

"I don't care. We'll figure it out, even if we have to climb in stasis boxes ourselves." Adam snapped back. "You're the tech grade four, right? Right?"

He snapped his fingers, pointed to a forlorn tool locker. He strode over, tore open the door, and pulled out a couple of antigrav bars. "That one," he gestured toward the nearest ag shuttle. "Now."

A low siren began to hoot in the echoing landing bay.

—

Drew leaned heavily on his daughter's shoulder as they limped through the dim Common's dome. Every so often, he swiped at the blood on his upper lip that continued to sluggishly pool there.

"I can fuse that shut, you know," Kayla said.

"I'm L-Group," he replied. "It's just about done leaking anyway. Won't even have any discoloration by morning."

"Still be nice if you stopped long enough to wash your face and change your clothes," she snapped back.

Drew chuckled. "I've missed you so much,

Kayla."

"Are you saying I still sound like a three year old?"

"No." Drew knew that single word was bitter and sad but he couldn't edit it.

"I know, " she replied more quietly, her grip tightening. And he believed her.

"They got out, Matthew, Joshua, and Matthew. Earth bound ag ship?"

"Right on schedule," she replied. They walked along in silence for a bit. Drew breathed in the greenery, trying to appreciate the soft lighting, even the feel of real stones under his feet, but they gave precious little solace. To have it all done now, to watch the last pieces fall into place so cleanly, left him feeling oddly empty.

"How did you know he would let Adam direct them like that?" Kayla asked. "It seemed so much safer to sedate and store Matthew and Joshua on that ag ship. Let them be unpacked on Earth. Let the thing take its course."

Drew shook his head. "Shock. I've seen Joshua in shock before, so I acted on that. He's pretty malleable then. Sedating them would have been my first choice, too. But I can't separate them, not more than a quarter mile, and with Joshua conscious, they'll at least have a chance to stay together. And I need Adam there, to focus them, to put them in the right place at the right time, even though all he *thinks* he's doing is saving Joshua in the long run. We have to hit at the heart of the Company, or there is a chance they can turn it all aside. We have to strike true, medical techs first. Putting an injured Matthew right in their midst will do that, because Joshua will be right beside him."

"Were those four more bloody deaths worth that?"

Drew sighed. "All of them served their purpose. They lived L-Group. They died that way. Adam, well, he is thinking he's finally doing right by Joshua, helping him like this. He thinks he has a chance at repaying some pretty heavy debts. He's not going to let Joshua down this time. I know it."

He glanced down at his daughter and smiled then. "With all these humanitarian questions, you're sounding suspiciously like your mother," he said, raising one eyebrow in a hint of a smile.

"She wouldn't see the resemblance. She thinks I'm too much like you."

"Of course she would."

Kayla shifted her grip on her father. "Matthew's injection will take about four days to kick in. Then, his proximity with Joshua should start the template sequence. Two more days until Joshua is able to shed the virus. Five days before those infected start to feel the effects. That's still a lot of time for things to go wrong, Father."

Drew nodded. "But we need to confuse the Company. We need that time for the virus to spread to key personnel before they pinpoint their vector."

"Before they pinpoint Joshua."

He nodded.

"You do love him, don't you?" she asked quietly. They had reached a little bench beside the pond, and he let her settle him, not so much because he needed help but because he didn't want her to let go of him.

"Must be hard. All the people you've had to destroy in your life were the same people you love."

Drew shook his head, his lips tensing and working over his teeth. "I believe in the larger vision. Wholly. But yes, it's hard. Particularly with your mother."

"It was her choice to go with the rest of the NCPs when the time came," Kayla murmured. "I gave up trying to understand it, understand her, a long time ago. She says I'm L-Group, through and through."

"That's not a compliment, coming from her."

"I know. When she saw the echo of James in Joshua's face, I think it really shook her. That James would have chosen that route for his only son..." Kayla rested her hand on her father's shoulder, and he covered her hand with his own.

"She hasn't let him go, not after all these years." He hated himself for saying it, but needed to hear it out loud and cold. He had never been able to fill those shoes, much as he ached to. And then, duty had called him away and the years had accumulated to the point that he knew he could never have a second chance with her.

"No," Kayla answered him without a pause. "I don't think she ever will."

Drew looked up into the glassy triangles of the dome. The dim lights kept the stars from shining through, but that was OK. He wanted to turn his mind from ships and planets and black reaches that consumed those he loved. For a while it was good to just sit with his daughter, feel her hand on his tired shoulder and pray that his part in the larger story was done.

Chapter 23

I don't think often about motivations, maybe because L-Group constantly drilled into that a quick and decisive response to a given set of stimuli was the only way to function in the world. But I watch him out there sometimes, standing in front of his owner's stasis box on the half-empty container deck, and I wonder how to turn him back to me, how to motivate him to see me anew. Matthew Dennon had him for a few months; our roots go much deeper. Nonetheless, I am aware it will not be enough to put myself in front of him and be blunt, like an L-Group commander. Now, I must court him as the NCP has done and I have no idea how one proceeds with such things. But one thing I do know—I have the freedom now to try. And that feels spacious and remarkable.

Commander Adam 416
Historical Archives
Terrantata Research Library

Ag Transport Ship
Outbound for Company Central
Distribution Docks

Despite Joshua's fears, the ag ship did in fact sport two small crew cabins, an abbreviated sonic shower and toilet wedged between them. Food cubes, enough for two, would meet their nutritional requirements if not their taste buds. They also found a large inventory of water on one of the other shuttles. Joshua had stumbled over a simple medical diagnostic unit in the main hold, but nothing sophisticated enough to tackle Matthew's injuries. Still, it was more than he had hoped they would find within.

An enormous part of the vessel was empty; it hadn't been fully loaded when he and Adam had kicked in its over-rides and sent it out of Terrantata's orbit. It had been hard, those first hours, working shoulder to shoulder with Adam. And oddly familiar, because the L-Grouper didn't talk to him unless it was necessary and barely met his eye. They both tried very hard to be in different parts of the ship now, crossing only occasionally by the food locker or the bathroom. The vast size of the ship was good; it allowed him to shove the past down where he wouldn't have to look at it too closely.

It was a practice he knew well, after all.

Joshua stared down over the metal railing into the hold's belly. Four ag shuttles were lined up along the wall, with space for nearly ten more. What a waste of fuel this trip would be. He almost laughed at the odd thought. But then, contemplating the ag containers always brought with it an image of a bleeding Matthew laying sprawled and frozen in one, and he had to close his eyes with the ache of it, had to push it down before it crested over him yet again. Too much time here, too much of it alone. But he would find a way to fill it, poking carefully around the Ag ship's components, getting to know her inside and out.

He had escaped the plan Drew had for him at least. Not in the way he would have wished, or even dreamed, but it had worked. On a more populated planet, he and Matthew could fade into the background. Start again. Or start for the first time, really living a different kind of life.

The big trick would be to convince the Earth-based ag center to transfer the container with Matthew to a high-end med-lab. Things like that didn't happen in the ordered scheme of things. But he had time to figure out how to do that without word of the strange request making its way up the Company hierarchy. Bad enough that the ag ship was off schedule and coming in from Terrantata. He shook his head. There was nothing he could do about that yet. He was no pilot, and wouldn't have been trained for an automated vessel like this anyway. Still, time was on their side. He could learn a lot in a few months.

He'd found some tan and white crew clothes in the storage cubby beneath his bunk and, while they hung on him and were a little short at the sleeve and cuff, they were comfortable and warm. It felt a little strange, not wearing his black uniform, but not necessarily bad.

He leaned on the railing, his fingers interlaced, his forearms taking his weight, one leg crossed loosely over the other. The image of the dreamcatcher Drew had spoken of came to mind. He was wrong, though, his analogy a fallacy. Because each string of the ancient symbol would have to vibrate with its owner's conception of good and evil, dark and light. Drew's visions, as well as his father's visions-- those were the very ones his own dreamcatcher would see caught and held.

Caught and held until the spider of time

dictated what to do with them all.

Coming Soon:

Strands of Silk

Book II of the Dream Catcher Fallacy Cycle

About the Author

K.B. Nelson holds a master's degree in comparative religion and loves teaching yoga, qigong and adult education classes when she is not writing, crafting fiber art or running after the sheep in her backyard. "My grandfather once said he was a jack of all trades and master of none. I think I have managed to live into that same sentiment my whole life, and I can't say it has ever disappointed me." Kim has authored three non-fiction titles and five science fiction works and her poetry has appeared in both national anthologies and national magazines.

www.ingramcontent.com/pod-product-compliance
Lightning Source LLC
Chambersburg PA
CBHW060140260626
47160CB00001B/51